THE
OTHER SIDE
OF THE
DOOR

DOORS OF THE HEART BOOK 1

P.F.
SPENCER

For Jacqueline

When one door closes, another door opens...
— Alexander Graham Bell

"Will you walk into my parlor?" said the Spider
to the Fly.
— Mary Howitt, *The Spider and the Fly*

CHAPTER 1

Tuesday Morning, November 12, 2002

I OPENED one eye, wondering what had awoken me. It was still dark. Last night's storm, featuring high winds and torrential rain, seemed to have calmed down, and it was quiet in the house. Too quiet. When had the furnace stopped working? I was freezing.

I snuggled closer to Dale. His body radiated seductive heat.

He sighed, rolled toward me, and captured me with one long arm.

For a blissful moment, I thought about staying home today, just the two of us. Regretfully, I knew Dale would want to go to work today. He rarely could be persuaded to take a day off, especially when he was engrossed in a new architectural project. I kissed his stubbled cheek and sat up, fumbling into my robe.

"Uhhmmmmm," Dale groaned.

"The power's out again, Dale. I'm going downstairs to light the woodstove. Maybe I can make some instant coffee before you leave for work. I'll deal with the situation here and join you in the office later."

He sat up, yawning. "Okay. I'll be down soon."

We kept an antique oil lamp and matches on the dresser for emergencies like this. Dale would use its light to help him get ready for work.

Taking the flashlight from my night table drawer, I made my way down the dark stairway. Through living room windows streaked with rivulets of rain, I could see a faint brightening of the eastern sky.

In the kitchen, I lit candles, and the big wood burning stove in our family room. We had plenty of dry firewood; Dale had filled the woodbox last night ahead of the storm.

Back in the kitchen, I unplugged the automatic coffeemaker, filled the teakettle with water, placed it on the woodstove, and sat down nearby to wait.

Though power outages happened infrequently, they did happen. We talked about buying a generator after each blackout, but somehow we never actually had done so. Maybe today…

❧

Dale sped through his morning routine and within a few minutes he appeared in the family room, freshly shaved and dressed as usual in sport coat, button-down shirt, khakis, and loafers. His dark red hair was damp and plastered down as much as possible, though his irrepressible curls would spring up as they dried. His tie was hanging loose.

I pointed to the teakettle, eyebrows raised.

"Don't bother, honey. I'll pick up some coffee and breakfast in town."

Leaning toward me, he ran one finger gently down my cheek and brushed my lips with his. Reaching up, I pulled him close and answered his kiss with a deeper one.

He growled with pleasure, and whispered, "I love you, Sharon," as he pulled slowly away. Standing upright again, he refocused. "Sharon, I'll be in the office until about eleven o'clock, and then I'm driving to Westchester County for my luncheon meeting."

I looked up at him. "Meeting?"

He smiled and tilted his head. "Did I forget to tell you?" He knew I would forgive him almost anything when he smiled that special smile and tilted his head like that. "I'm meeting today with New York-Presbyterian's executive board about their proposed Hudson Valley Hospital expansion project. I've got some sketches to show them, and I have some other ideas to run by them, too."

"Oh, yes, you did tell me. I forgot." I laughed, shaking my head. After more than twenty years of marriage, I still found him irresistible. "You'll have to drive my car today. It's so new I've hardly had time to learn all its features. You'll be careful, won't you?"

Dale's Mercedes had been in the shop for the past few days because it had been involved in an accident last week. A speeding truck had come up behind Dale on a curve, and after rear-ending him and forcing him off the road, the driver had backed up and sped away. The damage was not heavy, but according to our mechanic, it was going to take more than a week for the replacement parts to come in. Since the accident, I had been driving us to and from the office in my new BMW.

"Of course." Dale shrugged. "I'll check it out as usual. You know my routine."

"Yes." I smiled back at him and shrugged my shoulders too. Dale always checked his car thoroughly before getting in, even crouching to look underneath. Each time I asked him why, he would grin and claim to be a spy. He was making a joke, of course, though I had never found it very funny.

"Don't worry about me, Dale. When the power comes back on, I'll get ready and phone for a cab to take me to the office. Tell Linda I'll call her later."

Already preoccupied with the day's agenda, he merely nodded. Thrusting his arms into his overcoat, he turned away and walked through the kitchen to the garage.

Linda, my office assistant, was a motherly, middle aged woman whose self-appointed mission in life was to take care of me. I knew she would insist on coming to pick me up. When I called her, I would have to tell her firmly not to bother.

At last, the teakettle whistled. As I spooned instant coffee into my mug, the lights flickered, went out, and then came back on. Almost immediately I heard the furnace rumble to life and the refrigerator softly begin to hum. I turned on the TV to check the weather. According to the local report, the daytime high temperature would be in the low forties with a cold precipitation all day, and the possibility of snow by nightfall. Great!

A half hour later, I was able to take a warm shower.

Under the soothing spray, I daydreamed about Dale. Two weeks ago, we had had a rare sunny and relatively warm Saturday. It was too beautiful to stay inside, so Dale and I went out to rake some of the millions of fallen leaves littering our front lawn. Suddenly, grinning wickedly, he grabbed a handful and chased me around the yard, trying to stuff it down the back of my sweater. Shrieking and laughing, we collapsed onto one of our towering red and gold heaps. Moments later, his sparkling green eyes darkened and he pulled me into his arms, his mouth closing hungrily on mine. After a long moment, we scrambled up and headed for our bedroom, trailing leaves. I shivered with delight as I remembered what came next.

Reluctantly, I turned off the water and toweled dry. It was time to concentrate on getting dressed for work. In my walk-in closet, I chose a pair of chocolate wool pants and a warm pullover sweater, patterned in shades of cocoa and tan. I tucked brown ankle boots into my tote to wear indoors at the office.

While I was there, I took a moment to decide what to wear this weekend. There was going to be a charity dinner dance at the Country Club on Saturday evening, and Dale and I would be hosting the cocktail hour. I selected a short, dark red velvet sheath with a deep v-neckline. It flattered my slim figure, and looked terrific with my pale skin and loosely curling, shoulder length dark hair.

There was only one problem: none of my dressy shoes were suitable. I briefly considered a pair of silver sandals with three-inch wedge heels, but decided they were too summery to go with the velvet. Maybe I could take the train into New York City one afternoon this week for a shoe shopping expedition. I liked that idea.

In the hall closet downstairs, I located my hooded, red wool coat and a matching pair of rain boots. I called Linda, and then the taxi company. The dispatcher promised to send a cab as soon as possible.

Twenty minutes later, the taxicab arrived. As I ran from the house to the car, a blustery north wind dashed cold mist against my face. When we finally arrived at the office, I paid the driver and hurried inside with relief.

Linda must have been watching for the taxi because she met me at the lobby door. Clucking over my damp coat, she whisked it away to dry. Soon, she was in my office to hand me a cup of freshly brewed coffee and hang my dry coat—how did she manage that so quickly?—in my closet. She reported the morning's events, chief of which was that Dale had driven away only a few minutes before I arrived.

‹❀›

Late Afternoon

My office phone was ringing. At first, I ignored it. Linda would get it.

I was trying to balance the books. Dale was usually good about giving me all his receipts, but I was having trouble with his October expense report. I was going over the figures for the third time.

On the fourth ring, I picked up the receiver in irritation.

"Dale Grant Architects. How can I help you?"

A deep male voice spoke into my ear. "This is Deputy Sheriff Dave Thomas. May I speak with Mrs. Grant?"

Puzzled, I answered, "This is Mrs. Grant."

"I'm calling from Memorial Hospital. I'm sorry to tell you, but your husband was involved in a traffic accident this afternoon. Could you please meet me here as soon as possible?"

"Is he…?" I began, but the line was already dead.

"Linda!" I ran to the closet in my office to grab my coat and pocketbook, and caught my reflection in the mirror behind the closet door. There was a stark contrast between my dark hair and shocked white face.

As I ran down the hall toward the main lobby, struggling to get my arms into the correct coat sleeves, I almost collided with her. She had been making photocopies of our latest proposal and was on her way back to my office with them. She saw my face and stopped short.

"What's wrong? You look like you've seen a ghost."

Turning and running with me to the lobby door, she held it open for me.

"I have to go to the hospital." I pushed open the outside door. "Dale's been in an accident. I'll call you as soon as I know more."

The temperature had dropped, and the morning's heavy mist had turned to sleet. The icy shards stung my cheeks and blurred my vision.

It was only three short blocks to the hospital, but my legs felt heavy, as though I were wading through thick mud. In my haste, I had neglected to put on my boots and take an umbrella.

Finally, damp, shivering, and frightened, I reached the hospital and hurried to the front desk where the Deputy was waiting for me. I recognized him now. He had lobbied for a larger Sheriff's Department budget at a recent Chamber of Commerce meeting.

I nodded to him and made an effort to pull myself together. "Where's my husband?"

"Please come with me." Taking my arm, he escorted me down the hall, pulled open a door, and walked me into a nightmare. Through the bustle and noise, bright lights, and strange smells, I saw a surgeon in green scrubs talking with Rob Miller, our family physician. Rob and his wife, Mary, were among our closest friends.

Rob wore a white coat over his street clothes, and was listening intently as the surgeon spoke to him.

Something was wrong. Rob had office hours on Tuesday afternoons. What was he doing here now? He glanced up and, as he spotted me, his expression changed from shocked concentration to sorrow. He moved toward me and took my hands in his.

"Sharon, my dear, I'm so sorry. Dale apparently lost control on a curve and hit a tree head on. He was semiconscious but still alive and mumbling when the medics brought him in. Do you know anyone named Vladimir?"

I shook my head in stunned silence.

"Anyway, the doctors here did all they could, but his injuries… And he'd lost too much blood. I'm just so… I just can't believe he's gone."

Abruptly, he stopped talking. After a moment, he took a deep breath, still tightly gripping my hands.

"Sharon, if there's anything Mary and I can do… Right now, I'm going to take you home."

Faintly, far in the distance, I heard someone scream. There was a spinning sensation in my head and the smells and clatter of the Emergency Room abruptly ceased.

Wednesday Morning, November 13

When I awoke, the room was barely light. I was at home, I realized, in the bed I had shared with Dale for most of our married years.

I reached for him, but his side of the bed was cold and empty.

Where was Dale? What time was it?

I struggled to sit up, but my head seemed too heavy for my neck. There was an odd buzzing noise in my ears and my muscles were aching. Confused thoughts swirled through my head.

"Oh, Mom… you're awake."

Our daughter, Ellen, was sitting across the room near the window. I could see snow falling through the glass. Snow? When had it begun to snow?

As Ellen approached the bed, I could see that her beautiful green eyes were red and swollen, and tendrils of her thick, dark red hair, so like her father's, were curling damply around her face. Why was she crying?

"But, why are you here? Why aren't you at school?" Ellen was attending Williams College in Massachusetts, Dale's and my alma mater.

"Dr. Miller called me last night and arranged an early flight this morning. I've been here for the past hour or so."

Reaching the bed, she sat on the edge and pulled me into her arms, laying her face against mine in a wordless embrace.

Abruptly, my memory returned. I gasped, hugging Ellen tighter. Surely this was only a terrible nightmare. My eyes filled with tears.

"Mom…" Ellen's tears mingled with mine.

After a long moment, she pulled away and got to her feet, wiping her eyes. "You've got to eat something. Maybe some coffee… um, or water? I'll get some water."

Sobbing now, I fell back, clutching Dale's pillow to my heart.

When Ellen came back, she handed me the water glass and gave me one of the pills Rob Miller had left to help me survive these first days of grief. Through the next hours, as I drifted in and out of consciousness, random memories surfaced briefly before sinking again, to be replaced by others. Desperately, urgently, I snatched at snippets of the life Dale and I had lived together, secure in the warm embrace of our love.

CHAPTER 2

November 2002 to March 2004

I HAVE only hazy memories of the days following Dale's death. There was a funeral service at our church and burial in the local cemetery. A few weeks later, a memorial service was held in Manhattan, attended by friends, colleagues, and many of his more prominent clients. The eulogies and the obituaries in the newspapers described Dale's seemingly charmed life and praised his talent and dedication to his family and his art.

I attended the services, accepted condolences, and even soothed tearful friends, but I was sleepwalking with shock. In my numbed state, I longed to hear his voice, his laughter, and especially to feel his touch.

After all the ceremonies were done, Ellen and I spent a week on Dale's family's farm. His now-elderly parents and his brothers were devastated. His mother was able to cry, though she tried to hide it from the rest of us. Mike, Sr., and Dale's brothers went about their daily chores in heavy silence, unable to express their burden of sorrow. They were glad to have us with them, but we could do little to ease each other's hearts.

Soon after we returned home, my grief turned to rage. Dale and I had argued in the past, but never with bitterness. Now my fury toward him surprised and frightened me. I was unsure whether I could bring myself to forgive Dale for leaving me alone like this, without even the chance to say goodbye.

And then, there were my physical needs. Our lovemaking had been rich, varied, and very exciting. How was I to survive without it. Without *him?* In saner moments, I wondered if these were selfish thoughts. But my anquish, and my anger continued. Where would I ever find another love like ours? How could that even be possible?

Ellen was an almost constant presence, felt if not fully acknowledged. I was too angry and miserably unhappy to offer her the solace she needed, though she never complained. Now a sophomore at Williams College, she spent as much time with me as she could without missing too many classes. She was hoping to study architecture in Cornell University's graduate program just as Dale had done. We had been planning to bring her into the firm as a junior partner as soon as she was ready.

Thankfully, Ellen had formed a strong bond of friendship with her college roommate, Suzanna Smith. They looked very much alike, and enjoyed doing many of the same things, but more importantly, Suzanna was a warm, levelheaded, and understanding young woman. Ellen had often brought Suzanna with her when she came home for weekends and school holidays.

When I eventually realized how much Ellen had relied on Suzanna to help her survive her terrible grief for her father, I tried to thank her for being such a good friend to Ellen. Suzi, as she had asked me to call her, simply replied that she and Ellen were like sisters, and that Ellen would have done the same for her.

Suzi had very little family. Her parents had died in a car crash when she was a small child, and her only close relatives were her widowed grandmother, who had raised her, and her older brother, who lived with his wife and children in Texas. While Suzi was growing up, she and her grandmother had lived in Long Island. Now elderly and ill, Mrs. Smith lived in a nursing facility in Texas near her grandson's home.

I was always happy to see Suzi when she came to visit. I had grown to love her for herself, not just out of gratitude for her support of Ellen.

❧

Gradually, over the next few weeks, as I began to emerge from my fog of grief and rage, I started to wonder about Dale's accident. Dimly, I remembered Rob Miller telling me that Dale had been semi-conscious—barely alive—and mumbling about a man named Vladimir when he was brought to the hospital. Now, I wondered, why on earth would Dale have been calling for this unknown Vladimir instead of for me or Ellen? Who was this man, and what was he to Dale? The questions played over and over in my head.

I phoned Rob Miller, but since he had not been there when Dale was brought to the hospital, he could tell me nothing further. That was frustrating. I requested a copy of the police report of the accident, but it only yielded more frustration. It contained nothing unusual or surprising beyond a cryptic line stating there was inconclusive evidence that the car had been tampered with. *Tampered with*? In what, and with whom, had Dale been involved?

The officer who handed me the report was unable to give me any further details.

"Could I speak with the policemen who responded to the scene?"

"Yes," he said. "But it will take a few days."

I nodded, defeated for now, and went home.

A week later, when I met with them, they were equally unhelpful.

The ranking officer shook his head. "No, ma'am. There was nothing unusual about the accident. It was just a routine traffic call."

"But, Officer, my husband was involved in another accident just days before this one. Couldn't there be a connection?"

Now, both officers shook their heads. "No, we think the first one was caused by someone who was drunk or high on something. With this one, there's no evidence that another vehicle was involved. The weather was bad, and if Mr. Grant was speeding even a little, he may not have been able to slow down or stop. Unfortunately, that happens all the time."

"You're absolutely certain the two accidents couldn't have been related in any way?"

"No ma'am, that first accident was just one of those things. And, I think the second one was probably as I've described. We're sorry for your loss."

I was stunned by their lack of concern. How could they so easily dismiss the possibility of a connection?

The lawyer I consulted saw no reason to pursue my misgivings. He counseled acceptance of the coroner's verdict of death by accident.

As days and weeks passed with nothing else suspicious coming to light, I began to wonder whether there really was anything to worry about after all. Assuming I would never find the answers to my doubts and questions, I finally convinced myself to put them out of my mind.

⁂

Depression descended again. I knew it was useless to cry, but there was no way to stop my tears. Getting out of bed each day seemed impossible, but gradually I began so understand why I had to do it. I had to pull myself together, for Ellen's sake, of course, and for the firm, but most of all for my own sake. Still, I have no idea how I managed to do it.

The office was in limbo, waiting for me to return. When I finally did, I discovered our financial picture was rosier than I had expected, given my weeks of grief stricken absence. Thankfully, none of our current clients had canceled their contracts outright after Dale's death. Several projects were now in the construction phase. There were also a few in the design stage, nearing completion and, hopefully, approval.

After meeting with our accountants and lawyers, and speaking with our staff, I decided we could go forward, though we would have to take on less ambitious work in the future. Our staff architects were perfectly capable. They lacked only Dale's genius and drive. They both assured me they would stay with the firm, at least for now.

When we began to talk of marriage, Dale promised me that he would be successful one day. Now, I learned how well he had kept his promise. Ellen and I would never have reason to worry about money.

The firm was equally well funded. I had always deferred business decisions to Dale. Now, I was in charge. I was determined to keep the company functioning until Ellen proved to herself—and to our future clients—that she was her father's daughter.

CHAPTER 3

March 2004

ONE DAY, more than a year after Dale's death, our receptionist put a phone call through to my office. I had given Linda the afternoon off, so it was up to me to answer it. Frowning at the interruption, I picked up the receiver. To my surprise, it was Barbara Jeffries, a former college classmate and study partner.

"Hey, Sharon," she said. "I hope I'm not calling at a bad moment."

"Barbara! It's been a long time. And, no, now's fine. I was just proofreading our latest proposal. I'm happy to be distracted for a few minutes."

"I'll come right to the point. I have something to ask you, and I want to do it in person. If I catch the four-thirty-five train from Grand Central Station that's due to arrive in your fair city by five-fifty, will you pick me up at the station and go for a bite to eat? I think you'll like my proposal. It's personal, not business."

Intrigued, I checked my watch. "Okay, I'll be in a black Volvo. See you at the station."

It would be great to see her again. Each evening, I closed the office after everyone else had gone for the day, and drove home to an empty house. Once there, time stretched endlessly. After a solitary dinner of whatever I could find in the refrigerator, I read, watched television, or answered emails. I tried not to eat or drink too much. Then, I cried myself to sleep, eventually.

The word "lonely" hardly covered my state of mind. It was bearable during the day, I had the office. My nights were a very different matter. I had even stopped writing in my journal. It was too painful.

My usual routine was doing nothing to raise my spirits or make me happier. A change—even for one day—would be very welcome.

Barbara Jefferies had been an English major like me, though she also earned a minor in Russian literature. Both Dale and Barbara were brilliant students, and both had received a full scholarship to Williams College in Massachusetts, where we had met each other. They were both farm children too, though her family's farm was far less prosperous than Dale's. As her parents were unable to help her financially, she worked in the college cafeteria at lunchtime and in a pharmacy in town three evenings a week. She had no money for a car, and walking back to campus alone after the store closed was not a safe option. Dale and I got into the habit of picking her up in his truck on the nights she worked. Eventually, she made friends with a co-worker with a car and began riding home with him. I gradually saw less of her, but I had never forgotten how her intelligence and sense of humor enlivened our study dates.

I heard from her regularly after graduation and, though as time passed we contacted each other less often, I still thought of her as a good friend. I was very curious to hear what she had in mind.

At five-forty, I left the office and drove the short distance to the station. I parked the car and waited. The train was late, as usual, but when it arrived and commuters began to emerge, I got out and stood on the platform. Within a few moments, most of the passengers were gone, but there was no one I recognized. At last, a tall, blonde woman dressed in a smart black wool coat stepped off the train. With surprise, I realized that this lovely woman was Barbara. The once-poor and often scruffy duckling had transformed herself into a gorgeous and expensive swan.

"Sharon," she exclaimed. "It's me!"

We embraced and stepped back to observe the changes the years had brought. I decided that time had treated her gently, and now I was very curious to hear why she had called me.

There was a small café with good Asian cuisine a few blocks from the station. It was early March, and though the evenings were still quite chilly, we decided to walk. A sharp wind was swirling around us, making us hurry to the café. The hostess seated us in a cozy booth, and we immediately ordered hot tea.

"Sharon, I think I may have told you some of this in our phone conversations. Forgive me, if I'm repeating myself." She took a sip of her tea. "So, after I finished school, I worked for several years as assistant executive director for a small environmental group whose headquarters was on the upper West Side. Do you remember me telling you that?"

"Yeah, actually, I do. That was after you earned an MBA from Pennsylvania University's Wharton School of Economics, on a full scholarship, not that I'm jealous or anything."

She laughed. "You're kidding, right? You have no reason to be jealous of me! So, because I really liked the organization, I stayed until about six years ago. By then, I'd begun to feel restless. I realized I'd learned as much as I could there, so one day, I finally listened to one of the recruiters who kept calling me. The company he was pushing was another non-profit, but this time it was a large healthcare company. They hired me, and I started in middle management, learning on the job how to be a successful fundraiser."

While she talked, I watched her in wonder. Where was the raw, country girl I remembered? Her hair had been a flyaway mass of sandy curls, her long, freckled face innocent even of lipstick. Her best feature had been her large, luminous hazel eyes. They flashed brilliant green when she was excited, deep marine blue when she was thoughtful, but dark, stormy gray, when she was angry. That had happened often during the first semesters we studied together, though she had learned to control her fiery temper by the time we graduated.

Looking at her today, I was finding it hard to recognize the gawky, sometimes rude and foul-mouthed girl I recalled in this lovely, sophisticated woman. Now, her hair was tamed and her attractive blonde pixie cut somehow softened her long face. Her makeup looked natural, and was artfully applied to enhance her beautiful eyes, subdue the freckles, and bring her other features into proportion. Her speech was refined as well. No rude words, so far, at least.

We gave our orders to the waiter, and Barbara continued talking as soon as he left us. "Sharon," she laughed ironically, "as my organization's Senior Vice President for Development, I've reached the pinnacle of achievement in non-profit fundraising. I have a corner office, two secretaries, a six-figure salary, and a condo apartment overlooking Central Park West. I saved every penny I made along the way to buy that apartment. Now all I need is someone to share it with."

I must have looked alarmed, because she immediately continued.

"Oh, I don't mean with you. I was thinking more along the lines of a man!" She chuckled softly, shaking her head sadly. "I don't have much free time, but I'm doing my best to meet Mr. Right. So far, I've met way too many Mr. Wrongs!"

Again, she reacted to my expression.

"It's okay, Sharon. I haven't been hopelessly hurt, though my ego has been thoroughly bruised."

That reminded us of a disastrous double date we'd once suffered through. I was with Dale, but she, well, the guy was just not what we had hoped he would be. We were laughing over that incident when, turning serious, Barbara paused for a moment to observe me directly. "Sharon, I saw the notices of Dale's death in the New York City papers. I was so sorry for your loss."

"I was in a pretty dense fog then, but I actually dimly remember receiving a card and flowers from you. I don't know if you were properly thanked, but I do want to thank you now."

Looking uncomfortable, she asked, "So, how are you doing, Sharon? I mean, how are you *really* doing?"

I knew what she meant.

"Well," I said, shrugging my shoulders and looking away, "I have good days and bad. I'm trying to keep busy, and of course, the firm helps with that. But as for a social life, I have none. A lot of the friends Dale and I had are history now. They were great as long as he was alive, but now… Most of them said all the right things at the time, but I haven't heard from any of them lately."

"Have you thought about seeing other men?"

I was shocked. "What? No! I can't imagine ever being ready for that."

"Well, the two reasons I thought of calling you were a) because of Dale's passing, and b) the fact that I'm without a man in my life at the moment.

I've got an interesting proposition for you. I'm just hoping you're ready to consider it seriously."

"You've got my full attention," I said. "What is it?"

Our waiter appeared with our food. Barbara waited until he had arranged everything to his satisfaction. Then he bowed and walked away.

"My boss recently discovered that a small group of our more affluent donors are avid birdwatchers. Several of them invited him along on an outing in Central Park last week, and he enjoyed himself so much that he's decided to take up birding as his new hobby. In the meantime, his wife's sister and her husband took a river cruise in Russia last summer and came home raving about the terrific time they had."

She shrugged, smiling ironically. "So, I guess it was inevitable: my boss has come up with the brilliant idea of sponsoring a river cruise in Russia later this year for a group of, counting spouses, about two-dozen of our birdwatching donors. He knows I learned about birds in my first job, and he's aware of my passion for Russian literature. Therefore, he insists I lead the tour. It's for two weeks at the end of August and the beginning of September. Our group will fly to Moscow and board a river cruiser. After sightseeing for a few days in Moscow, we'll motor up various waterways to St. Petersburg, where we'll spend another few days."

I opened my mouth to speak, but she held up her hand to stop me.

"Here's the deal: you'd be my guest for the entire cruise, including sleeping accommodations on the river cruiser, meals, tours, and transfers. You'd only have to pay for airfare, souvenirs, tips, and other incidentals. We may have to share a cabin, but I've been told we might be able to each get our own at no additional cost if the cruise isn't fully booked. What do you say?"

"Russia, wow! It's a great opportunity, but wait, Barbara, why me? Why aren't you taking someone who's closer to you? Not to mention, I'm not a birdwatcher!"

"I've tried," she said, laughing ruefully. "In fact, I've asked almost everyone I know—my mother, my sisters, my cousins, my close friends—and nobody is free for the entire two weeks." She sighed dramatically. "Basically, I'm grasping at straws here. I thought I was going to have to go alone, but then in a moment of inspiration, your name popped into my head. I remembered how much fun we had in college when we studied together. It's a long time ago now, but I think we'll find that we can still get along just fine."

I nodded in agreement.

"We're planning a couple of birding field trips outside of Moscow and St. Petersburg, and there will be a Russian ornithologist with us on board the ship, but you wouldn't have to get involved if you didn't want to. Most of the time we'll just be sightseeing. I don't think you'd be bored. The people in our group are recreational birdwatchers, not professionals or scientists. Since they're also big donors, I'll have my hands full trying to make everybody happy. As my guest, you wouldn't have anything to do except have fun. You could just enjoy yourself."

I must have looked sceptical, because she repeated, "Really, I'm serious. You could decide for yourself how much involvement you want in our activities, but you'd be welcome whatever you chose to do. Mostly, as I said, we'll just be sightseeing."

"Well," I said, frowning, "it sounds really interesting, but I'll need to talk with Ellen and the office staff before I decide. It's a long time to be away."

"Listen, why don't you talk to the people you need to discuss this with and get back to me? I'll need to get your answer in about two weeks. Okay?"

"Sure," I nodded. "Thanks, Barbara. This is exciting. I've always wanted to visit Russia, but with Dale gone…"

"I know. Just call me as soon as you can," she said.

After we finished our meal, I walked Barbara back to the station. A Manhattan-bound train was waiting on the track when we arrived, and we hurried onto the platform for one last hug before she boarded. The doors closed and it pulled out with a wheeze and the clatter of wheels. Despite the cold wind, I stood for a moment gazing down the tracks as the train's red tail lights faded from view.

CHAPTER 4

March to July 2004

THE NEXT day, I called Ellen at school. She was in class, of course, but she called me back later when she checked her messages. She sounded preoccupied at first, but when I mentioned my meeting with Barbara, her attention sharpened.

"Russia, huh? Didn't Daddy go there a bunch of times?"

"Yes, but I don't know if he did any sightseeing. He certainly never talked about it, or about the people he met. He always made a face when I asked questions, and said it was a dreary country."

"Oh, too bad, Mom. If you had some names, you could look up some of the people he worked with."

"Well, I could check our archives, but I think I'll pass. Wait a second, are you telling me you think I should go?"

"Of course you should go! This is just what you need. Plus, here's a chance to meet new people." She giggled. "Ughh! I'll bet they'll drag you off to see Lenin's tomb!"

"Uh oh, you're probably right. Thanks, darling. I'll think seriously about going. But I'll need to talk to the people in the office first. The trip's only for two weeks, but I don't feel comfortable leaving them for so long."

"They'll be fine. It'll be good for you and I'm sure they'll tell you to go."

In the office next day, I called a general staff meeting for late morning. When I came into the conference room, the buzz of conversation abruptly stopped. I noticed anxious looks being exchanged. It looked as though they were expecting to hear bad news.

I shook my head, smiling sheepishly. "I'm sorry. I should have realized you'd be worried I was going to announce layoffs or even the firm's closure. Nothing could be further from the truth. Instead, I need to ask your advice."

The atmosphere in the room suddenly changed, and everyone looked at me expectantly. After I told them about my invitation to go on the Russian river cruise, they enthusiastically urged me to accept.

Afterwards, Linda followed me back to my office and closed the door. She hugged me tightly and when she let me go, there were tears in her eyes.

"I don't think you have any idea how worried we've been. Not just for our jobs, but for you. We have been trying for weeks to figure out some way to get you out of the office for a change of scene. This trip is exactly what you need. Whatever I can do to help you get ready, I'll be glad to do it, and everyone else feels the same."

Later in the day, I met with our two architects, Charles Shaw and Richard Hanford. After we went over their current projects and discussed future proposals, I thanked them for their loyalty. They were perfectly competent to oversee the office while I was gone, and I told them so.

After they left my office, I sat for a while thinking about the staff's response. While I was relieved they were encouraging me to go, I no longer had an excuse to stay. Was I emotionally ready to make this journey without Dale? Was it too soon?

My head was beginning to ache. I decided to try to put these questions out of my mind for now.

The next morning, when I awoke, I realized I had made my decision. I would go. I might be lonely without Dale, but I needed to take this first, important step toward self-reliance.

When I called Barbara to tell her I had decided to go, she shrieked her approval. She faxed a copy of the itinerary to my office, and gave me contact information for the tour company handling the trip.

I began making lists of things I had to do before leaving: bills to pay, people to notify, and dozens of other details. According to the tour company, my first order of business—after I had sent them a deposit for my airfare—was to apply for a Russian entry visa. The paperwork would take several weeks and had to be submitted according to strict guidelines.

Fortunately, my passport was in order. Next, I checked my wardrobe for suitable clothes for city tours and river cruising. I would need a mix of smart and casual summer weight pants, skirts and tops. Also, I needed to bring a cocktail dress, rain gear, comfortable walking shoes, at least one cardigan or long-sleeved pullover sweater, and a light jacket for cool nights. I needed to go shopping.

The tour company sent a list of recommended guidebooks as well as books on Russian history and culture. At the bookstore, I chose one of each. I decided to devote at least an hour each week to learning more about Russia. I was glad both thick books contained many color photographs.

One evening, a few days after I decided to go on the river cruise, I took off my clothes and stood in front of the full-length three-way mirror in my dressing room. I would celebrate my forty-sixth birthday just before the start of the cruise. Though I was not completely over the hill, I was no longer a young woman. Swimming and tennis dates at the club with friends had helped me stay in shape over the years, but I had stopped going there regularly since Dale's death. There were too many memories and some of our former friends had avoided me. That had hurt, but looking at myself now, I could see I had hurt myself more.

My diet had deteriorated appallingly. Some nights, my dinner consisted only of ice cream, or something equally unhealthy. Now, I noticed, my muscles were growing slack and I was developing a midriff bulge. My thick, shoulder length, dark-brown hair, badly needed shaping. Thankfully, though I peered closely, there was, as yet, no sign of gray. My heart-shaped face had gained a few new lines, especially around my blue-green eyes and the mouth Dale had always called "kissable," and my complexion looked dull and dry. It was time to take myself in hand.

Next day, I called my hair stylist in New York City to schedule a shaping. I also made an appointment for a manicure, pedicure, facial, and spa massage. I asked Linda whether there was a good gym in our town. She told me there was a co-ed gym for serious body-builders, but she and her daughter went to one for women only. She offered to take me there that evening after work.

I left the office on time for once, and followed Linda to the gym. Inside, everything was brightly lit and decorated in vibrant shades of pink, from pale to hot. The friendly young woman behind the desk introduced me to the personal trainer, who gave me a tour of the facility.

After my tour, I decided to join. There were about four and a half months before I was due to leave for Russia. If I made a real commitment to work out with the trainer three times a week, I could get into reasonable shape before the trip began.

I discussed my diet with the staff nutritionist. She suggested some guidelines for better nutrition, and together we made a shopping list for the grocery store. By the time I was ready to leave, Linda, *sans* daughter tonight, was just finishing her workout. I thanked her and told her I would see her in the morning.

For the first time in what seemed like ages, I felt energized. I realized I had not focused on my own needs for a very long time. It felt good.

≪≫

Over the next several weeks, I worked with renewed enthusiasm. Everyone in the office seemed to notice my better spirits. The entire atmosphere felt lighter.

I closed the office by six o'clock on the nights I went to the gym. After working out with the trainer, showering, and changing into clean clothes, I shopped for fresh fruits and vegetables at the organic market next door. Then, I hurried home to prepare my solitary, but no longer quite so lonely, dinner. I put my favorite music in the CD player, and sometimes, I even danced around the kitchen to the beat.

Ellen, just finishing her junior year at Williams, landed a summer job at a distinguished Manhattan architectural firm. Because her roommate, Suzi, would be interning with a public relations firm located only a few doors up the street from Ellen's office building, they decided to share a sublet studio apartment for the summer. Ellen came home most weekends, and together we went for long walks or to see a movie. Often, Ellen brought Suzi with her. They were rarely apart for very long.

I was happy they were so close. They were full of plans to go hiking, fishing, skiing, and double-dating, but their friendship was forged in tragedy as well as fun. While Suzi had helped Ellen survive her father's sudden death, Ellen had traveled to Texas with Suzi to visit her grandmother—battling colon cancer—twice, so far.

As time passed and the date of my departure approached, I grew more and more excited. My gym visits were beginning to pay off, and I found that I enjoyed shopping for the pretty and practical clothing I needed for the trip. I donated Dale's black suitcases to a local thrift shop, and replaced them with a three-piece set in a cheerful yellow and orange print. They were brighter than I normally would have chosen, but they would be easy to spot on a busy airport carousel.

I hired a house sitter through an agency, and asked her to come a few days before I was due to leave. I wanted to familiarize her with the house, and show her how to set and disarm the alarm system.

My airline and cruise tickets arrived along with massive amounts of tour materials. Everything was spelled out in minute detail, but I refused to be overwhelmed by the sheer volume of information. I learned the name of our ship—the *River Sprite*—though I had no idea how to pronounce the name in Russian.

CHAPTER 5

August 2004

DURING THE second week in August, I suddenly realized my Russian entry visa had not yet arrived. I made a panicked call to the tour company, but they assured me that this was not unusual. They would investigate. I hung up and tried to focus on last minute details in the office. Finally, I gave up and went home, skipping my usual workout with the trainer at the gym. After a solitary dinner and a boring evening in front of the television, I decided to go to bed.

I opened the windows in the bedroom. After the heat of the day, a fresh breeze fluttered the curtains, and outside, crickets chirped loudly. High clouds scudded across the face of the full moon, its pale light playing over the thin blanket at the foot of my bed. The night was so beautiful. Suddenly, loneliness gripped me, and grief overwhelmed me. It had been a long time since I had cried for Dale with so much anguish. I finally fell asleep with tears still on my cheeks.

I was dreaming. I knew I was, but it was all so real...

1976-78

It was a miracle that Dale and I met at all. Was it fate? Maybe, though I have never really believed in fate, or chance, or coincidence. But looking back on it, I do believe it must have been all those things. Serendipity, certainly.

On our first day of classes at Williams College, Dale and I were assigned to the same Freshman Biology section, and happened to sit next to each other in the big, amphitheater-like lecture hall. I took no particular notice of him then, though he told me later that he had definitely noticed me.

At our first Biology lab session, we met again. This time, we each had been assigned a specific seat at the stone tables that furnished the room. As it turned out, Dale's seat was directly across from mine.

The professor read our names aloud, and Dale looked closely at me when I responded, his head slightly tilted and a wide grin on his face. I smiled briefly back at him and returned my attention to the blackboard where a lab assistant had chalked our first assignment. I tried to appear nonchalant, but my heart was beating rapidly. Beneath a thatch of long, thick, curly, dark red hair, intense green eyes sparkled with humor and intelligence. Light freckles splashed across his straight nose, and his smile radiated friendliness. I thought he was the most attractive boy I had ever seen.

After class, I gathered my books and made my way to the door. Outside, in the hallway, he was waiting for me. He was over six feet tall, I noticed, and nicely built.

"Sharon," he said. "That's my mom's name, too. Can I give you a lift to the Student Union? My name's Dale, Dale Grant."

Over the next few weeks, we saw each other in class and, often, in the Student Union. A group of our classmates met there informally each afternoon. We often joined them when our classes were over for the day, and spent hours discussing the new information and ways of thinking we were being exposed to. We were very young and earnest, though not always so serious. There was quite a bit of laughter and rowdiness.

I turned down his offer of a ride to the Student Union on the day we met, but after several weeks, I began to accept rides in his battered pickup truck. Dale was enormously proud of it. Raised on an upstate New York dairy farm, he earned the money to buy it by pumping gas during his high school summer vacations and doing odd jobs on the weekends through the rest of the year, though his farm chores had to be completed first. Its black paint was scratched and worn, and its fenders were slightly dented, but he kept it running as smoothly as an expensive sports car.

At the beginning, Dale and I studied our biology lessons together as part of a small group of our classmates, but we soon began meeting in the library most evenings by ourselves. After a few hours in adjoining carrels, he walked me back to my dorm. We walked slowly, laughing and talking flirtatiously until just before the eleven o'clock curfew when I had to go inside.

Gradually, we began spending more and more time together. We discovered our August birthdays were only five days apart. The more we talked, the more we found we had in common.

Among the many things I admired about Dale was his talent as a sketch artist. He carried a charcoal pencil and sketchpad with him wherever he went, and during our Student Union discussions, drew caricatures of our friends and professors. They were funny, never malicious, and much admired. He gave them away freely. Most of us felt it was an honor to receive one.

Dale had entered college planning to study physics, but one day early in our first semester, an art professor saw him sketching a building on the campus and stopped to critique the drawing. Their conversation convinced Dale to drop a physics class and substitute an entry-level course in architecture. Thanks to the art professor, Dale found his true vocation. For him, architecture blended art and science in a deeply satisfying way.

Before the end of the term, he was accepted into Williams's demanding art history and practice program, which allowed him to study the history of architecture while learning design techniques and procedures. Though he was a whole semester behind, his professors worked with him and he quickly caught up.

Dale's scholarship paid for tuition, books, and room and board, but personal spending money would have to come either from his parents or a job. He wanted to ease the financial burden on his family, so for him, there was no choice. Despite his difficult schedule, he made time to work several hours a week in a clothing store in town, unloading cartons and stocking shelves.

I decided to major in English literature, and though I was challenged by the volume of work required, I enjoyed most of the readings we explored. I was part of a group of people I liked and admired, and Dale and I were together as often as our schedules permitted.

Over the next two years, I took my time with Dale. I refused to let him get too close, though it was obvious that he wanted badly to get closer. Often, he would take my hand or throw his arm casually around my shoulders. I felt a physical tug whenever he touched me, but I knew I needed to go slowly.

I had a pressing reason to do that, and I was extremely reluctant to share it until I felt I needed to do so. I found that need at the end of the Columbus Day weekend during our junior year at Williams.

As usual, after my last class on Friday afternoon, I went to the Student Union to meet Dale. That afternoon, he and I had planned to eat an early supper together before he left to drive to his home in upstate New York for the three-day holiday.

He had been fighting a nasty head cold for several days, but I could see he was much worse. His forehead was burning hot, and he was shivering. There was no way he could drive all the way home, he was too ill.

I had to decide what to do. His roommate had already gone away for the weekend, and Dale was too sick to be left alone. He was living in a male only dorm, and I would not be allowed in his room to take care of him. Taking him to my room was also out of the question, even if it had been allowed, since my roommate was planning to stay there all weekend.

Over Dale's protests, I called his parents. They promised to meet us halfway if I could drive Dale's truck. I agreed to try driving it around the campus, and if I thought I could make the trip, I would call them back and arrange a meeting place.

I had learned to drive a car with a manual transmission while visiting a friend's chateau in France, and had even driven on the left side of the road in England. I now had a New York State driver's license, but no car. I had never attempted to drive a truck, but as it turned out, Dale's was easier to handle than I had feared.

I called Mr. and Mrs. Grant, and they suggested we meet at a diner in Little Falls, New York, a small town a few miles east of Utica. I helped Dale climb into the passenger seat, where he promptly fell asleep. On the way out of town, I stopped at a gas station to fill the tank and get a road map. I found Little Falls on the map, and restarted the truck.

Dale's body slumped against mine, and with the motion of the vehicle, his head fell on my shoulder. Carefully, hoping not to wake him, I drove through the late afternoon dusk into early evening darkness.

Eventually, we approached Little Falls. I found the diner easily and as I pulled into the parking lot, a middle-aged couple left the restaurant and hurried toward the truck.

Sharon Grant, Dale's mother, was just as Dale had described her: small and gray-haired with a sturdy body and a down-to-earth manner. She opened my door to help me out—I was shaking with relief and fatigue—and took me directly into her arms.

"Sharon," she said, "we've heard quite a bit about you. I can't thank you enough for making this trip. Dale's pretty stubborn. I'm sure he tried to talk you out of it."

"Oh, Mrs. Grant," I shook my head. "I don't know what you've heard about me, but Dale was too sick to argue very much. He fell asleep before we even left the campus, and he stayed asleep until just now, when I turned off the engine."

Meanwhile, Mr. Grant had opened the passenger door and helped Dale, who was burning with fever and half delirious, out of the truck.

"Honey," Mr. Grant called softly, "Dale's in a bad way. Let's get him into our car and get him home."

As Dale's mother went around the truck to his side, Mr. Grant added his thanks to his wife's.

"Now you mustn't think of driving back to the campus tonight," he said. "You come home and spend the night with us. We'll talk in the morning. Don't worry about the truck. We'll see about picking it up sometime tomorrow."

"Are you sure you have room for me? I don't want to put you to any trouble."

"Trouble? You're no trouble!" With Dale safely in the backseat, Mrs. Grant came back, took my arm, and began walking me toward their car. "You just come home with us. We'll put you in the guest room where you can be comfortable, and we'll have that talk in the morning."

I was too tired and anxious to argue. Dale was taking up most of the backseat, but I was able to squeeze in next to him.

Mrs. Grant had come prepared. She put a cold compress on Dale's head—ice from the diner wrapped in one of her kitchen towels—and tied it in place. She gave him aspirin and made him take the tablets with warm sweetened tea. He sighed, and fell back asleep, his head again on my shoulder.

I devoured the hamburger and fries the Grants had ordered for me from the diner's menu, and a few hours later, we turned off the main road onto a long gravel drive leading to a large white farmhouse. Lights were shining from the windows, and the house seemed to glow in the darkness.

Mr. Grant half carried Dale upstairs to his room while Mrs. Grant led me to their cozy guest room, which contained a double bed covered with a colorful quilt.

There was a bathroom across the hall.

"Most everything you'll need is in there, but I think you could use these." Mrs. Grant handed me one of her nightgowns and a toothbrush still in its wrapper.

"Thanks so much, Mrs. Grant. I really appreciate this."

"It's nothing. Have a good night's sleep and we'll see you in the morning. Good night, dear."

Minutes later, I was ready to slip into the soft bed. I fell asleep almost immediately.

Sunlight streaming through the guest room windows the next morning woke me to the tantalizing aroma of coffee, scrambled eggs, bacon, and freshly baked homemade biscuits. I was famished.

I washed my face, put yesterday's clothes back on and, following my nose, arrived at the kitchen table just as Mr. Grant was about to sit down. He gallantly pulled out a chair for me.

"Now, both of you just sit down and eat while this food is hot," Mrs. Grant said. She handed each of us a full plate and joined us at the table with a plate for herself. Everything was delicious. It was all I could do to keep from wolfing it down.

I had cleaned my plate and was buttering a second biscuit when Mr. Grant asked, "Ready for some more coffee?"

I nodded enthusiastically, and Mrs. Grant jumped up to pour it for us.

Mr. Grant stirred milk and sugar into his cup. "Doc Hardy, our family doctor, came by early this morning on his way to the hospital. He says Dale has an ear infection, something he's never had before. Doc gave him some medicine and left a prescription for more. He thinks Dale's fever and infection will be gone after a few days on the medicine, and then he can go back to school."

Mrs. Grant sat down again and sipped her coffee. They looked at each other and then Mr. Grant said, "Now, Mrs. Grant and I talked it over and we want you to stay for the entire weekend. Do either of you have classes on Tuesday?"

I shook my head.

"Good," he said. "Dale should be on the mend by then, and you can take your time driving back."

I opened my mouth to protest, but Mrs. Grant put her hand on mine and said, "Honey, we insist. It'll give us a chance to get to know you a little, and I'm sure you could use some rest yourself. I know how it is when you're away at school. You probably don't eat right or get enough sleep. We don't want you getting sick, too."

I relaxed slightly, realizing suddenly how at home I felt here and how grateful I was for their generous hospitality. "Thank you. I'd like to stay."

Mrs. Grant was soon up again bustling about the kitchen, scraping plates and stacking them in the sink, ready to be washed. I got up to help and she showed me where she kept the kitchen towels, talking and laughing with Mr. Grant and me all the while.

As I dried the last dish, Dale's two older brothers, Mike, Jr. and Hank, appeared. They had finished their chores and now they wanted to meet me before they drove away to pick up Dale's truck in Little Falls, and fill his prescription.

The brothers, both in their thirties, were red-haired and looked very much like their dad, although Mr. Grant's hair had receded and was turning gray. All three were tall, broad shouldered, and good looking like Dale, but without Dale's... I searched my mind for the right words to describe him. The only ones that seemed to fit were spirit, and dash.

Mike, Jr. and Hank looked at each other and then grinned at me. "Now we know what we have to do to get a chance to drive Dale's truck. Get him sick and get his girlfriend to drive him halfway home," Hank teased.

"You know, until now, no one has ever been allowed to drive it but Dale himself," Mike, Jr. added. Everyone laughed except me. My cheeks had begun to burn, a sure sign my face was turning red.

"I'm not Dale's girlfriend. We're just good friends."

There was more laughter, while I continued to blush in silence.

"Oh, you boys!" Mrs. Grant chuckled, glancing at me with sympathy. "Go on now, get out of here and leave Sharon alone!"

After the brothers left, Mrs. Grant took me upstairs to Dale's room to see how he was doing today. He was sleeping easily, and his head was slightly cooler.

When we came downstairs again, Mr. Grant said, "How about a tour of the farm? Have you ever visited a dairy farm before?"

I shook my head. "I've never been on any kind of farm before, but yes, thanks. I'd love a tour."

Though it was primarily a dairy operation, there were a few goats and pigs, a coop to house a rooster and a dozen or so chickens, a large kitchen garden full of late season vegetables and flowers, and a small orchard. Acres of neatly fenced pastureland, dotted with cows, stretched in every direction.

The dairy barn was huge and immaculate. In fact, every area of the farm I saw, including the farmhouse, was extremely neat and well kept. I was impressed. I had driven through upstate New York before and remembered few farms looking as prosperous as this one.

When we arrived back at the farmhouse, Mrs. Grant said, "You'll need some clean clothes for the next few days. Here, try these on for size."

I took the small pile of clothes gratefully.

"Go on now. Go wash up and try on these things. I'll be doing our laundry on Monday, so you'll have your own clean clothes again on Tuesday."

"Thank you, Mrs. Grant." I knew I would feel much better after showering.

Dale's old jeans fit reasonably well if I rolled up the pant legs. Mrs. Grant had loaned me some of her own tops, another of her nightgowns, and a sweater of Dale's. Everything was clean and fresh, scented with a hint of lavender.

When I reappeared downstairs still fluffing my long hair, Mrs. Grant invited me to sit at the big kitchen table and drink a cup of tea with her. Gently, she began to question me about my family background and my plans for the future. Was I enjoying my studies at Williams? What were my impressions of Dale?

I was nervous at first, knowing how little I wanted to divulge. Gradually, I relaxed. I could tell she was questioning me because she loved Dale and wanted to protect him. Though I was still claiming we were "just friends," I was aware that our mutual affection was changing into something much deeper.

Nevertheless, I was not ready to talk about my growing feelings for Dale or my family's financial or social status. I hated the thought of lying to Dale or to his parents, even by omission, but I was afraid. Now that I had seen Dale's home and met his family, there was no denying the enormous difference in our backgrounds.

In the end, I put her off with half-truths, and turned the conversation as quickly as I could.

"Tell me about Dale and your family. Have you always lived here on this farm?"

She smiled broadly. "I was born here, and Mike was raised on a farm nearby. We were school friends as kids, and as we grew up, we fell in love. My parents died soon after we were married and, since I was an only child, I inherited this farm."

"What happened to Mr. Grant's parents' farm, not that it's any of my business?"

Mrs. Grant shook her head and patted my hand.

"No problem. Mike has several brothers and sisters, and when their parents got too old to work the farm, the kids sold it and used the money to buy their parents a home in town. Later, they *moved them into a nursing facility. They're both gone now, of course."*

"So, you raised Dale and his brothers here on this farm?"

"That's right. Now, of course, Mike, Jr. and Hank are married with families of their own. They both have houses in town, but the boys help their dad work this farm. You know, Dale's more than a dozen years younger than Hank and almost seventeen years younger than Mike, Jr. So, he was almost like an only child."

"Tell me about Dale. Was he always a good student?"

She smiled proudly.

"Oh, yes. Hank and Mike, Jr. did well in school, but Dale was something else. He was so bright, he scared us, and by the time he graduated from our big central high school, he was kind of like a superstar. He was captain of the varsity football and basketball teams and co-captain of the track team. In his senior year he was elected student body president and homecoming king, and was president of his award-winning debate team. He gave the valedictory speech at graduation, and won a full scholarship to Williams College, along with several other academic and sports awards.

"Wow. I had no idea. He hasn't told me any of that."

"We didn't cut him any slack either. He achieved all that while completing all his farm chores before and after school. And during the summers, he worked at odd jobs and at the gas station."

"He did tell me about that. That's how he was able to buy his truck."

"That's right." She sighed, and a look of regret crossed her face as she stared down at her folded hands. She looked up at me again. *"Mike and I realize he won't be coming back to work this farm. He'll be doing something else. We're sad about that, but we know that whatever he does in the future, he'll make us proud."*

⚮

The weekend flew by. I helped Mrs. Grant as much as she would let me, setting the table, drying the dishes, and chopping vegetables for dinner. Outside, she showed me how to feed the chickens and collect eggs. In her garden, I picked the last few green tomatoes. Together we wrapped each one in newsprint and stored them in the cellar to ripen over the next several weeks.

Evenings were quiet, yet far from boring. Mrs. Grant was knitting a sweater for her youngest granddaughter, but when Mr. Grant finished reading the local newspaper, she put away her work and cleared the table for board games. Music from the stereo played softly in the background while we competed fiercely at Scrabble and Monopoly.

Dale refused to stay in bed on Sunday. He insisted on eating his meals at the kitchen table with us and spent the rest of the day reclining on a sofa in the family room, reading and watching television. By Monday, he was outside doing chores with his brothers. After lunch, he took me on a walk through the fields and demonstrated— comically—how to milk a goat.

Later, we sat across from each other on a wooden glider near the kitchen garden.

"I have something to show you." Shyly, as the glider swayed to and fro, he took a folded paper from his wallet and handed it to me.

"Oh, Dale." It was a portrait he had drawn of me, and from the clothes I was wearing, apparently done soon after we met. I stared at my likeness in wonder. "You've flattered me. I'm not nearly that nice looking!"

"No, that's exactly how I see you. You are beautiful." He looked deeply into my eyes. We held hands on our way back to the farmhouse.

Early Tuesday morning, Dale declared himself fit to drive us back to Williams. Leaving the farmhouse after expressing my thanks to Mr. and Mrs. Grant for their hospitality, tears filled my eyes. I had loved every moment of my visit.

We drove away with a large picnic basket on the front seat between us, filled with Mrs. Grant's delicious cold roast chicken and homemade potato salad, her special dill pickles, sweet and juicy apples from the orchard, and slices of her mouthwatering three-layer chocolate cake. There were jugs of sweetened tea and well water, and a tin of cinnamon sugar cookies for a late afternoon snack.

At noon, we reached Little Falls. A few miles later, Dale turned into a roadside rest area so we could eat lunch.

The picnic tables were deserted, the small grassy area inhabited only by two chattering squirrels. They scampered away as we carried the heavy picnic basket to a table beneath a tall sycamore tree. Most of its leaves had fallen, and the fitful sun shining through the bare branches warmed our shoulders as we sat side by side at the table.

Before I could open the picnic basket, Dale turned to me and pulled me against his chest. I stiffened and began to try to push him away. He only held me tighter.

"Sharon," he began, pausing briefly to kiss the top of my head, "I can't believe how you took charge and brought me home. I'm very grateful. Where did you learn to drive a truck?"

I struggled to draw breath to answer, my nose mashed against his shoulder.

"I'd never driven a truck before, but I needed to get you home, and..."

He held me away and looked down into my eyes.

"You are really something. What would I do without you?" He shook his head. "I hope I never find out. You know, I'm in love with you, Sharon."

His brilliant green eyes were focused on my mouth.

"Please, Sharon..."

Before I could answer, his lips closed on mine. Heart pounding, my arms twined around his neck. I clung to him with all my strength, my defenses shattered. I wanted his kiss to go on forever.

"Y-Yes, I do know," I stammered, as we finally pulled apart.

I paused a moment to gather my scattered thoughts, the happy excitement of a moment ago turning to fear.

"But, there are things you don't know about me, and they could change the way you feel about me."

"Nothing you could possibly tell me could make me change how I feel about you!"

He spoke emphatically, but there was a note of doubt in his voice.

"Dale, please, you have to listen! We can't go on together until you do."

I had kept my financial and social background hidden from everyone I met at school. It was one of the benefits of attending a small out-of-state college like Williams. No one seemed to recognize my name, or tried to take advantage of me.

I had been dreading this conversation, but now was the time to tell the truth. I began at the beginning.

"Dale, my father was born into a wealthy New York family involved for several generations in banking and politics. He wasn't interested in a banking career, or any other occupation, either in business or the arts. He was never given any real responsibilities, and almost never took the time to visit the large, comfortable office his family's bank provided for him. As long as the bank's trustees sent his generous monthly allowance on time, he was happy to spend it without any thought at all about where it came from. Luckily, there were other relatives to run things and keep the bank's investments and other operations growing and making money.

"My mother was from an old Southern family whose fortunes had been declining since the Civil War. They were slowly sinking into what could be *called 'genteel poverty,' and by the time she met my father, they had almost run out of ways to hold off their inevitable bankruptcy. Mama was a small, pretty blonde who saw no reason to pursue higher education, even if her family could have afforded it, since she had no ambition to be anything but a rich man's wife. Unfortunately for me, she also had no inclination toward motherhood."*

Dale grunted in surprise at that, but said nothing. He nodded his head for me to continue.

"It probably came as a very unpleasant surprise when Mama discovered she was expecting me. After a difficult pregnancy, I was born in a private hospital in Manhattan.

"My parents hired a nurse named Marina to take care of me during my baby- and childhood. Knowing that she could return to her former life as soon as she recovered, Mama handed me over to Marina before we left the hospital."

"Was this Marina good to you?"

I smiled, remembering. "Oh, yes! When I was old enough to understand, Marina told me she'd fallen in love with me the moment she first held me in her arms and I stopped bawling. The feeling was completely mutual. I loved her with all my heart. I called her Mimi, which was, in fact, my first word."

"Ah, that's better." For the first time since I began, he smiled back at me.

"So, our little household consisted of me, Mimi, our cook and housekeeper Trudy, and her husband Bill, who served as our butler, chauffeur, and handyman.

"I hardly ever saw my parents. Travel was the one passion they shared and they spent most of their time vacationing in exotic locations with their friends. Now and then, they'd come home for a little while to shower me with presents, but then they'd fly off again before I had time to get used to them."

I paused for a minute to take a deep breath. Talking about my family was no fun.

"Anyway, as long as my parents were traveling, life went smoothly in our little household. Trudy and Bill were kind and gentle with me. I followed Trudy around as she dusted and vacuumed the apartment and she called me her 'little helper,' though I'm sure I got in her way much more often than I helped her. Bill drove Mimi and me to the playground in Central Park, on shopping trips, and to my favorite place—the Bronx Zoo. He always had a nod, a wink, and a special smile, just for me.

"Mimi was patient, loving, and wise. She had an unlimited supply of hugs, kisses, and smiles for me, but she was never shy about telling me 'No!' when I needed to hear it." I stopped for a moment, smiling as I remembered. *"And then, in terms I could understand, she'd explain why she'd said no.*

"I attended a private kindergarten and elementary school, took lessons on our antique grand piano, and learned the basics of ballet from a stern former ballerina who, before she defected to the United States, had danced with a famous Russian ballet company.

"I always read above my grade level, but I really didn't care very much about school. My grades were only so-so. Although I practiced when I was reminded to, I had no real talent for the piano, and because I was tall for my age and clumsy, my ballet teacher knew I would never be a dancer." I shrugged. *"But, the lessons continued.*

"Then, when I was twelve, my parents announced they were going to send me to an English boarding school for girls. I was shocked and tried to refuse to go, but my tears and anger had absolutely no effect on them."

"Wait. You went to an English boarding school?"

"Yeah. Before I left, Mimi had a long talk with me. She said almost all of the people I had met so far were of my own economic and social background. As I grew older, she warned, I would meet some who were less fortunate. While few of those individuals would try to take advantage of my wealth and position, there were some who would. She cautioned me to guard my heart against people who would befriend me because of what they thought I could do for them. She suggested that I not make instant friends, but wait, watch, and trust my instincts while assessing people."

"That was good advice. I hope she wasn't envisioning someone like me."

"She would have been very pleased with you!"
He took my hand, and held it in both of his.
"Let me continue. I'm almost done."
"Okay." But he kept hold of my hand.

"At school in England, I was lonely at first. I began to study harder, and my grades improved. Gradually, keeping Mimi's advice in mind, I made a few good friends, and for the first time, I began to play organized sports. I loved soccer and doubles tennis."

"Were you any good at them?"

"Better at soccer than tennis, but I had a great time playing both."

"I'm sorry, I wasn't supposed to interrupt."

"That's okay. Here it gets sad."

"Sad?"

I nodded. "When I came home from England at the end of my first term at school, I discovered my parents had replaced Mimi, Trudy, and Bill with a cold, silent butler. I cried bitterly and pleaded with Father to rehire them, but he claimed to have no idea where they were or how they could be contacted. When I was older, I tried to find them on my own through domestic agencies, police and hospital records, and any other way I could think of, but I've had no luck. I finally decided that they preferred—or maybe, were warned—not to be found. I couldn't believe they'd deliberately turned their backs on me, though."

Dale shook his head. "Wow, it's no wonder you feel the way you do about your parents."

"Sometimes, when they were planning to be in their penthouse apartment, they ordered me to travel home for school holidays. I very much preferred spending them in England or France with my friends' families, since my parents and I were essentially strangers. I was ill at ease

*around them and, I'm afraid, I behaved pretty
badly. I was resentful, and answered rudely when
they asked a rare question about school, teachers,
friends, and clothes. I'm ashamed to say it never
crossed my mind to ask them about their lives.
That was selfish and, maybe, a missed
opportunity."*

*"Sounds to me like you treated them they way
they deserved."*

*"Thanks for trying to stick up for me, but if I'd
tried harder, maybe we could have repaired some
of the damage." I shrugged.*

*"Well, anyway, when it was time to decide
which college I was going to attend, I refused to
consider Bryn Mawr, or Wellesley, or Smith as my
parents wanted. Instead, I argued for a large
public university, an idea they found horrifying.
We were at an impasse for weeks, but eventually
we compromised on Williams College. It wasn't
an Ivy League, or rather, a Seven Sisters school,
but they liked the fact it was a small, but
competitive, liberal arts college. They also liked
its location in Massachusetts' beautiful Berkshire
Mountains. They hoped I would meet the 'right
people' there."*

*"Well, I can guess how they'd feel about me.
I'm definitely not the 'right' sort of person."*

*"Stop it! You're definitely the 'right' sort of
person for me." He squeezed my hand.*

*"I could hardly wait to start my new life as a
college freshman. New doors would be opening,
and soon I'd be a grownup. I'd finally be able to
make my own decisions about my future. I was*

sure that things were about to change for the better.

"Father offered to buy me an expensive sportscar to drive around the campus, but I turned him down. I thought a car like that would send the wrong message. He also wanted me to fly home between terms, but I refused that too. I take the train home instead, but you already knew that.

"So, as you can see, our backgrounds are very different, and maybe now you can understand why I never told you much about my childhood. I'm sorry. I never wanted to keep all this from you, but I was worried."

I closed my eyes. I wanted to avoid looking directly at him. I hoped he'd be fair, but a small part of me was afraid I might see anger or disgust at my deceitfulness in his eyes or, much worse, greed. Finally, I stole a glance at him.

He was gazing out over the fields across the road. He sat motionless for several long moments while I waited, alternately hopeful and hopeless, for him to respond.

Finally, he turned to me again, shaking his head.

"Your family's money means nothing to me, though I understand why you were worried that it might. I have no intention of living on your parents' money. Not ever. I plan to be very successful one day, though it'll probably take a while until I've achieved my goals."

He took a deep breath, his dazzling green eyes probing mine. "I have only one question: do you love me enough to marry me, even though we'll *have to struggle financially at first?" He watched my face closely, waiting for my answer.*

I closed my eyes again and bid Mimi a silent goodbye in my heart. Now was the time to act on what it was telling me to do. A future without Dale was unimaginable. Opening my eyes and gazing into his, I saw only love.

"Yes, Dale. With all my heart."

His strong arms encircled me. He kissed my forehead, my eyelids, and both cheeks before repossessing my mouth. If his first kiss, before I began my story, left me dizzy, this one left both of us breathless with desire.

It was a long time before we moved apart again. We ate his mother's lovely food without really tasting it. We were too busy planning our future together.

Before we left the picnic area, I promised to marry Dale as soon as we graduated. In lieu of a diamond, he gave me his high school class ring to wear on a chain around my neck. One last kiss and we climbed back into the truck.

As he put it in gear, he assured me that we would overcome our parents' objections. We knew there would be many objections to overcome.

$$\approx$$

August, 2004

When I awakened the next morning, my mood had lifted. Dreaming about Dale, his family, and that pivotal weekend, seemed like a gift. I chose to believe he was giving his stamp of approval on my trip to Russia. I drove to the office singing cheerfully along with the radio.

Soon, the tour company representative called. My missing Russian visa had been shipped yesterday via an overnight carrier.

I found the package on my doorstep when I finally got home from the office and the gym. With relief, I opened it and tucked the document into my passport. Now I was ready to go.

CHAPTER 6

Thursday, August 26
Day 1

THE DAY of our flight, I awoke before dawn and took my coffee onto the terrace to watch the sunrise. This had been one of the small joys of my married life. During the warm months, when he was home, Dale and I would often sit here in silence, sipping our coffee, waiting for the sun to appear. Once it grew lighter, we would turn to each other and begin to talk over our plans for the day. Whatever the conversation, my husband's hand caressed mine.

He often told me how much he loved me, but the little things—the touch of his hand, the casual arm around my shoulders, the smile he reserved just for me—made me feel cherished. Might he have strayed during his long trips away from home? I never asked. I knew, in my heart of hearts, that he loved me deeply, just as I loved him.

I gave myself a mental shake. It was time to return to the present.

Tomorrow afternoon, their time, I would arrive in Russia. How amazing. It really was a small world after all.

I sat a little longer, taking pleasure in the beautiful morning. The sun glinted off the surface of the pond, and birdsong competed with the brook's splashing water. During one of our recent telephone conversations, Barbara told me that birds were beginning to fly south for the winter. She thought I would probably notice more of them than usual stopping by to rest in the woods and to drink and bathe in my pond. She was right.

Inside again, I called Ellen one last time.

"Hi, darling. Today's the day. I just wanted to tell you how much I love you. You'll be all right?"

"Mom, of course. Now, don't worry about anything. Just have a great time. I can't wait to hear all about it. And, Mom, I love you too." She hung up before I could reply. No sentiment today. No tears.

The tour company had instructed us to arrive at the airport at least two hours before takeoff. I needed to leave at noon if I was going to make the drive to New York City's JFK Airport in time. At ten o'clock, the house sitter arrived. She wished me luck and disappeared into the guest suite on the lower level where she would be staying while I was gone.

At the airport, I found a spot in the long-term parking lot. Lifting my bags from the trunk, I saw the terminal shuttle approaching. The driver loaded my gear into the bus and I climbed aboard.

This was the first time I had traveled by air in the almost two years since Dale's death. I had flown alone several times during our marriage, meeting Dale in some exotic location for a few days of rest and relaxation. I had treasured the luxury of stepping off a plane and feeling his arms sweep me into a welcoming embrace. Meeting him like that had done wonders for our marriage, and helped keep me from feeling too lonely for him while he was overseeing big projects over long periods of time.

As we approached the terminal, I came out of my trance and started to gather my belongings. I had put one of my fat Russian guidebooks and a paperback mystery in my tote to read on the plane.

Inside the crowded terminal, I joined a check-in line snaking in slow motion across the floor. Eventually, I made it through security and headed for the gate. I found two seats together and waited for Barbara. Within minutes, she arrived, large coffee in hand. Excitedly, we hugged each other. Then, sitting down, she pulled today's *Wall Street Journal* out of her tote, and began to read.

At last, our plane was called. Barbara and I grinned at each other as we rose and began to gather our belongings. Our adventure was about to begin.

"Sharon, I'm going to put on my name badge now. There may be some of our group on this flight, and if there are, I'm sure they'll want me to start my official tour leader duties as soon as they see me."

"Well, if you don't mind, I won't put mine on until I have to."

"Fine with me."

For the next two weeks, we were all supposed to wear our tags every day, both on board our ship, and on land during the sightseeing excursions the tour company organized for us. Since, as Barbara had said, I had nothing to do but be a tourist, I could do as I pleased for now.

When our plane rose into the sky, the sun was shining brightly, but very soon we flew into dusk, followed swiftly by the dark of evening.

CHAPTER 7

Friday, August 27
Day 2

WE BOTH dozed as we flew over the Atlantic and Western Europe, waking as we touched down at the Frankfurt airport for a two-hour layover and a change of planes. Dawn was breaking. Our short night was over.

In the terminal, we grabbed a light breakfast and coffee in the food court, and wandered through the Duty Free shops. They displayed tempting jewelry, smart gadgets, and brand name perfumes, among others, but we agreed it would be best not to buy any souvenirs or gifts at this point.

Soon we boarded a new plane for the second leg of our long journey. Barbara dozed, but I was too excited to sleep.

In the Moscow airport, we found our luggage and followed other passengers down a long, narrow, ramp-like corridor into a large ground floor waiting area where we would be processed through Customs. We pulled out our passports, entry visas, and customs forms and joined one of the two long lines of people waiting to see an agent.

Unlike most of the other airports I had seen, granted, not that many, this one was dark and drab. There was no attempt at cheerful decorations, not even colorful posters or advertisements. The signs were only in one language: Russian, and there seemed to be no one to welcome us, answer questions, or give us directions. Worse, there was very little ventilation in the hot and stuffy waiting area, and no chairs or benches for the elderly, or anyone else who might need to sit. I was disappointed. It was not a good first impression.

At last, it was my turn to show my papers. A stern-looking clerk slowly read and re-read every word and compared my face to my passport photo several times. She finally decided I was who I claimed to be, and waived me through. Barbara was next, and finally, we both were able to exit the terminal.

Outside, we found the bus our tour company had arranged to take us to the *River Sprite*. When it was almost full, the driver closed the doors and headed to the wharf on the Moscow Canal where our ship was docked.

This was our first chance to see something of Moscow. I watched excitedly as we passed subway stations, parks, shopping areas, and rows of apartment buildings, some with potted flowers and vines trailing over terrace railings. Except for the Russian signs in the unfamiliar Cyrilic alphabet, it could have been any western city.

It was the evening rush hour, and traffic was fierce. Sleek and powerful sports cars, sedans, and huge SUVs were overtaking us on both sides.

"Wow! Look, Barbara. Did you expect to see this many European and American cars?"

"No, and look at all these super-long limousines. Their windows are so darkly tinted you can't see who's inside. Maybe they're those Russian billionaires I keep reading about."

"Probably. I'm guessing that all the shabby looking little cars we're seeing are *not* owned by oligarchs. It's good to know that some regular Russians can afford to own cars."

At last, the bus driver negotiated a blind turn into a narrow alleyway leading to our dock, and there was the *River Sprite*. She was larger than I expected, long and narrow, shaped to fit through the many locks we would be traveling through between here and St. Petersburg. It was obvious that the ship was not new, but she was clean, and her white paint sparkled in the afternoon sun.

At the reception desk, we showed our passports and cruise tickets and picked up our cabin keys. Barbara introduced me to the members of her group who had been with us on the bus, and we waited until they received their keys. Several of our party had already arrived on earlier flights, and the rest would be here before dinnertime.

Finally, Barbara unlocked the door to our cabin and we stepped inside.

"Well," Barbara chuckled as she looked around, "it's not a palace, but it looks like there's enough room for both of us. Let's check out the bathroom."

"Oh boy," I said, as I peered behind the door. "It's tiny, and the whole bathroom is the shower. That's one way to save space!"

The main room of the cabin held a twin-sized bed built into the wall on the right, and across from it, installed sideways, there was a fold-down bunk similar to a Murphy bed. Above both, there were several storage cabinets. Reading lamps were attached to the wall at the head of each bunk, and there were overhead lights near the corridor door and in the bathroom. A small table stood beneath a round porthole between the two bunks, and a tiny closet with just enough room to hang a few items was located next to the bathroom.

A beam of light, shining through the porthole, lit one side of the cabin and glanced off a full-length mirror attached to the outside of the closet door, temporarily blinding me.

I rubbed my eyes, and looked around the cabin again. The bedding was far from deluxe, but the mattresses felt comfortable enough when we sat down to test them. Industrial carpeting covered the floor. The designers had made an effort to color coordinate the paneled walls, carpet, storage cabinets, and bedding in shades of beige and pale green. The overall effect was neat, efficient, and even attractive in an austere way. Nothing was brand new, but everything was very clean.

There was a sharp knock on the door. It was two members of the Russian crew with our luggage. We thanked them and began to unpack and put away our clothing and gear.

"Oh, boy," Barbara groaned. "My boss bought this spotting scope specifically for me to bring, but where am I going to put it?"

The scope was large and bulky and there was a separate telescoping tripod, both of which were wrapped together in protective packaging. It defied our efforts to shove it under the fixed bunk, out of the way. Besides, according to the instructions from the tour company, we were supposed to stash our empty suitcases there.

Barbara sighed. "I'm responsible for this albatross. I can't let anything happen to it, but it takes up way too much room. But, of course, I'll be thrilled when we are actually using it."

"Forgive my ignorance, but what is it for?"

"It magnifies distant birds so it's easier to identify them, especially unfamiliar birds."

"Oh. Well, I hope it'll come in handy."

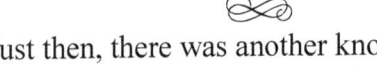

Just then, there was another knock on the door.

"Hello. I'm Maddy, your cruise director," said a cheerful, middle-aged woman in a lilting European accent. "I'm here to inform you that there is a mandatory orientation meeting for half of our passengers at six o'clock this evening. Please make sure everybody in your group comes to the Sky Bar on the top deck, three flights up from here. See you soon."

She gave us a mock salute, and as we closed our door, we could hear her knocking on the one across the hall.

"That's just twenty minutes from now," said Barbara ruefully. "I guess I'd better go tell the rest of our group."

She went off with her list of room numbers in hand, leaving me to finish putting away my things and get ready for the meeting. The dim lightbulb in the bathroom proved to be a bit of a challenge, but there was still enough sunlight to see myself in the full-length mirror.

I took stock. I had slept poorly the night before we left—I had been too excited—and then woke up before dawn. After our long overnight flight, my eyes were puffy and my clothes were wrinkled. I shrugged. There was nothing I could do about it now. I took out my name tag and put it on. It was time to join the others for the orientation.

As I stepped out into the hall, I was overcome by a familiar, nagging sense of guilt. I had never expected to take a trip like this without Dale. I knew I was doing nothing wrong, but ever since I had agreed to go, I had been unable to let go of the feeling that I was being somehow unfair to Dale's memory.

Now, running up the open, circular stairs, I decided that it was time to put those guilty feelings behind me once and for all. If I had to face the rest of my life without Dale, I would need to go forward as bravely as I could. Maybe this would be the beginning of a brand new life.

Comfortable couches and chairs lined the outside walls in the Sky Bar, under enormous panoramic windows. A handsome dark wood bar, complete with padded leather barstools, was at the back of the room, its mirrored backdrop reflecting shelves full of exotic bottles.

According to the literature the tour company had supplied, the *River Sprite* could accommodate about 240 passengers when fully booked. Though the Sky Bar was fairly large, I could see why we had been split into two groups. Tonight, several rows of folding chairs had been placed in the middle of the room. Latecomers would have to stand.

I found a seat not far from where Barbara was sitting with several members of her group, and one of Maddy's helpers handed me a packet of papers. I scanned them quickly. They contained the general information we would need during this voyage: safety procedures, dining room and gift shop hours, instructions for changing money on board, how to contact the ship's doctor, and other essential information.

The meeting took just thirty minutes, with Maddy leading us briskly through the listed items and describing the amenities on board. Every evening, she promised, an itinerary for the following day would be slipped under our cabin doors, giving us mealtimes, land tour departure and return times, the day's scheduled activities on board the ship, and other interesting data—the daily weather forcast, for instance. Besides making us all feel welcome, I found Maddy's cheerful, no-nonsense manner infinitely reassuring.

At the end of the meeting, Maddy instructed us to go to our respective decks for a mandatory safety drill. She assured us that this was a serious exercise and that attendance would be taken. When the drill was completed, she invited us to go to dinner in the Volga Dining Room, located on the deck just below the Sky Bar.

As I waited my turn to descend the stairs, I looked through the wide glass doors opposite the Sky Bar to catch a glimpse of the large open deck at the front of the boat. I could see at least a dozen white umbrella tables and chairs, and there were clusters of lounges scattered about as well. It looked inviting. I was already looking forward to sitting there and watching the scenery glide by as we cruised slowly toward St. Petersburg.

The crew quickly and efficiently guided us through the safety drill. It was reassuring to know where to find life vests and which lifeboat to board, but I very much hoped we would never actually need this information.

The Volga Dining Room was at the rear of the boat, with a large kitchen between it and the Neva Dining Room at the front. Named for the two most famous rivers we would be navigating, the passengers who would be dining in the Neva this evening were now upstairs in the Sky Bar, taking their turn to listen to Maddy's orientation. After tonight, all our meals would be served in both dining rooms simultaneously, with the passengers split evenly between the two.

Ivan, our server tonight, was a polite young man from the Don River Valley south of Moscow. We soon discovered that many of the wait staff were from that area. Ivan spoke fluent English and smiled pleasantly as we settled ourselves at the various tables in his area. There were at least seven other waiters bustling about, serving water and taking orders for our first meal on board.

We were given two choices each of appetizers, main courses, and desserts. I chose a crisp green salad to start, followed by perfectly grilled chicken and vegetables, served with roasted potatoes. For dessert, I had chocolate mousse topped with what tasted like real whipped cream. The food was delicious and had been plated with as much artistry as I would have expected in a fine Manhattan restaurant. It was a very welcome surprise.

I shared a table with three single women traveling together who turned out to be from towns not far from my own in upstate New York. Good friends and travel partners for many years, they were part of a group sponsored by the New York City Public Library. According to the passenger list I received with the rest of my travel documents, I would be meeting people who were with university, military, and union groups, as well as some who were traveling alone. It was an eclectic mix of people.

Dinner over, I was ready to find my bed. I said good night to my new acquaintances and headed downstairs to our cabin. I was inside only a few minutes before the promised itinerary for the next day was pushed under the cabin door. I read it through, and decided what clothes I would need. Tiredly, I changed into pajamas and prepared for bed. At last, I sat down on my bunk to brush my hair and read a few pages in my novel.

Half an hour later, Barbara came in.

"I've tucked everybody in for the night, figuratively speaking. I'm bushed. Did you enjoy dinner?"

I nodded.

"Mine was yummy," she said. "Where did you wind up sitting? You know, you're welcome to join us any time."

"Thanks. I may take you up on that once in awhile, but I expect I'll meet a lot of interesting people during this trip. I don't want you to worry about me. I'm fine on my own. But since you asked, I ate with three women who are practically my neighbors at home. Small world."

I yawned. "Are you as sleepy as I am? The bathroom, such as it is, is all yours. I'm done in there for tonight."

Barbara grinned, grabbed her nightclothes, toothbrush, and toiletries, and headed into the tiny bathroom. I have no idea when she came out. I was already asleep.

CHAPTER 8

Saturday, August 28
Day 3

FORTUNATELY, I had packed a battery-powered alarm clock. When it went off next morning at six-thirty, I peered through the porthole window to find the sun was just coming up. I was tempted to roll over and ignore the alarm, but then I remembered that this was our first full day in Moscow. I sat up, rubbed my eyes, and swung my legs to the floor. Barbara had insisted that I sleep in the fixed bed, while she took the fold-down bunk.

Barbara groaned. "I didn't sleep at all last night! The ventilation system at the foot of your bed creaked and whistled all night. I could hear it even through my earplugs. Do you mind if we turn it off?"

I made a face. "Well, do you think that's a good idea? It will get really warm and stuffy in here without it. And if I can't breathe, I can't promise I won't snore louder than the noise of the vent."

"It didn't keep you up?"

"No, I'm a pretty sound sleeper. I didn't hear a thing."

"Well then," she said, "how would you feel if I asked Maddy to give me a different cabin, if there's one available?"

"I'd miss you, but it's okay. Look, with your own cabin you'd have room for your huge spotting scope and, here's the really good part: we wouldn't have to share that postage-stamp bathroom!"

"Good points! I'll go see Maddy right after breakfast."

Somehow, we managed to get ready by seven-fifteen and arrived in the Volga Dining Room to find it only partially full. I guessed we were not the only passengers finding it hard to get up this morning.

Our breakfast, served buffet-style, was lavish and beautifully presented. Long tables were loaded with a vast array of hot and cold foods. As passengers filled their plates and sat down, the waiters brought pots of coffee and hot water for tea to our tables. We soon discovered we would be treated to this kind of breakfast buffet every morning of our voyage.

We filled our plates, and found seats with others from the birdwatching group. Ivan, our waiter from last night was nowhere to be seen, but Alexander, another smiling young man from near the Don River, poured coffee, made tea, and kept our water glasses and cream pitchers filled. Everything was delicious and I ate every bite. I was going to have to watch that. If I kept eating this way, I would have to buy a new wardrobe in St. Petersburg.

Barbara finished first and excused herself, giving me a significant look. I nodded a silent good luck. As I drank my coffee, I saw the three women I had met last night. On my way out, I stopped to chat with them. We were assigned to different sightseeing buses, but we promised to look for each other later.

Just outside the dining room, I noticed a small showcase filled with beautifully designed necklaces, earrings, bracelets, and cocktail rings, mostly of Baltic amber. The women behind the counter were doing a brisk business. I made a mental note to check prices later.

On the way back downstairs, I decided to explore a bit, since we still had a little time before we were due to leave on our first tour. Besides the Sky Bar at the the top of the ship, and the big open area opposite it called the Sun Deck, there were card and meeting rooms, a well-stocked gift shop, a more intimate bar called the Panorama Lounge, a beauty salon, a sauna, and a small library/TV room filled with assorted paperbacks other passengers had left behind, and furnished with comfortable chairs. At the moment, the TV was tuned to CNN International, now showing a weather forecast for western Europe.

When I returned to our cabin, I found Barbara repacking her suitcases.

"Hey," she said. "Maddy gave me a cabin on the next deck up, number 217. Come visit any time."

"Wow, that's great. I hope the ventilation system in there is quieter."

She grinned. "Me too, but if it's not, I can shut it off without bothering anybody."

Grabbing the last of her belongings, she closed her suitcases and started for the door.

"I'll be back in a few minutes to get the scope," she said. And with that, she was gone.

I looked around and decided that this was a much better arrangement. Now I would have the whole cabin to myself. I no longer had to share the bathroom, and if I wanted, I could stay up late reading without disturbing Barbara.

Would I feel lonely without a roommate? After almost two years of living mostly alone, I was pretty sure I could handle it.

It was time to go. I left my cabin key at the reception desk and, with the other passengers, waited for our sightseeing buses in a large parking lot across from our ship's berth. I was assigned to bus number three, along with the rest of Barbara's group.

Soon the buses began to arrive and open their doors. Maddy and her assistants were with us to make sure there was no confusion. Quickly, the first two buses were filled and on their way, and it was our turn. Waiting for us on board were two local women who were to act as our guides, and there was a man too, now standing at the bottom of the steps, waiting to assist us up into the coach.

As we pulled away and joined the traffic on the main road into the city, the female guides, Olga and Rina, both of whom were small, middle-aged blondes, took turns giving us background information about Moscow and the sights we were going to see. The man, whom I thought was nice looking but not particularly handsome, smiled at me as he took a seat across the aisle from mine near the back of the bus.

Our first stop was the Kremlin. Olga said, "*Kremlin* is a common word in the Russian language. It means fortress and though the Moscow Kremlin is the most famous one in Russia, every city, town, and village in the country has one."

Like a huge, lopsided triangle, Moscow's Kremlin dominated the skyline above the Moskva River. Inside its walls, we drove slowly past the Grand Palace, the Armory, and the State Palace.

Rina, whose turn it was to speak, said proudly, "The State Palace was built during Khrushchev's time as Premier. It was originally used for Communist Party and diplomatic gatherings, and also as a second stage for the Bolshoi Ballet. Today it is used mainly for concerts and other popular performances, and as the home of the Kremlin Ballet company. It can seat up to 6,000 people and is the largest concert hall in Russia."

The Palace's austere glass and concrete architecture was a stark and jarring contrast to the rest of the lovely Russian Gothic buildings in the Kremlin. Cathedral Square was rimmed with gold domed churches, mostly preserved as museums, lavishly decorated inside and out with fifteenth and sixteenth century iconic art.

Almost as an afterthought as we passed it, the guides pointed out the building in which Russian

President Vladimir Putin's office was located. According to Olga, Lenin's office had been in the same building.

While in the Kremlin, we toured the Armory. Inside, there were crowds of people, each group clustered around their respective tour leader. Rina took the lead, motioning to us to form a tight circle around her. "You must stay close to Olga and me, so you can hear our commentary, and more importantly, not be left behind!"

None of us wanted that to happen.

Olga told us that although the Armory had once been a royal arsenal, it had long ago been converted into one of Russia's most important museums. She and Rina led us first through an immense and magnificent collection of royal clothing and possessions, including the 190-carat Orlov diamond, one of the largest in the world.

I was amazed at the incredible wealth of the collections. We walked through huge rooms filled with ancient weapons and armor, precious religious art and artifacts, ornately gilded and jeweled carriages, a treasure house of gold and platinum nuggets, and, finally, they showed us a display of Russia's famous Fabergé Eggs, housed in a glass showcase.

During the entire tour, the guides kept us entertained with irreverent and amusing stories about the various Czars and Czarinas. I laughed with the others, but the sheer magnitude of the opulence surrounding us left me feeling slightly queasy, as though I had eaten a too-rich meal.

At the end of our tour, we re-boarded our buses and headed back to the *River Sprite* for lunch. At one point, I looked over my shoulder and found the Russian man who had helped us back on the bus looking my way. He was tall, at least four or five inches above my five-feet-nine. Slim, but powerfully built, he had short dark hair, cut military style, and expressive black eyebrows like bird's wings. He was wearing what seemed to be the standard uniform for male tour-guides in Moscow: a black, long-sleeved sport shirt tucked into black chino pants, though I noticed he filled out his clothing better than most.

Meeting my eyes, he smiled slightly and nodded his head. Our eyes held for a moment and, to my surprised confusion, I felt my cheeks grow warm. Was I blushing? I looked quickly away and turned back toward the front of the bus, feeling ridiculous. Why on earth would I blush just because a friendly stranger smiled at me?

In a few minutes, I was able to concentrate on the scenery again. We were passing through a business district that seemed to buzz with energy. Lunchtime pedestrians crowded the sidewalks. Restaurants and shops of all kinds seemed to be doing a thriving business.

As we traveled away from the city center, we passed residential neighborhoods, Metro stations, schools, public parks with playground equipment and sports fields, and small strip malls that included all kinds of stores. In several places along the sides of the road there were colorful beds of flowers, planted in intricate designs resembling Oriental carpets.

Our guides, who had been mostly silent on our ride back to the ship, suddenly noticed we were passing a flower market. Olga said, "In all Russia, the schools are still closed for summer recess, but they will open again for the fall term in a few days. It is a Russian tradition for our children to bring bouquets of flowers to their teachers on the first day of classes."

Rina asked, "Do you do that in your towns on the first day of school?"

I had never heard of that being done in the United States, but it sounded like a charming idea. Maybe we *should* do that at home.

Soon, we arrived back at the bus parking lot at the docks. The dark-haired man jumped off the bus and waited at the bottom of the steps to help us off. As he took my hand, I felt again the small jolt of electricity I had tried to ignore the first few times he had helped me on and off the bus. This time, I found the courage to look up into his wide-set eyes. They were cinnamon brown with gold flecks. He was smiling, and his eyes were sparkling.

I swallowed hard, ducked my head, and mumbled a quick "Thank you." My heart was pounding as I hurried toward our riverboat's gangway. I felt my cheeks heating again. What on earth was the matter with me?

Lunch was simple; a cup of borscht, a ham and cheese sandwich on dense Russian black bread, and a warm fruit tart topped with a small scoop of vanilla ice cream for dessert. Despite its simplicity, the meal was delicious and beautifully presented. I was eating lunch today with retired Marines and their wives. I gathered they had served together somewhere overseas. They must have had a very good time wherever it was, judging from their almost continuous laughter.

We were free to spend the afternoon however we wanted, though our group needed to be back on board by late afternoon. We were scheduled to "meet the Captain" at a cocktail party at five-thirty and I would need time to shower and change into the cocktail dress I had brought for this occasion. I was looking forward to dressing up a little.

Despite my brave declaration that I would be fine by myself on this trip, I was feeling a bit lonely after our morning tour and lunch with strangers. Of course, I knew from the beginning that I would be on my own during most of this cruise. It would have been fun to have a close friend to chat and compare impressions with, but Barbara was unable to fulfill that role. She needed to devote almost all of her attention to her birders.

As for them, they were polite to me, but they were mostly couples. They had not shown any inclination, so far, to invite me, an unknown single woman, to join them. I had little in common with them, after all.

I considered my options for the afternoon. I could go back into Moscow by taxi, lounge on the Sun Deck outside the Sky Bar, or stay in my cabin reading or napping. I decided to find Barbara and ask what her group was doing.

"A few of us are going to share a cab and go back into Moscow to visit Old Arbat Street."

"Oh, from the descriptions I've read about it, that sounds like fun. Do you mind if I join you?"

"Of course not. Meet us at the gangway in five minutes."

We left our keys at the reception desk and asked for directions to the nearest taxi stand. It was close, only about a block away.

The driver's English was broken, but understandable. "I haf cousin in Cleveland. You maybe know him?"

We looked at each other. Barbara, as nominal leader of our tiny group answered. "No, sorry. We don't live in Cleveland."

"Oh, well. I just ask. Maybe some day I get lucky, you tink?"

Old Arbat Street was as described: a pedestrians-only shopping mall full of color and activity. Getting out of the taxi, I looked around in anticipation. We joined a crowd of strolling people enthusiastically shopping, people-watching, and enjoying the street performers. There were classical, jazz, and rock muscians; dancers, some wearing colorful costumes; artists displaying their work; and shops and stalls selling a vast array of antique and modern goods and souvenirs of all kinds. Along the way, there were statues of famous Russians, including the poet Alexander Pushkin and his wife. Restaurants were full, even now at mid-afternoon.

Though we admired dozens of interesting items, we decided not to buy anything so early in the trip. At one point, I looked over my shoulder and thought I spotted the man from our bus strolling behind us. When I looked again a few minutes later, he was nowhere in sight. I decided I must have been mistaken.

All too soon, it was time to go. We splurged on ice cream and took a taxi back to the boat.

Back on board the *River Sprite*, I showered, brushed my hair, and reapplied my makeup. After I stepped into my black cocktail dress and slipped on low-heeled black pumps, I surveyed myself in the full-length mirror, turning this way and that. I was pleased with the overall effect. My hard work at the gym had been well worth the effort. I put on my diamond stud earrings and took out the heart-shaped diamond necklace Dale had given me for our twentieth anniversary. Smiling in remembrance, I fastened it around my neck and tucked a jeweled clip into my hair.

The cocktail party was held in the Sky Bar. With his full white beard and round belly, the Captain reminded me of Santa Claus. He smiled broadly as he greeted us, but it soon became obvious he spoke very little English. He bowed and deferred to his first mate, a younger man whose English was fluent.

Tiny shot glasses of vodka covered the bar. I looked around in surprise. Unlike other cocktail parties I had attended, there were no canapés or other appetizers to blunt the effects of the alcohol. Most of our group was present, and we stood together, awkwardly making conversation. After a suitable interval, we drifted outside onto the Sun Deck where we could relax.

After dinner, we returned to the Sun Deck. The evening was warm, with a gentle breeze. We sat down at an umbrella table and ordered drinks from the bar. A few minutes later, Anatoly

Sorkin, the group's Russian ornithologist, appeared.

Barbara was immediately attracted to him, I saw. It was not surprising. They did, after all, share an interest in birds, and as a Russian schoolboy, he was sure to have studied the literature she found so enthralling.

As I watched her lean toward him though, I realized his looks probably appealed to her most, at least at this point. His thick, wavy blond hair was streaked with gray, and hung almost to his shoulders. He was tanned and fit, probably thanks to years of field research and, though not exactly handsome, his lean face was friendly and open with an attractive smile. He looked to be in his late forties, just the right age for Barbara. I hoped they would become friends on this trip and, if she wished, perhaps a little more.

As eager birders began to ply him with questions, I slipped away to stand by the railing. The water was dark and lapped gently against the ship. I was alone and, for once, not thinking of Dale. I was remembering a pair of smiling brown eyes with dancing gold flecks. I gave myself a mental shake. We would soon be gone from Moscow, leaving Mr. Brown-Eyes far behind.

CHAPTER 9

Sunday, August 29
Day 4

WHEN THE alarm rang the next morning, I awoke feeling refreshed. Once again I had slept through the noise of the ventilation system, and in fact, the gentle whistling had lulled me to sleep. On my own, I sped through my morning routine of showering and dressing, and entered the dining room exactly at seven o'clock.

After breakfast, we boarded our buses for our morning tour. Our group was assigned to the same bus as yesterday, with Olga and Rina to guide us. Their male assistant sat, as usual, at the back of the bus. His name, we found out today, was Nikolai.

Our first stop was the one Ellen and I had dreaded: Lenin's tomb in Red Square at the foot of the Kremlin wall. The buses dropped us off near the entrance to the Square and we waited in a long line weaving back and forth between roped stanchions. Eventually we arrived at a security gate where we were made to leave our backpacks, pocketbooks, totes, cameras, and other belongings.

At last, we were ushered through the gate and entered the tomb. In single file, we slowly descended a dimly lit staircase on one side of the tomb, passed in front of Lenin's body lying in state on a raised glass-enclosed platform, and climbed the steps on the other side back up to street level. I wondered, as so many have done before me, whether the body we saw was really Lenin, and not a wax model.

The contrast between the bright sunlight outside and the dim lighting within the tomb made it difficult at first to see the uniformed soldiers stationed at intervals along the way. The line was kept moving at all times. No one was allowed to stop, and the noise level was low, barely above a whisper.

When I emerged into the light again, I blinked and took a deep breath of relief. I found the whole experience strange and profoundly depressing. As I collected my camera and tote bag from the officer at the security gate, I realized that other visitors seemed to have been affected in the same way. There was very little conversation.

Next, we gathered around our guides in the middle of Red Square. Rina said, "The word 'red' in Red Square's name has nothing to do with Communism. In the Russian language the word red means beautiful." That meant, of course, that every time someone called a Communist "a dirty Red," they were actually calling him "beautiful." How ironic.

We had half an hour to walk around Red Square on our own. Barbara and I took photos of each other to send back home, and at one point I spotted Nikolai, lounging on the rim of a fountain with a cigarette. His eyes met mine and he smiled broadly. I gave him a quick answering smile and looked away. I could feel my cheeks warming again.

I spent the rest of our time admiring the colorful and ornate St. Basil Cathedral, skirting tombs of other important Russian politicians, and taking a quick look at the contents of a natural history museum housed in a former church. One entire side of the square was taken up by GUM, the famous department store once ineptly run by the Communist state. Today, I was amazed to discover, it contained a giant indoor flea market. I glanced around inside, but was not tempted to linger.

Back on the buses, we drove to a Metro station in downtown Moscow. Nikolai and the two women guides led us inside for a short ride on the city's famous subway system. Muscovites are proud of their subway, said to be one of the most beautiful and efficient in the world. My guidebook showed photos of marble walls and crystal chandeliers in some stations. Unfortunately, we saw nothing so ornate in our visit today.

We rode a steep down-escalator into the depths of the station. The noise, heat, and the stoic commuters seemed familiar, reminiscent of the days when I regularly rode New York City's subway system. Off the escalator, we lined up in groups on the platform. Soon a train pulled into the station and the doors opened.

Nikolai touched my elbow and murmured, "Hurry, madam."

He stood near me as the train doors closed and we hurtled down the dark tracks to the next station. We stayed on the train through two more stops and when the doors opened at the third station, Nikolai guided me back onto the platform. After a quick head count proved we were all there, he and the other two guides escorted us onto an equally steep up-escalator and out onto the street. Around the corner, our buses were waiting to take us back to the *River Sprite*.

After lunch, we had just over two hours of free time before leaving again for an early dinner at the Marriot Royal Aurora Hotel. I decided to stay on the ship to browse in the gift shop and sit outside in the sunshine.

In the late afternoon, the buses dropped us off directly in front of the hotel. Nikolai helped me down with the broad smile I had come to expect, and I reacted as usual. Then, I paused for a moment to admire the building's handsome Russian Gothic exterior. We had been told this was one of the most exclusive hotels in Moscow, perfectly located within walking distance of Red Square, the Kremlin, and the Bolshoi Theater.

Inside, I gazed around the opulent lobby at what seemed like acres of gleaming marble on the floors, walls, columns, and almost every other surface. The decor was elegant and luxurious, but so much marble left me feeling a little chilly.

The hotel staff escorted us upstairs and into a beautiful dining room where the maitre d' welcomed us. I found a seat at one of the tables set for four. After a few minutes, Joan, Marcia and Sara, the three women I had met on the ship, joined me.

Joan, a retired high school mathematics teacher, sat next to me. "How are you doing, Joan? Are you enjoying being in Moscow?"

"My friends had to convince me to come. I didn't think I would like it at all. In books and movies Moscow is usually described as dark and dreary, or snowing and freezing cold, and always—I don't know—somehow sleazy."

"Well, I'm sure we won't see any of the corruption and crime I've read about while we're here," said Marcia, an elementary school speech pathologist. "After all, they want our money. So, all that will be carefully hidden from us."

"But, on the other hand, I've been really surprised at the energy of the city," I said. "The gorgeous weather we're having helps. Everything looks better when the sun is shining and the temperature is in the 70s. How did you feel about seeing the Kremlin and Red Square?"

Joan laughed. "Well, I never expected to set foot in either of them in my lifetime. I had to keep reminding myself that KGB agents probably weren't going to march up and arrest me as an American spy!"

I smiled. "Did you hear the guide, Olga, I think, say that Vladimir Putin's office was in the same building as Lenin's? I wonder if he's using the same room?"

Marcia shook her head, laughing. "If he is, maybe we need to start worrying about him. Do you think he'd be affected by Lenin's ghost? But seriously, it's pretty amazing to be here. I've gotten a better sense of the history of both the Kremlin and Red Square—bloody history!"

"But don't you think, if Putin keeps doing what he's doing right now, Russian policies might become more mainstream, both economically and politically? Maybe then we could stop thinking of Russia as our enemy," said Sara, a professor of economics at a private college near her home. "Hopefully, the Cold War is over the good. The question is, does he really intend to stay on his present course?"

"I hope so," I said. "But here's our waiter, and we haven't looked at our menus yet."

We made our choices and the conversation turned to lighter topics. Joan was sleeping better, she said, and though her knee ached occasionally, she was able to keep up with the guides.

The three women were obviously quite fond of each other. Marcia and Sara teased each other continually and kept Joan amused. It was thoughtful and generous of them to invite me to join them.

"Tomorrow," I said, "while you are visiting the Tretyakov Art Museum, I'll be travelling with our little birdwatching group to a nature preserve outside Moscow. I'm not a birder, but I'm looking forward to seeing a little of the countryside beyond the city limits."

"Oh, I envy you," said Sara. "But I wouldn't want to miss the art museum."

When dinner was over, we found our buses waiting in front of the hotel to take us to the world famous Moscow Circus. Nikolai swung down the steps at our approach and waited to help us back on board. As he took my hand, he said, "I hope you enjoyed your meal, madam."

I shivered slightly as I had each time he touched me, and murmured something inane as I escaped up the steps. I had never blushed so often in my life, and it was years since I had admired a man other than my husband.

Wait! Was I *admiring* Nikolai? How embarrassing!

The circus was held in a large theater in the round. As we filed in, we passed groups of costumed performers posing for photos with a few of the circus animals, and stands selling snacks, drinks, and souvenirs. It was almost eight o'clock and I was surprised to see so many family groups, some with very young children. Then I remembered that school had not yet begun. This visit to the Circus was probably a special treat for the whole family.

Our seats were high up in the circular hall. I had read good things about this circus, and when the show began, I was thrilled by the excellent trapeze artists, acrobats, animal acts, and clowns. Their reputation for excellence was well deserved. It was good to hear the children laughing as "oohs" and "aahs" echoed around the hall.

When the performance was over, we re-boarded our bus to return to the *River Sprite* for the night. As we took our seats and the bus began to roll, I felt Nikolai's eyes on me.

At last, we reached the dock. As he helped me down, he said, "I will not be with you tomorrow morning. I hope you will have a pleasant day. I wish you a good night."

Surprised, I murmured, "Thank you. Good night, Nikolai."

Slowly, I boarded the ship and went along the corridor to my cabin. I was disappointed he would not be with us tomorrow, though I was reluctant to examine why I felt that way. He was just a tour bus guide, right?

It took me a long time to fall asleep.

CHAPTER 10

Monday, August 30
Day 5

THE NEXT morning, my alarm chimed an hour earlier than usual. Rubbing sleep from my eyes, I raced to get ready on time. We had been warned to wear long pants and boots, or at least closed shoes, for our hike in the Nature Preserve. If we arrived back in time to visit the Tretyakov Art Museum, there would be no opportunity to change clothes. Optimistically, I slipped a pair of sandals into my tote for later.

True to his word, Nikolai was nowhere to be seen. Our two female guides were gone as well, replaced by Anatoly, our Russian ornithologist. He told us he was currently working at a nature preserve in the southeastern part of Russia, near the Chinese border, studying the effects of climate change on the birds of that region. He was originally from Moscow, however, and was familiar with the area's native birds.

Traffic was heavy, but grew lighter as we drove through the outlying suburbs. Just before we reached the city limit, we stopped in front of a large apartment building. A small, middle-aged man was waiting for us. He climbed aboard and Anatoly introduced him as Dr. Pavel Kozlov, manager of the nature preserve we were going to visit.

We soon left Moscow behind, travelling east on a straight, two-lane highway. The preserve was more than an hour away, Dr. Kozlov explained, asking us to call him Pavel. He pointed out interesting sights along our route and told us a little about the small towns we drove through.

The birders were eagerly questioning both Pavel and Anatoly, and checking their binoculars and cameras to make sure they were in working order. Barbara had lugged the giant spotting scope aboard, and several of the men promised to carry it for her and help set it up.

I was sleepy, and at first, I listened with only one ear. However, the birders' enthusiasm was contagious, and I started to pay closer attention to our surroundings. Soon we began to see brightly painted dachas on either side of the road. Some of them, I was delighted to note, looked as if they belonged in a Victorian storybook. The small buildings, most not much larger than a garden shed, were surrounded by gardens in full bloom. Though the plots were tiny, I could see vegetables, flowers for bouquets, and fruit trees loaded with apples ripening in the late summer sun.

Just before we turned off the highway onto a dirt road hardly bigger than a track, we passed the most beautiful dacha of all. It was painted a sunny yellow, with delicate white gingerbread trim outlining its steeply pitched roof, decorating the front door, and framing each window. Its picture-book garden was filled to bursting with flowers in a rainbow of colors. All too soon we had driven past, and I made a mental note to look for it again on our return trip.

We bumped along the unpaved track until the bus could go no further. Gathering our gear, we piled off and crowded around Pavel and Anatoly. After a brief consultation in rapid Russian, the two men set off down a nearby path with the rest of us trooping along behind.

The path became increasingly muddy. It had rained heavily the previous night and the ground was still quite soft. I was glad I had obeyed the instruction to wear sturdy, closed shoes.

After a five-minute walk, we came to a wide lake. Pavel told us a chain of lakes, ponds, creeks, and springs ran through the preserve, which meant this sanctuary had more diversity of native animals, birds, and plants than many other Russian preserves.

Anatoly spied some birds in the water across the lake, and Barbara and her helpers quickly set up the spotting scope. When I took my turn to look through the powerful lens, the birds seemed almost at arm's length.

While most of the group continued to admire the birds through the scope, a few of the non-birders—mostly spouses of the avid birdwatchers—followed me along another path toward a meadow I could see a short distance away. In the clear morning light, we could see the field was dotted with wildflowers blooming among grasses waving in the light breeze. We recognized red and white clover, blue chickory, bright golden black-eyed-Susans, and even some dandelions. It was fun to see the Russian equivalents of what we thought of as our North American wildflowers.

We rejoined the others and followed them to the edge of a forest, and then to a huge field of tall native grasses. Just as we were about to hike back to our bus, a flock of cranes appeared and glided down to feed among the grasses. Viewing the cranes in their native habitat was the highlight of the excursion for most of the birders.

As our bus turned back onto the highway, I admired the yellow dacha once more. Working quickly, I managed to take a shot or two with my camera before we passed it. I wondered to whom it belonged, and where they were today, though since this was a Monday, they were probably at work.

In contrast to the ride to the preserve, the birders talked quietly amongst themselves, or dozed, as the bus returned to the city. I was watching the time. We might be able to visit the art museum after all. I changed my shoes in anticipation.

As we pulled into the parking lot across from the docks, I saw another bus waiting to take us to the Tretyakov. Our two city guides were inside the coach and Nikolai was there to help us on board. As we drove away, Nikolai, who was sitting across the aisle, turned to me, his wing-like eyebrows raised.

"Did you enjoy the countryside?"

"Yes," I said. "I'm not really a birdwatcher, but I loved walking in the preserve. It's beautiful. I thought the dachas we passed were lovely, too. Some of the gardens were overflowing with the most gorgeous flowers and so many fruit trees were full of ripening apples."

"I am sorry I could not travel with you today." He was gazing intently at me.

"Well, you're here now," I said boldly, surprising myself.

"Yes, I am."

Uncomfortable now, I looked away, my cheeks heating. After a moment I decided I wanted to continue our conversation after all. When I turned back to him, he was still watching me. I took a deep breath.

"Just before we turned off the main highway, we passed the most beautiful dacha."

I described it in detail. He nodded.

"Yes." He smiled broadly, the gold flecks sparkling in his eyes. "I know it. I have travelled on that road before, and have admired it too."

"Do you own a dacha here?"

"No." Still smiling, he shook his head. "I live in St. Petersburg, where I am a professor of English Literature at the University there."

"What are you doing here?"

He was serious now. "I spend my summers working for the tour company. My salary and tips help me to afford to live in St. Petersburg."

"Oh!"

The bus had arrived at the art museum and there was no more time for conversation. As I descended the steps, I stumbled slightly and he caught me in his arms. I slowly raised my eyes to his. He was smiling down at me.

"Watch your step," he said, chuckling softly.

Mortified, I walked away with as much dignity as I could muster. I could feel his eyes on me as I entered the building.

The Tretyakov was a revelation. It was filled with treasures by artists who were almost unknown outside of Russia, at least to me. There were paintings in every genre from early religious icons to twentieth century works. As always, I was most drawn to the Impressionists, but here were artists of whom I had never heard. The paintings seemed at least as good as familiar works by well-known Western masters like Monet and Renoir, two of my favorites.

Outside in the bright sunshine, the bus was waiting to take us back to the boat for lunch. We had been advised to tip our Moscow guides today, as we would be leaving them behind when we left the port in Moscow early this afternoon.

I had enjoyed listening to the two women guides, but it was especially awkward tipping Nikolai. I was sorry to say goodbye, and he seemed to feel the same sadness at our parting.

Again, I held my head high and kept my back very straight as I walked away from him to the *River Sprite*. I told myself he probably flirted with someone in every tour group who came through Moscow. I was already missing him.

I went to my cabin to put away my jacket and walking shoes, and change my khakis for a light cotton skirt. The day was growing warmer, and I was uncomfortable wearing pants in hot weather. I refreshed my lipstick and ran a brush through my hair. I sighed. No more gold-flecked brown eyes smiling at me.

As I tucked my hair behind my ears, I noticed I had lost one of my earrings. Dale had bought them for me from a Manhattan street vendor in the long ago days before Ellen was born. The small silver hoops probably cost less than ten dollars at the time, but they were priceless to me, and I had worn them often. I quickly searched the clothes I had just taken off, my jacket, my tote, the floor inside my cabin, and even the corridor outside. I could have lost it at any time today. It was gone, I realized sadly, forever.

I went back inside the cabin, put on a different pair of earrings, and slipped my book into my tote. I decided I would stay with our group for a while, and then steal away to a table on the narrow side deck outside my cabin. I would read a bit and watch the scenery drift by while we motored upstream.

It was time to eat. Slowly I climbed the stairs to the Volga Dining Room.

Running steps echoed behind me as Barbara came panting up.

"I'm late. I was supposed to commandeer a table for ten, but I got sidetracked by one of the birders who wanted to complain about the nature preserve. Apparently, he thought it was a waste of time. He checked off only two birds on his life list today!"

She frowned, "He'd traveled in Russia two years ago. Why he thought he'd see so many more birds today, I really don't know!"

I smiled and shook my head in sympathy. I was glad *I* didn't have to deal with her group's complaints!

We entered the dining room together, Barbara already looking for her birders. Standing just inside the door, dressed in a well-tailored sports jacket and dress trousers, was Nikolai. He smiled broadly and gave a small bow when he saw me.

I stared, open-mouthed. What was he doing here?

Finally, I found my voice. "What are you doing here?" I croaked, trying without success to clear my throat.

"I am your Russian teacher for the duration of this voyage. I hope you will join my classes." There was a huge grin on his face. He was very pleased to have given me a surprise.

I stood looking at him, dumb again, until he took pity on me.

"Enjoy your lunch, madam." He nodded to Barbara, who had been observing this byplay with curiosity.

"What's going on between you and Nikolai?" she demanded as she pulled me away.

"Nothing… Nothing at all!"

My voice was barely working. I coughed, and tried again to clear my throat. "Let's eat! Can I join you today?"

"Sure. Come on. I see Anatoly has saved a table for us."

She looked back and shook her finger at me as she led the way to the table. "But you'd better tell me what's going on."

I sat down, but I had a hard time focusing on the conversation, and for the first time since we arrived on board the *River Sprite*, I could only push the food around on my plate. I was conscious of Nikolai's eyes on me, even though he was sitting some distance away. Several times I looked in his direction—my gaze was involuntarily drawn to his—only to encounter his smile. He seemed to be enjoying my discomfort.

Finally, the meal was over and people began to drift away. I grabbed my tote and headed for my cabin where I planned to stay until I could calm myself.

I had been inside only a few minutes when there was a knock on my door.

My heart beat faster. "Who is it?"

I was hoping it was Barbara, coming for a talk with me, but somehow I was sure it was not.

"Nikolai. I have something for you."

I stood, hestitating, by the door.

"What is it?" I held my breath.

"You must open the door so I can give it to you."

He sounded so reasonable.

I opened the door a few inches. He stood in the corridor, holding out his hand. In his palm lay my lost earring.

"I found this in the parking lot when we returned from the art museum. You have lost it this morning?"

"Yes! And you found it? How did you know it was mine?"

"I have seen you wear it before today." He was grinning again.

"I was sure it was gone forever. Thank you so much for bringing it to me."

"It is my pleasure."

Somehow, he was inside my cabin with the door closed behind him. Before I could move, he took my hand. His warm brown eyes darkened, and I shivered.

"Forgive me," he said. "There is something I must do."

I was moving into his arms almost before he finished speaking. Inevitably, or so I told myself later, I raised my lips to his.

There was a knock on the door.

"Hey, Sharon, open the door. I need to talk to you."

It was Barbara, at the worst possible moment.

Nikolai backed away from me, and opened the door.

"Hello, Miss. Excuse me, I was just returning some lost property to your friend."

He turned and disappeared down the corridor.

Barbara stood in the doorway, looking from my red face to Nikolai's retreating back.

"Okay, what's going on here?"

"N-nothing."

"Nothing?" She stood arms akimbo, eyebrows raised. "You can't expect me to believe that. Just look at your face. Something's going on all right, and I want to know what! I feel responsible for you. You're a grown woman, but it seems to me that you're a complete novice when it comes to men other than your late husband."

Trying desperately to clear my throat, I finally whispered, "Really, it's nothing. He, I... It's complicated."

"Okay. *Life* is complicated. Just start at the beginning."

"Every time he touched me getting on and off the bus, I got a shivery feeling, almost like an electric shock. At first, I thought it was just coincidence, but it kept happening."

"Oh? Well! What else?"

"I thought I would never see him again after we said goodbye to our guides and left the bus today. I was beginning to think about him too much, so I thought, well, that's it! I'll never see him again. Then, then..."

Now I was talking too fast. "He was there... in the dining room when we came in for lunch. I couldn't believe my eyes!"

I collapsed on my bunk. My face was still hot, and I was close to tears.

"Why are you so upset right now?" Barbara demanded.

"Just before lunch, I discovered I had lost one of the earrings I was wearing today. Dale bought them for me years ago and I wear them a lot. I was so sad to have lost one."

"So?"

"Nikolai found it. I'd lost it in the bus parking lot. Just before you came by, he gave it back to me. But that's not all. He was about to kiss me and I wanted him to. I was already walking into his arms when you knocked."

Now, Barbara was grinning, trying not to laugh.

"Okay. I can understand, now, why you're upset. He's probably the first guy you've noticed as a man in a long time, right? But Sharon, he can't seduce you right here on the ship. He isn't allowed to fraternize with the passengers. If he got caught, he'd get fired."

She leaned in, gave me a swift hug, and smoothed my hair back from my face.

"What a relief. I was worried he had threatened you in some way." She sighed, and shook her head. "Don't worry too much about this. Enjoy a little flirtation. It can't hurt you to lighten up a bit, but don't lose your heart. You know there can be no future with Nikolai, right? Look Sharon, you'll be home before you know it, and when the time is right, and you finally do meet a man you can plan a future with… Well, who knows?"

"What if the others in our group notice something?"

"Nonsense. They're so busy throwing themselves at Anatoly they'll never notice anything you're doing. I'm actually jealous of the time he gives them, though of course, that's why we hired him. But, he's very attractive, and we do have a bit in common. Oh, well. A little flirtation can't hurt, right? Huh. Maybe I need to take my own advice."

I nodded, and mumbled something vague. I was far from sure a little flirtation with Nikolai would leave my heart unharmed.

With a light pat on my knee, she left the cabin.

Finally alone, I began to calm down. She had given me good advice. There was no point in working myself up like this. In ten days or less I would be on my way home. I would never see this man again, whether I wanted to or not.

Now I had a decision to make. I could carry on a light flirtation, or ignore him completely from now until we left for home. Could I do that? I would soon see. I was not going to hide away in my cabin.

I splashed water on my hot face, brushed my hair again, and straightened my clothes. Picking up my tote, I locked the cabin door and headed upstairs to the Sun Deck.

Anatoly, sitting at an umbrella table off to one side, was just beginning a talk on Russian water birds. The birders had moved their chairs as close to him as possible, and were hanging on his every word. I rolled my eyes at Barbara and she covered her mouth to hide her grin.

Not having a particular interest in Russian water birds, I drifted away. There was a small noisy group enjoying after-lunch cocktails in the Sky Bar, and the rest of the Sun Deck was crowded with passengers relaxing in the sunshine. Some were reading, some dozing. At one table, a group of women were playing Canasta, and four serious Bridge players sat at another. Not seeing anyone I wanted to join, I wandered around to the shady side deck and found an unoccupied table.

I was about to pull my novel out of my tote, when I found another book in the bag. Along with the other tour materials, we had been given a small guidebook that described our voyage in detail, kilometer by kilometer. Numbered markers on the shore corresponded to descriptions in the book of the towns we would visit and other interesting sights. I must have been carrying the little blue book with me every day so far without realizing it.

I oriented myself with the book and traced this afternoon's route from the Moscow Canal into the Volga River. According to our itinerary, we would be stopping at the provincial town of Uglich tomorrow afternoon. I found descriptions in my guidebook of Uglich's highlights: the Transfiguration Cathedral and the Church of Prince Dmitry on the Spilled Blood. That one sounded a little scary.

I was about to read about poor Dmitry when I noticed the shade I had been enjoying had moved. Blinded by a sudden ray of sunshine, I got up to find another table. As I turned around, I bumped squarely into someone and dropped my guidebook.

"Oh, I'm so sorry!" I blinked my eyes, trying to restore my sight. Bending over to pick up my book was Nikolai.

"It's you!" I could feel my face burning again.

"It is I who am sorry. I did not mean to startle you."

He pressed the book into my hands, and looked intently down into my eyes.

His deep voice was low. "I want to apologize for upsetting your friend. I hope all is well between you, but I cannot apologize for what almost happened. I believe there is a connection between you and me, and I believe you feel it also. Is this not correct?"

He stood before me, waiting. There was an unreadable expression on his face, but his formal, accented English was crystal clear.

I cleared my throat. "Nikolai, I will be going home in less than ten days. What connection can there possibly be between us?"

"It is true our time is short. Should we not take as much for ourselves as we can?" He was standing so close, his breath stirred my hair. I caught a trace of his scent, musky and faintly sweet.

"Sharon… Do you permit me to call you Sharon?"

I nodded, dazed.

"Please, Sharon. Have dinner with me tonight."

"Where? In the Volga Dining Room?" I was surprised.

"No, I will bring food to your cabin. Our cook will make a delicious meal. Please, Sharon."

"Won't you be missed at your table?" At lunch today he had eaten with several members of the ship's Russian crew.

"No, we eat at different times. It is not difficult to arrange this."

Still bemused, I asked, "When would you come?"

"You agree!" He seemed overjoyed. "I will bring food at seven o'clock."

He took my hand and pressed my open palm to his heart.

"Tonight," he whispered and was gone.

Stunned by what had just happened, I sat down in the nearest chair and stared at the riverbank opposite. What I saw there—dense, dark green forest, a romantic castle ruin, a picture-book village, lush sunlit meadows—was a blur. I was lost in a dream, or was it a nightmare? What had I gotten myself into?

What did I know about this man? There had been a very short biography of him, just a few lines, in the activities brochure we had been given when we boarded the boat. "Nikolai Petrovich Novikov is a professor of English Literature at the University of St. Petersburg. He will teach a series of beginning classes in the Russian language during our cruise. At an hourly rate to be determined, he will be available for private language instruction and sightseeing tours of the towns we visit during this voyage." There was no other information about him.

Was he the kind of man who singled out a woman traveling alone to seduce on each cruise? Was I to be his victim on this one? Was I afraid of his charm? Of him?

Was I afraid of him? Or was I afraid of how he made me feel? Hungry for something I could not yet identify, or more truthfully, something I was unwilling to put a name to? My situation was hard to believe. I was a 46-year-old woman, a widow, a sophisticated woman who had had an idyllic marriage of more than twenty years. Yet, here I was, behaving like a sex-crazed teenager over this stranger. I refused to think about Dale. I was unwilling to analyze what he might have thought about what I was about to do.

There was an emergency button in every cabin. If it was all too much and Nikolai refused to leave if I wanted him to, I could press the button. The resulting scandal would be ugly and unfortunate, but I would be rescued. *If,* I needed rescuing.

Eventually, a loud group of passengers carrying drinks came around to my side of the ship and sat down at nearby tables. Checking my watch, I was shocked to realize how much time had passed. The afternoon would soon fade into evening.

I rose quickly and headed for my cabin. I had better shower and change into something comfortable. Sexy? I ran down a mental list of my wardrobe. I had brought a sleeveless chocolate brown sheath with a vee neckline as an alternative to the black dress I had worn to the Captain's cocktail party. The vee was deeper than I usually wore, but it was flattering. If I was committed to dinner with Nikolai, I might as well dress for it.

As I got ready for whatever was going to happen tonight, I was surprised to realize I no longer had any fears or doubts. I was even singing Beatles songs in the shower, something I had not done since Dale died. Who was I kidding? If Nikolai showed any reluctance to seduce me tonight, I would seduce him.

I continued to hum as I dressed. I applied makeup sparingly in the tiny bathroom mirror, and brushed my hair into an elegant up-do. I wondered how long it would remain atop my head.

At seven o'clock on the dot, there was a soft knock on my cabin door. Nikolai. I checked my lipstick once more in the mirror and smoothed my hair.

"Come in," I said softly as I opened the door.

Nikolai stood in the hallway, balancing a tray holding several covered dishes. An older man and woman, walking past my door, looked in curiously.

"Here is your dinner, madam. Will there be anything else?"

He glanced at the nosy couple. He was trying to protect my reputation.

Playing along, I took the tray from him.

"Thank you. That will be all."

He pretended to close the door, and the couple continued on their way.

As soon as they were out of sight, Nikolai stepped into the cabin.

"That was unfortunate. I am sorry."

"Don't worry, it's all right," I said, distracted. I was looking around for a place to put the tray.

Nikolai took it out of my hands again, and set it on the little table under the porthole. He turned to me, the intensity of his gaze setting the gold flecks gleaming in his brown eyes.

"Sharon. I have been waiting for this for so long."

He moved toward me. Now his eyes were focused on my lips.

"You are beautiful."

I took a shaky step backwards. He followed, pinning me against the bathroom door.

Gently, he touched my cheek. I caught his scent again and without another thought, I raised my face. Then I was in his arms, his mouth searching mine. With amazement, I heard myself uttering soft, urgent cries against his lips. Reaching up, my arms circled his neck. I slipped one hand into the silken dark hair at the back of his head, and pulled him closer. After a long moment, he raised his head and softly kissed my forehead and cheeks.

"Do you wish to eat first?" There was no need to ask what the alternative would be.

I shook my head. Food could wait. He was all I wanted at this moment.

Taking my hand, he led me to the bed. He carefully removed the pins holding my hair in place. As my curls tumbled down, he buried his face in them and groaned in pleasure.

"I have been longing to do that," he said. Then, he slowly turned me around and I heard the sound of my zipper. In an instant my dress was puddled at my feet. He unhooked my bra and I felt the exquisite touch of his hands as they cupped my breasts.

I gasped in shocked pleasure. He nibbled my ear and ran kisses down the side of my neck to the tender spot just above my collarbone. He turned me back around then, and eyes sparkling, he bent to kiss my breasts.

I clutched his shoulders, then began to fumble with his shirt buttons. He briefly moved aside to rip it off and then turned back again to gather me into his arms.

Later, when I was alone, I tried to remember each kiss and caress, but they all mingled into a breathtaking tangle of sensation. He was magnificent. Hard muscle, soft mouth, the coarse dark hair of his body, the sure touch of his hands. I was drowning in wonder. Awash in emotion.

During pauses to catch our breath, I heard whispered Russian. Nikolai, or Niko as he asked me to call him, nervously translated when I asked him what he was saying.

"I do not wish to frighten you. I am saying how beautiful you are, how you make me feel, how much I want to spend every moment I can with you. I know I cannot, and that you might not welcome such attention from me." He looked down at me, a slight smile twitching the corners of his mouth. "But, your enthusiasm for our activities tonight makes me believe you might not chase me away, yes?"

I laughed. "No, I mean yes. I am very enthusiastic about our activities tonight. And, no. I will not chase you away. But, I think we should stop and eat our dinners. We can continue our activities after we eat, right?"

"Yes. Let us do so. Quickly."

We sat side by side on the bunk, sharing the tray between us as we ate our cold, but still delicious dinners. I loved the sound of his voice. It was deep and musical, with a slight British inflection mixed with his Russian accent. He seemed as intensely curious about me as I was about him.

"Niko, were you born here in Moscow? And tell me a little about your family, if you want to. Of course, you don't have to tell me anything."

"But I wish to. I wish to tell you everything about me. Well, perhaps not everything." He smiled. "I must keep some secrets, no?"

I nodded, laughing. "Sure. Keep your secrets, and I'll keep mine. Not that I have so many. My life is pretty much an open book."

"Well, then. No, I was not born in Moscow, but in St. Petersburg. My parents died when I was very young, and I remember little of them. My younger sister, Raisa, remembers nothing of them. She works as a technician in a laboratory at the University in St. Petersburg. She is divorced with one child, a daughter, Eva, who is eight years old. I see them as often as possible, and try to help them when they need me. It is sad that there are no grandparents."

"How about you, Niko? Do you have children? Or, maybe I should ask first if you've ever been married?"

"No to both questions. I have little time to be with young women, and I cannot see a time for marriage, even in the future. Teaching and summer travel on the river cruises keep me too busy for serious romances. Until now." He squeezed my hand and kissed me, a long, thorough kiss. We ate a few more bites of our food.

"Do you enjoy teaching? Tell me about your classes."

"Yes, very much. I teach classic English literature, novels, short stories, and poetry of the eighteenth and nineteenth centuries. English is not the first language for most of my students, and when one suddenly grasps the meaning of what they have struggled to read and understand, it is wonderful to see, as though the sun has shone through dark clouds. Sometimes, there can be other problems with students, but I enjoy that too. Working closely with them, the problems can often be solved."

He put our tray on the floor and pulled me back into his arms. "Now it is my turn. Sharon, why did you come to Russia?"

"My husband was an architect. He designed several projects here and in St. Petersburg, but I couldn't get him to tell me much about Russia and the people he met here. That made me curious. He might have brought me with him one day, if he'd lived. But he didn't. So, when my friend, Barbara Jeffries, invited me to come on this trip as her guest, it was an opportunity I didn't want to miss."

"Have you known her many years?" Sighing, he wound strands of my hair around his fingers. He seemed fascinated by my curls.

"We were college friends, and we've kept in touch since then."

"Do you have children?"

"A daughter. She's away at college now."

"You are too young to have a daughter of such age." He kissed my throat and reached lower. There was no more conversation.

'...too busy for serious romance, until now' sounded like a line. He probably said that to all the women he seduced.

I was under no illusion what we shared was *love*, but the emotional current between us had lifted what might have been awkward or ordinary sex to something that felt much more important. He had kissed away my tears as we were beginning to come down from our first impossible high.

I lay in Niko's arms for a long time after we had exhausted each other, each of us breathing in the other's scents, each caressing the other. Finally, he groaned and, kissing me thoroughly once more, rose to put on his clothes.

"I must return to my cabin and sleep. Tomorrow morning I am to teach my first Russian class of this voyage. I cannot fall asleep in mid-lesson. You will join us, yes?"

"If I don't oversleep," I yawned, smiling. Then, more seriously, "I'll be there. I wouldn't miss it."

"Good. Then tomorrow afternoon, when we reach Uglich, I will take you on a private tour of the village."

"You can do that?" I was surprised. "Don't you have people signed up for your paid private tours?"

"No. And, I will take no money from you." He reached into his jacket pocket and pressed the envelope containing the tip I had given him that morning into my hands.

I hesitated. I knew he needed money, but he seemed truly determined not to take *my* money.

"On the ship," he continued, "I have little free time, but when we reach St. Petersburg, I will have more freedom. I will make as much time to be with you as I can."

I slipped out of bed and into my robe, and walked with him to the door. I opened it and peered up and down the corridor to make certain no one was coming.

"What should I do with our tray?"

"I will put it outside your door. It will be picked up before morning."

He did so, and then held me tightly for a moment and whispered against my lips, "Until tomorrow."

Then he was gone.

CHAPTER 11

Tuesday, August 31
Day 6

WHEN THE alarm sounded the next morning, my first waking thought was of Niko. Stretching lazily, I discovered I was a bit sore in familiar places—places no man had touched since Dale. No. I was not going to think about Dale.

By the time I showered and dressed, the faint aches were gone. Only the glow remained. *Niko*. I would see him soon.

He was not at breakfast when I arrived. I loaded a plate and found my three new friends, Joan, Marcia, and Sara. They were almost done, but welcomed me warmly, and asked how I was enjoying the trip so far.

"I'm having a great time," I said. "I'm enjoying meeting new people and the scenery along here is beautiful."

"We were hoping you were all right," said Marcia. "We didn't see you after lunch yesterday."

"Oh!" I swallowed, hoping I was not going to blush. "I didn't see you either. Did any of you get to the gift shop yet?"

"Well, we've all been looking, but so far only Sara has bought anything," Joan said. "I'm trying to find a special present for my granddaughter, but I haven't found it yet."

"She's been trying, all right," said Sara, "but finding the perfect gift for a 16-year-old isn't very easy. My nieces are younger, and much easier to buy for." She began a long, heavily descriptive tale about the Russian nesting dolls she had bought for them.

Relieved I had successfully turned the conversation, I listened as Joan and Marcia interrupted Sara's story and all three began to tease each other. Meanwhile, I devoured my breakfast. I was hungry this morning.

Soon after they left, Barbara spotted me as she was leaving the dining room, and sat down beside me.

"I didn't see you last night at dinner. Did you and Nikolai manage to spend some time together?" She eyed me with curiosity.

"I can't talk about it yet, but the answer is yes."

"Oh, well… good. Maybe there's hope for me." She laughed ruefully, and with a congratulatory pat on my shoulder, she left the dining room.

The smiling Ivan, our usual waiter, filled my teacup with hot water. "Will there be anything else, madam?"

That was a familiar phrase. I grinned, remembering Niko delivering our dinner tray last night. "Thanks, Ivan. No, that's all."

I sat for a few minutes, enjoying my tea and watching the passing scenery through the wide windows. This morning, there was dark, dense forest, unbroken by clearings or signs of civilization. The sun slanted over the tops of the trees with the promise of another warm and sunny day. So far, rain had fallen only on the night before we visited the nature preserve, while I was sleeping.

I glanced at my watch. I had only a few minutes to get ready for Niko's Russian language class. I swallowed the rest of my tea and ran down to my cabin.

≪≫

I tried to steady my nerves as I walked up the winding stairs to the Sky Bar. How would I feel seeing Niko this morning after last night's "activities?"

He stood at the front of the room with a stack of papers in his hands. Folding chairs had been set up in rows with an aisle in the middle. I found a seat at the end of a row and looked around. Almost all of the seats were taken and more people were hovering at the door.

"Come in, come in," he urged them. "Welcome, everyone. Please take a seat and we will begin."

Carefully avoiding meeting my eyes, Niko began distributing the handouts he had prepared. A moment later, he gave me enough for everyone in our row. Following his cue, I kept my head down. I took one and passed the rest of them on without looking up at him.

As it turned out, Niko was a very good teacher, patient but firm with anyone who tried to waste time with irrelevant questions or comments. I was impressed by how easily he controlled the class, which must have been very different from the classes he taught at his university.

He began by introducing the Russian Cyrillic alphabet, which contained what seemed to be part of the Greek alphabet mixed with a few familiar English letters. He pronounced each character and asked us to repeat the sounds. Then he showed us how they combined to spell familiar words a traveler would need to know, such as 'restaurant,' 'Metro,' and 'men's and ladies' restrooms.'

On another page, there was a long list of common phrases, and when he came to 'I love you,' his eyes found mine and held my gaze for a long beat. He smiled slightly. Predictably, my face warmed.

I must confess, I was concentrating more on Niko himself than on his lesson. What was it that made him so attractive? He was not classically handsome, and those winged black eyebrows were more devilish than angelic. His large eyes were wide spaced and deep set, shaped like fat, slightly up-tilted almonds. His nose was narrow, but long, with the hint of a hook, his high cheekbones jutted just enough to create shallow hollows on his lean cheeks, and his square chin was firm and strong. Maybe it was his lips that held me most in thrall—they were full, wide, and expressive, covering even white teeth.

I tilted my head to observe him better. At one or two inches over six feet, his body was long-limbed and graceful, perfectly proportioned. His head was balanced on a long, strong neck, and he had a superbly toned upper body and muscled legs.

Nodding slightly, I decided it was not his looks alone, but the whole package: looks, intelligence, personality, a keen curiosity, and a dry sense of humor. I wondered why I was so sure of all this on such short acquaintance. I had no explanation for that, but despite meeting him so recently, I felt I already knew him intimately.

When the class was over, I made sure to be the last person to leave.

As I passed him, Niko touched my arm. "I will meet you at the bottom of the gangway when we dock at Uglich, yes?"

I nodded, smiling, and left the room. My arm was tingling where he had touched it.

We were scheduled to dock at Uglich at two o'clock.

We had half an hour before the next activity was to take place, a lecture by Madame Yelena Slosky, a Moscow University professor. She had been an aide to former Russian Presidents Mikhail Gorbachev and Boris Yeltsin, and for a short time to the current leader, Vladimir Putin. She was scheduled to present a series of hour-long talks over the next few days on various Russian topics. I decided to attend her first lecture, which was on Russian royalty, and then it would be time for lunch.

Though I went more to fill the time than because I was interested in the subject matter, the time sped by. Madame Slosky was an outstanding speaker with a sly, surprising sense of humor. She made what might have been a very boring topic come alive.

At lunch, I found a seat with our party and listened with half an ear as Anatoly spoke about Russian birds of prey. I hoped not to run into any while we were here. As a group, they sounded dangerous.

At last, the meal was over and I escaped to my cabin to change into walking shoes. I smiled at my reflection in the mirror as I reapplied my lipstick. I half hoped it would be kissed away, though since we would be with other tourists, that would not be happening. I picked up my sunglasses and left the cabin.

Niko was waiting, as promised, at the bottom of the gangway. He nodded formally to me and we fell into step. He kept his hands in his pockets as we walked away from the quay toward the town.

Along the way, Russian vendors were selling souvenirs, and I was amused to note there were several groups of musicians, each playing different American tunes. "America the Beautiful" vied with "Dixieland," and further along there was a four-piece ensemble playing "The Star Spangled Banner."

When I remarked on it, Niko said, "Do not be surprised by this. Everyone is trying to make a living in any way they can. This is especially true in the small towns and villages, even ones tourists are permitted to visit. Good jobs are difficult to qualify for and the others pay very little."

He was serious. It was the first time he had spoken to me about the lives of ordinary Russians.

Several questions about those ordinary Russians came to mind, but I would have to wait until tonight to ask them. Now, we were approaching the ruins of the old Uglich kremlin.

"Many of the historic buildings in the old town have been destroyed," Niko said, "but, luckily, several have been preserved. The kremlin's moat has also been preserved, and as you can see, it now provides a picturesque harbor for small boats."

We stayed for a moment to admire it. Then, Niko pointed toward a green-domed church, perched at the moat's edge.

"This is the Transfiguration Cathedral." I nodded. "We will stop in here now to see the icons, and then later, there will be a surprise."

"A surprise?"

"Yes." He looked down at me, smiling broadly. "I hope you will enjoy it."

The cathedral had a high vaulted ceiling unsupported by columns, quite a feat of engineering when it was built in 1713. Inside, every square inch was covered with brightly painted icons and religious scenes. Off the nave in a museum-like anteroom, there was a collection of more icons and other religious articles. They looked very old and were probably quite valuable.

"This cathedral is still used for religious services. We are lucky. Today there are none. We can admire the beauty of the decorations in peace."

But not for long. Soon, tourists began to crowd inside. Niko touched my arm and we escaped through a small door at the rear of the anteroom into a narrow alleyway outside. With no one in sight, he pulled me into a quick embrace.

"Next, we will visit the Church of Prince Dmitry on the Spilled Blood," he whispered, brushing my lips with his, and reluctantly releasing me. We could hear people laughing nearby.

We followed the alley to the main street and walked a short way to the front of Dmitry's church. As we began to climb the steps to the door, I looked at Niko and said, "I was wondering about the name of this church. There must be a story behind it, right?"

"Yes. Dmitry had the misfortune to be Czar Ivan the Terrible's only living heir. Boris Godunov, a Russian noble who was serving at the time in Ivan's court, wanted to become Czar himself. He knew eliminating nine-year-old Dmitry would help him achieve his goal, so he ordered his men to kill him. Dmitry was murdered on this very spot.

"Uglich's bell alerted the townspeople, who killed some of Godunov's men. He and the rest of his men were brought to trial, accused of arranging Dmitry's death. But, he already must have been gaining power, because the court pardoned all of them. The judges declared Dmitry had had an epileptic seizure and stabbed himself to death with his own knife.

"Of course, this was nonsense, but Gudunov was not satisfied with his pardon. He celebrated his victory by taking revenge on the townspeople of Uglich and even punishing the bell. He had it whipped, and then sent it to Siberia with its clapper removed. Eventually it was returned and we will see it inside the church."

"Poor Dmitry. He never had a chance."

"We will never know what kind of ruler he might have been, but by dying as he did, people worshiped him as a martyr and he was later canonized. He became St. Dmitry. This church was built to commemorate his death. Sadly, Godunov was later elected Czar, so his plot was successful."

Dmitry's church vaguely resembled a birthday cake, with a cheerful red, white and blue exterior. Inside, every surface was brightly decorated. In addition to an unusual fresco of Adam and Eve with neither clothing nor fig leaves, the legend of Dmitry's death was portrayed on the walls of the tiny nave. And, there was the Uglich bell, back home after its long exile in Siberia.

Soon, we left the church and walked toward the Transfiguration Cathedral's tall bell tower, topped by an elegant gold dome.

"We must hurry," Niko said. "In a few minutes, it will be time for your surprise."

Just before we entered the Bell Tower, Niko whispered, "Tonight, in your cabin at seven o'clock, yes?"

I nodded, smiling.

Inside, I rejoined our group and took a seat on one of the wide benches against the walls of the tower. An invisible door cut into a wall opened and more than a dozen monks entered in single file, dressed in dark red robes. They stood in a line, and at some unseen signal, began to sing. Their unaccompanied voices mingled and soared around the small chamber and up into the vaulted ceiling. It was a beautiful and otherworldly sound, a little like recordings of Gregorian chants I had heard, but different, more Asian in tone and feeling. The fine hairs rose on the back of my neck, and I shivered. I had never been so moved by religious music.

In wonder, I looked toward Niko who was standing against the wall near my bench. He met my eyes and smiled.

All too soon, the monks bowed slightly and marched out. It was time to return to our ship.

Niko left before me, walking quickly back to the *River Sprite*. I waited inside the bell tower until the last musical note, shivering in the air, fell silent, and everyone else had stepped outside. I wanted to savor the intimacy of this experience, and the precious time I had spent with Niko in Uglich.

Finally, I walked out of the tower into the late afternoon sunshine. Along the path through the old town and back to the ship, vendors were selling wristwatches, nesting dolls, enameled boxes, wooden toys, needlecrafts, and other souvenirs.

I stopped to admire a display of small trinket boxes made of birch bark. The carved designs were exquisite, and precisely done. If I had not seen the artist at work, I would have believed they were produced by machine. I bought an oval box for Ellen, decorated with delicate vines and tiny flowers across the lid and around its edge. I chose a square one for myself, with a forest scene carved into the top and a stylized leaf design around the sides of the lid.

As I strolled slowly back to our ship, I nodded and smiled at various vendors and other passengers I recognized, but avoided being drawn into conversation with anyone. This time, I made sure to give generous tips to the Russian musicians, still valiantly playing American tunes.

Back on board, I took my novel and went to the Sun Deck to find a lounge chair. The late afternoon air was clear and warm and the sun was still bright. We would be leaving Uglich's port at six o'clock, an hour before dinner. Tomorrow we would dock at Yaroslavl, a much larger town than Uglich, according to my guidebook. Tonight there was to be a folk music concert after dinner. I hoped no one would notice my absence. I would be in my cabin with Niko.

Just as I began to doze over my book, Barbara, Anatoly, and several of our group came out of the Sky Bar carrying drinks. They called to me to join them, and I decided it would be a good idea to do so. It might be easier to explain my absence at dinner and the concert—should anyone ask—if I had a drink now.

I ordered a vodka martini and carried it back outside, taking a seat on the edge of the group. They were in the midst of questioning Anatoly about a small yellow bird they had seen near the harbor in Uglich. No one expected me to participate in their discussion, though I listened politely.

Barbara gave me a meaningful glance and moved over to sit beside me.

"How are things going with you and you-know-who?" she asked in a low voice. "I saw you walking together in Uglich."

I was grateful she had not mentioned his name.

"Okay, I guess." I paused to sip my drink. "I don't know quite how to take his interest in me. I'm enjoying it while it lasts, but I don't think for a moment he's serious."

"What makes you so sure? Has he hinted there's a wife and a dozen children at home?"

"No. He's mentioned a sister, and she has a daughter, but he says he's never been married."

"Ah…" She grinned. "Then, do you think he has a girlfriend in every port?"

"Not necessarily. He spent time with me in Uglich."

"Well, then… Every port except Uglich?"

I laughed. "He probably picks out a woman to romance on every voyage. On this one, I'm it! But, I've decided to relax and enjoy whatever it is while I can."

"Good attitude. Oops, Anatoly's looking this way. I'd better go rescue him."

I finished my drink and ordered another. Eventually, one of the men glanced at his watch and announced, "Hey, it's six-thirty. We'd better go freshen up before dinner."

His wife hooted. "Ha! You're fresh enough already!"

There was general laughter and the scraping of chairs as the group trooped off to find their cabins. I sat on for a few minutes, putting my drink aside untouched. There was no need to rush. I had only to brush my teeth and change into something easily removed. The last thing I wanted was for too much alcohol to blunt my enjoyment of what was to come.

Promptly at seven, there was a knock on my door. Niko stood there with our dinners on a tray and a wicked grin on his face.

"Madam, here is your dinner. Is there anything else I can do for you?"

There was no one passing by in the corridor this time. There was no need to repeat last evening's charade.

"Yes, please come in." I was trying not to laugh too hard. "My zipper is stuck. Maybe you can help me?"

He put the tray down on the bedside table as before, and turned to me. "Now about that zipper…"

His arms came around me and his lips found mine. And time stopped.

His hands and mouth, though gentle as they stroked and probed and kissed and sucked, brought me to a height of pleasure I had never expected to share with a man other than Dale. In return, I seemed to know exactly how to produce the same response from him. The usual descriptive devices—crashing waves, exploding fireworks—were useless to explain what happened when we were together like this. We were shipwrecked in a strange and astonishing land.

Gradually our breathing returned to what passed for normal with us. Niko gathered me into his arms and rocked me gently. I stroked the bunched muscles in his powerful shoulders and arms while he murmured Russian endearments into my hair.

"We should eat," he whispered, finally. "Like last night, our food will be cold, but I must eat if we are to do this again tonight."

I laughed. "Oh, yes. Please, let's eat." I definitely wanted us to do this again tonight.

Later, when he left me, I went with him to the door, looking out first to make sure no one was passing in the corridor. The hallway was empty. In an old-fashioned, courtly gesture, he drew my hands to his lips and kissed each palm in turn. Then, he was gone, leaving me trembling in the doorway. I would see him again tomorrow morning. No, today. It was after midnight.

I fell asleep easily, but instead of a peaceful night's rest, after my strenuous "activities" with Niko, I dreamed about Dale and our life together. I tossed and turned, forced to relive our happiness—and the realization that it was gone— all over again.

⤬⤬

1978 to 2002

I finally told my parents of my engagement to Dale during my senior year at Williams. Predictably, they were furious and threatened to cut off my monthly allowance if I persisted in such an unsuitable liaison. I ignored them.

At last, our big weekend arrived. Dale was graduated summa cum laude, and won a major architectural design award, which thrilled his family and made me almost burst with pride. Though I won no prizes, I was excited to receive a cum laude diploma.

Our wedding was held the next day in the campus chapel, crowded with our friends. My parents, having proclaimed I was marrying beneath me, refused to attend either my graduation or our marriage ceremony. Though Dale's parents still worried he might be making a mistake marrying someone from a background so different from his, Sharon and Mike came, along with Dale's brothers and their families, and lovingly wished us well. They gave us a small gift of money we used to help pay for a short honeymoon on Cape Cod.

That week in late May on the Cape set the tone for our marriage. We found passion and pleasure in each other's bodies, and never having visited the Cape before, we spent several hours each unseasonably warm and sunny day sightseeing. We rented bicycles and rode from town to town, stopping now and then to walk hand in hand along the sandy beaches and watch the waves roll in. We were blissfully happy.

Well before graduation from Williams, Dale had applied for admission to the Cornell University Graduate School of Architecture, requesting financial assistance. A few weeks before graduation, we learned he had been awarded a full scholarship. When we returned from the Cape, we drove to Ithaca, found a small furnished apartment near the campus, and set up housekeeping.

Both of us worked full-time that summer. I took a secretarial job I hated, but the salary paid for our essentials. It also taught me most of what I needed to know about running a well managed office and navigating my way through the inevitable office politics. While he earned his graduate degree, Dale worked at whatever part-time jobs he could fit into his schedule.

Shortly after we moved to Ithaca, I received a letter from my parents' attorney. Because I had married against their wishes, they were washing their hands of me. They would leave their fortune to charity. I was instructed neither to contact them nor to expect to hear from them again.

I was dismayed at the finality of this step, though not really surprised. Now, I owned nothing but my college clothing and the books I had begun to collect. Though he found it impossible to imagine how my parents could do such a thing, Dale took it rather well. In fact, he was probably secretly relieved. It was up to us to support each other.

Dale worked hard at his studies and, with the help of one of his professors, he was awarded a coveted internship at a prestigious New York City architectural firm. The company's president, Robert Morton, noticed Dale's promise, and became his mentor.

After Dale received his Masters degree, Morton hired him as a draftsman and we moved into a tiny studio apartment in mid-town Manhattan. I began working for a weekly environmental newspaper, headquartered in a drab basement in the East Village. I doubled as reporter and copy editor. It paid little, but I loved the unexpectedness of the job. Many of the people I interviewed were rising stars in the increasingly controversial environmental movement.

As Dale was assigned more challenging work, his salary increased. We left our little studio and moved uptown into a larger, one-bedroom flat.

By the time Morton retired, Dale had risen in the firm to become a junior partner and had begun winning architectural awards, bringing additional fame to the firm as well as to himself. Increasingly, he was asked to design projects in Europe, South America, Asia, and the Middle East. I worried about his travels, fearing plane crashes or other foreign disasters, especially since there were sometimes long stretches of time when I was unable to contact him. To my relief, he always returned safely, claiming he never had any problems while overseas.

One of his first foreign projects was in the Ukraine. Though we spoke by telephone several times at the beginning of the project, later I had no word from Dale—and was unable to reach him—for more than three weeks. I was frantic. I had no one to turn to other than friends who were sympathetic, but who could do nothing to help me.

Dale's office was equally unhelpful. They had not spoken with him directly, though they believed the project was progressing well. Be patient, they advised. The Ukraine was not like the United States. Disruptions of telephone service, electricity, and transportation systems were commonplace. Dale would call me when he could.

Naturally, I was furious when I finally heard from him. He listened patiently, but brushed off my tearful raging with infuriating nonchalance. He promised to make it up to me when he returned, but it was another month before he came home again.

I was so grateful to have him back safely, my anger quickly drained away. This was only the first of many such communication breakdowns. I finally accepted that they were simply a part of his job, just as the money he made and the international prestige he was earning were other parts.

However, I could never get used to the silences, though he always had a plausible explanation as to why I had not been able to reach him, and why he had not called me.

Six years after our marriage, our daughter Ellen was born. I decided to stop working for the paper toward the end of my pregnancy, though I hoped to continue writing, perhaps trying my hand at poetry or even fiction. With a tiny baby who demanded round the clock care, my urge to write was beaten down by exhaustion, though I kept a journal handy to record midnight musings and Ellen's milestones.

The months passed and Ellen thrived. Soon, with toys and baby equipment everywhere, our uptown apartment began to seem cramped. We moved again, this time to a two-bedroom flat in the same building. Then, when Ellen was two, I inherited some money from my Aunt Martha, my mother's older sister. According to Mama, Aunt Martha also had made an unsuitable marriage. Though they were childless, she and her husband had been happy, and had been financially comfortable.

Long a widow, Aunt Martha had encouraged me to follow my heart. Because of her support, Dale reluctantly agreed to let me use the money for our benefit. Her legacy was small compared to my parents' fortune, but it was enough to use as collateral to set Dale up in business for himself, and to purchase our first house.

While Dale wound up his commitments to Morton's firm, we spent weekends hunting for the perfect community. We finally found it, north of New York City in Putnam County in the Hudson River Valley, within a relatively easy commute to Manhattan. It was a historic and picturesque village with a New England flavor. We chose it for our home and Dale's architectural practice because, quite simply, we fell in love with it. The house we bought was an older Dutch colonial with a wide veranda, just blocks from the space we rented, and eventually purchased, for Dale's offices.

Over the next few years, our lives settled into a comfortable pattern. Dale's practice grew and we added more staff. Seemingly overnight, Ellen, a chubby toddler when we moved to town, became a tall, skinny "big" girl, with tousled dark red curls and scraped knees. I began working part-time in Dale's offices, making sure to be at home in the afternoons when the school bus dropped Ellen at our corner. When Dale was home from his travels, we played tennis and swam at the local Country Club. Occasionally, we entertained clients there.

In our spare time, Dale and I worked together on plans for a house of our own design. Much as we loved our Dutch Colonial, it had been built in 1899 and had a somewhat inconvenient layout with odd nooks and steep, narrow stairs. While those were the very features we loved when we first bought it, over time they lost much of their charm. The house had been kept in good condition by all of its owners, especially Dale, who was careful to preserve its character whenever we repaired or redecorated any part of it. We were sure another family would find it as attractive as we had.

Dale and I often talked about what our new home would be like, what materials to use, and how to furnish it. We agreed that the house should be welcoming but private, airy yet cozy, spacious but not too big.

We began searching for the right property. One day, we drove down a shady lane near the edge of town in response to a real estate ad in our local newspaper.

As we got out of the car, Dale grabbed my hand and pulled me with him to the top of the hill that capped the middle of the four acre property. We slowly turned around, looking in all directions. Toward the street, there were magnificent old trees. On the opposite side, the ground sloped gently down to a small stream splashing merrily into a sizeable pond. The nearest neighbors were out of sight. We hugged, laughing excitedly.

"I'll have to find out about the stream. If it floods regularly, we'll have to pass."

"But, Dale, isn't the hill high enough to keep us safe?"

"Maybe. We'll have to find out where the source is and whether it actually floods or not. Then we can make an informed decision. Of course, I'll also have to find out if the price is negotiable, if there are any liens on the property, what the taxes might be, whether there are water and sewer lines out here, and a lot more."

In the end, he received positive answers to all his questions, and the sellers agreed to lower their asking price.

I was ecstatic, already picturing the three of us happily living there.

Dale designed a three-story contemporary-style house for us, built into the natural slope of the land. At the front of the house on the main floor, there was a spacious living room and a separate dining room. Behind them, there was a powder room, and a large kitchen, separated from the family room by a long counter and barstools.

The family room stretched across the entire back of the house, with huge windows that framed the view of the pond and stream. Dale included a large, European-style wood-burning stove on one side wall, backed by beautiful gray stone, heavily veined with russet, from a local quarry.

Upstairs, the master suite had a luxurious bath and two walk-in closets. Our windows overlooked the terraced garden, brook, and pond.

Across the hall were Ellen's bedroom, another full bathroom, and a large all-purpose room with space for a drafting table, computer desks, and plenty of storage for files and my needlework projects.

On the lowest level there was a sizeable guest suite, and a heated three-car garage, linked to the street by a curving driveway.

Off the kitchen/family room was a wide flagstone patio, with steps leading down through terraced gardens to a smaller, secluded stone patio near the pond. With all the windows planned for the house, I looked forward to watching the views change as season followed season.

Thirteen years after our marriage, we started construction. When it was finally completed, it was everything we had envisioned.

I always told people I helped design the house. That was an exaggeration, though I spent many happy hours choosing furniture, paint and upholstery colors, window coverings, art, and other decorative accessories. But as Dale's designs for the house evolved and matured, I began to understand what made him such a respected and sought-after architect. He had an intuitive and sensitive ability to understand not only what his clients needed, but also what they might have dreamed of, if only they had his genius.

The years passed and no more children came, though our doctors found no conclusive reasons for infertility. We enjoyed being Ellen's parents and watched her progress with pride. She was bright, athletic, and popular with her classmates.

Between working in Dale's office and keeping up with Ellen's activities, I had plenty to keep me busy while Dale was away, and when he was at home, we made the most of our time together. We were active members of our community and enjoyed the friendships we made. We took the train into the city for celebratory dinners, Broadway shows, concerts, museum visits, and shopping trips.

Like most long-married couples, we had had our disagreements, but we had shared a strong physical and emotional bond. We knew how lucky we were, and we had each treasured our full and happy life together.

It had been almost idyllic, but now it was gone—so suddenly it might never have existed at all.

CHAPTER 12

Wednesday, September 1
Day 7

I HAD forgotten to set my alarm, and when I awoke, later than usual after my disturbed night, there were dried tears on my cheeks. I was unsure whether I had simply been dreaming, or if I had experienced a nightmare. I showered in a daze, and had just enough time to grab coffee and a buttered roll before racing to catch the bus into Yaroslavl. By the time I spotted Niko, waiting at the bottom of the steps, as usual, to help our group on board, I had begun to shake off my sadness.

Niko managed to look friendly but aloof when he saw me, as though he were greeting someone with whom he had not spent the better part of the past two evenings. I tried to match his casual air, but it was very difficult to achieve when he took my hand to help me up the steps. We both felt small jolts of electricity each time we touched.

I found a seat toward the back. Niko sat directly behind me, with the rest of our group sitting ahead of us. We knew it was necessary to keep up the pretense of casual friendliness in case any of the other passengers turned around and caught us behaving inappropriately. Nevertheless, at one point he leaned forward to caress the nape of my neck and squeeze my shoulder. I shivered with desire.

In Yaroslavl's Old Town, we saw interesting medieval wall paintings, but while I admired the architecture of the churches and the monastery we visited, I was less impressed with their over-the-top interior decorations, which seemed garish to my eyes. At the monastery there was an elaborate display of hand bells of different tones, each attached to a thin rope. A young monk held the ends of the ropes like a puppeteer, expertly manipulating them to produce a short but lovely concert.

The part I enjoyed most was our walk along the river embankment. Our guide described it as one of the most beautiful of the Volga River promenades. I believed her. It was easy to imagine elegant ladies strolling arm-in-arm with their lovers, pausing now and then for a romantic *tête-à-tête* in the graceful little stone gazebos built into the ornate balustrade. At either end of the promenade there was a small circular garden, planted with colorful annual flowers and herbs in quaint Victorian patterns.

Our tour ended with a musical presentation held in the ballroom of a formerly grand mansion. There were impressive Russian paintings hanging on the walls, but as in the Tretyakov Art Museum in Moscow, none of the artists were familiar to me.

We were seated in rows of folding chairs and as we waited for the concert to begin, I admired the architecture of the enormous room and its decorations, especially the ornate crystal chandeliers hanging far above us.

At last, a mixed voice chorus filed in, took their places, and sang two unfamiliar classical pieces, directed by a middle-aged woman who accompanied them on the piano. Then, as an unexpected treat, a well-known Russian opera singer, who was vacationing nearby, made his entrance. He was quite good, a tenor with a wide range and excellent intonation, singing sometimes alone and sometimes with the chorus.

His encore was a poem by the famous Russian poet Alexander Pushkin, set to a hauntingly beautiful folk tune. The singer portrayed sadness and hope with his fluid voice. Though the words were in Russian, I was deeply moved by the beauty of the music. Niko, who was standing against the wall at the end of my row, caught my eye and nodded in empathy.

In the confusion of leaving the concert hall and finding our bus again, Niko took the opportunity to squeeze my hand. "That last song was one of Pushkin's most famous poems. Later I will tell you the story behind it."

Back on board the ship, it was lunchtime. I was ready for it. My sketchy breakfast was a distant memory.

In the dining room I found my three friends, Joan, Marcia and Sara. We chatted about the morning's visit to Yaroslavl, sharing our impressions and bemoaning the lack of shopping opportunities there as opposed to the ones in Uglich.

Then Joan said, "We haven't seen you at dinner the last two nights. Are you all right?"

I quickly swallowed a mouthful of potato salad. "Sure. I guess I was done before you came in, or came after you left." I felt my face begin to heat.

As coolly as I could, I explained. "I've been trying to avoid a couple in our group who seem to want to spend every moment with me. She's really interesting and funny when she's not with her husband, but he's a terrible bore. That's why I've been laying kind of low."

I was sorry to mislead them, but I was not about to confess I had been having amazing sex with a member of the ship's crew.

After lunch I browsed in the gift shop. I wanted to bring back gifts for Linda, my assistant; the architects, Charlie and Rich; and our other staff members. I also wanted to find something for my personal trainer at the gym. All of them had been so kind. First, they had encouraged me to decide to go to Russia, despite my objections. Then, once I had made up my mind to go, they had listened patiently to all my plans. Bringing back a small gift was the least I could do for them.

I wanted to pick out something special for Ellen. I had seen and was considering a pair of Baltic amber earrings for myself, rich drops in a plain sterling silver setting. But Ellen, with her dramatic coloring, deserved an important necklace, or possibly a necklace and earring set. I knew I would recognize the right pieces when I saw them.

I glanced at my watch. It was almost time for Madame Slosky's lecture on Russian political history.

I spotted a seat near the front and discovered I was sitting next to a couple from our group. Cindy and Ted were from a small town near Toronto, Canada. Before their retirement, she had been a librarian and he was Dr. Ted, a podiatrist. Both were avid birders and had traveled the globe adding to their life lists. They shared a droll sense of humor, and often had us laughing during bus rides and long waits in lines.

Serious for once, Cindy asked, "How did you like the tour this morning?"

"It was interesting, but I was struck by how much peeling paint we saw during the drive to the Old Town."

"I noticed that too," Ted said. "Looks like the Communists spent very little money on maintenance, though it's more likely due to Soviet incompetence."

I nodded. "Yes. Even the Russian Orthodox Church seems to have spent little or no money here. I found it very surprising when our guide mentioned that many of the churches we visited were built by rich families for their own private worship."

"I was surprised, too!" Cindy shook her head in mock wonder. "Imagine having that much money!"

"Huh! It's hard to imagine." I shook my head, too. I was remembering Niko explaining how difficult it was for most ordinary Russians to make a living. I was beginning to see how right he was. Since we had left Moscow, most of the wealth we had seen was from the Eighteenth and Nineteenth centuries, and had been in the hands of the nobles.

Cindy made a wry face and whispered, "I've seen enough icons to last a lifetime! Of course, we're just getting started. I'm sure we'll see lots more, eh?"

I nodded. "I'm sure you're right, but what did you think of the concert?"

"It was great!" Ted said. "Did you notice the blonde soprano in the first row? Not only was her voice heavenly, but she had the face of an angel!"

Ted often exaggerated a bit, but in this case, I had to agree.

"Yes, she was almost better than the tenor, though he was very good too, I thought. Their duet was divine."

Cindy nodded. "Yes, indeed! I think that concert was the highlight of our trip so far."

It had been a very good concert, but I remembered the choir of monks in Uglich, and my awed delight. That had been pure magic.

"Ah, here comes Madame Slosky."

The next forty-five minutes flew by as Madame Slosky entertained us in her usual style. She told us the Russian word "soviet" meant a governing council, so when Lenin proclaimed "Land to the people, peace to the people, power to the Soviets," he was really saying power to the *people*. However, she noted that while certain people had grabbed all the power, the rest of them had been given none.

During the Stalin era, Madame Slosky said, "about sixty-five million people, or about half of the present day population of Russia, were 'eliminated,' a polite word for genocide."

A few minutes later, she remarked, "Khrushchev, who was famous for pounding the table with his shoe at the United Nations, banned many books and liked to call himself 'a self-made man'." Madame Slosky remarked dryly, "Well, that took the responsibility away from God!"

Before I knew it, the lecture was over. I reached for my tote and scrambled to my feet. With a hasty wave to Cindy and Ted, I fled to my cabin. I had less than fifteen minutes to get ready for Niko's next Russian language class.

I waited until I knew I would not be the first one to arrive in the makeshift classroom in the Sky Bar.

"Good afternoon, madam," Niko murmured with a smile as I walked into the bar. Fifteen or twenty people were already seated and there were more behind me.

"Everyone please take a seat, so we can begin."

It was easy now to imagine him as an English professor in his university classroom. Though his English sounded a little old-fashioned, it was perfectly correct—unless he was excited, as I had reason to know.

When everyone was seated, he handed out a printed sheet with more Russian phrases, first in

Cyrillic and then spelled phonetically in the English alphabet. We read through them, carefully pronouncing the unfamiliar words.

All too soon, the class was over and people began to leave. There was no way to have a private word with Niko. He was trapped near the door, mobbed by people with questions.

I slipped through the crowd around him, and found a seat on the almost deserted Sun Deck. We had been cruising since lunch. According to our itinerary, we would continue to do so all of tomorrow and part of the following day until we reached Kizhi Island.

I put my guidebook away and opened my novel, but I soon began to feel sleepy. I leaned back in my deck chair and closed my eyes for a short nap, but sleep was impossible. Thoughts of Niko and our relationship—no, our affair!—filled my head. My eyes popped open, and I sat up in defeat.

I truly believed Dale would have wanted me to find happiness with another man, eventually, if something happened to him. However, it was less than two years since he had died. He might have expected a longer mourning period, given how blissful our marriage had been. Or, maybe I was just feeling guilty because of last night's dream.

I sighed, deciding to put these thoughts out of my mind, and simply be grateful for his company, not to mention the marvelous sex I was enjoying with Niko.

I settled back, opened my novel, and promptly fell asleep.

The next thing I knew, the barman was bending over me, calling, "Madame, Madame."

I startled awake, and blinked. The barman said, "Excuse me, Madame. It is almost time for dinner."

I thanked him, and grabbing my book and tote bag, I hurried back to my cabin.

Niko arrived, as usual, exactly at seven o'clock. He quickly set our dinner tray down on my bedside table and pulled me into his arms, kissing me hungrily.

His hands cradling my face, he rained kisses from forehead to chin, then back to possess my mouth. His lips dipped lower, and once again we were swept away.

CHAPTER 13

Thursday, September 2
Day 8

THE NEXT morning, I awoke at dawn, well before my alarm was due to sound. I thought I could hear the sound of a helicopter lifting off, but decided I must be mistaken. Outside my porthole, I could see nothing but a dense, white curtain of fog. We had left the Volga River far behind and were now somewhere on Lake Onega.

Since I was up so early, I decided to join the daily stretching session on the Sun Deck, led by one of Maddy's assistants. I had been very lax about aerobic exercise on this trip so far, though I was getting plenty of another type of exercise.

There were about twenty people in the class, and the not-too-strenuous workout was fun. I glanced up at the sky as I left the deck. The fog was already beginning to lift.

Back in my cabin, there was just time for a shower before breakfast and Madame Slosky's next lecture.

According to my guidebook, Russia was far ahead of most other nations in women's educational and professional equality. That had surprised me. Now, Madame Slosky explained why: by the end of World War II, there were six to eight Russian women for each man, because so many Russian soldiers had been killed in the fighting. Women were welcomed into the professions and other high-paying jobs because that was the only way the country could survive.

In other ways, however, she claimed Russia was still stuck in medieval times, and she had little faith the corruption and general incompetence of local and national politicians would ever improve. I did notice she mentioned nothing even slightly critical about Mr. Putin, currently in his second term as Russia's President. She probably was being wise, given his KGB background, though he claimed to have put such past associations behind him. She also mentioned none of the troubles with rebellious members of the former Soviet Union, the Ukraine, for instance, and particularly Chechnya, after years of guerilla warfare, terrorist activity, and bloodshed.

At the end of her talk, I returned to my cabin shaking my head over her omission of Russia's troubles with Chechnya. I thought that was very odd, because yesterday CNN International had begun TV coverage of a dreadful situation in Beslan, an industrial town in southern Russia near their border with Chechnya.

At breakfast this morning, several of our group who had seen the initial news coverage described what had been reported: Yesterday was the first day of the school year in Beslan. Just after the opening ceremony in the town's School No. 1, dozens of masked men wearing explosive belts and carrying guns stormed into the building and took hostage the more than eleven hundred people in attendance, including students, teachers, parents, small children, and infants. The men— Muslim separatists and Arab mercenaries—were demanding Russian troops be withdrawn from Chechnya or they would blow up the school and everyone in it.

With sadness, I remembered our Moscow guides telling us Russian children traditionally brought flowers to their teachers on the first day of school. This year, the first school day in Beslan had been horrific. Starting today, I knew many of us would visit the TV room to watch CNN's coverage whenever we could snatch a few minutes. I sent up a silent prayer for the quick release of the hostages. How would the government in Moscow respond, I wondered?

≋

When I returned to my cabin there was a folded note on the floor just inside the door. I picked it up, took it over to the porthole, and sat down on the bed before opening it. It was addressed to me in unfamiliar handwriting: bold and angular, written hurriedly in black ink. With a sense of foreboding, I unfolded the paper.

The note was from Niko. I thought, Oh, boy. Here it is… he doesn't want to see me again.

I was wrong, if I could believe what I was reading. He wrote "in haste." He had been called away on an "emergency," though he did not explain what the emergency was. He was to be airlifted off the ship early this morning before breakfast. I was not to worry; he was "in no danger." *Danger?* He would be back as soon as possible. In the meantime, he would "treasure the memory of our time together" and "was longing to return to my arms." It was signed "with love, N."

My first reaction was fury. Was this was how he removed himself from an awkward sexual entanglement? Despite the lies in his note, was our relationship, or whatever it could be called, only physical, something he could turn on and off on a whim?

I threw the note onto the bed, and stalked into the bathroom to splash cool water on my face. Well, I would show him. I would go to lunch and participate in all the rest of the day's activities without giving him another thought. I would have fun!

By the time I had climbed halfway up the stairs to the Volga Dining Room for lunch, I realized my anger was completely misplaced. If I was calling what we had only an affair, why would I expect anything more than a physical relationship from him? On the other hand, maybe it was true he cared about me, at least a little. Removing himself from the ship before the end of the cruise was a drastic way to end an affair. He would lose the balance of his salary for this cruise, not to mention his share of the tips the other passengers and I would distribute at the end of the voyage. He had told me he depended on his salary and the expected tips to help support his own existence, as well as his sister's. She had been recently divorced and needed him to help feed and clothe her daughter.

Did I believe him? Maybe.

I sat with Barbara's group at lunch. They were engrossed as usual in questioning Anatoly about Russian birds and discussing whether there had been more habitat destruction here than in other parts of the world. It might have been interesting if I were not so preoccupied with my own thoughts. At least, none of our group expected me to participate in their birding conversations.

With one ear on the voices around me, I picked at my lunch and watched the sparkling water of the lake flow past the big dining room windows. The shores of the wide lake were out of sight for now. There was not a cloud to be seen. Today was as usual, warm and sunny with a soft breeze.

During lunch, Maddy, our cruise director, made an announcement on the PA system. "Our Russian teacher has had to leave the ship because of an emergency, I will stand in for him at the scheduled Russian lesson this afternoon. We very much hope he will return soon, possibly by tomorrow evening."

After lunch I sat for an hour in my cabin, rereading Niko's note and waiting for the next Russian language class. Despite his absence, the lesson went well with Maddy in charge. I was surprised at how quickly the time passed. I hoped the rest of the afternoon and evening would too.

I scanned the list of the day's activities, but found very little that sounded tempting. In an hour, there was to be a cooking lesson in the Volga Dining Room. We would learn how to prepare *pelmeni*, a traditional meat-filled dumpling. Under normal circumstances, I might have skipped this, but today it sounded as good as anything else on the agenda.

I spent the intervening hour in the TV room. The news on CNN was bad. The hostage situation in Beslan was ongoing, and the journalists' reports were increasingly grim. The scene had become a battle zone as the Russian Army tried to gain the upper hand. Meanwhile, there were clips of anguished family members, tearfully waiting for news of their loved ones, and begging on camera for their release. The coverage was heartrending.

The cooking lesson was more of a demonstration, though we were each allowed to pinch the dough of a dumpling together, pre-stuffed with a mixture of minced beef, chicken, pork, and onion. We dropped our little dough pouches into boiling water and in a few minutes, we were each given one to sample. It was bland. Maybe it only needed the right dipping sauce. Barbeque? Teriyaki? Honey mustard? Since I could imagine no scenario in which I might actually prepare and eat *pelmeni*, I decided to forget the whole thing.

Next on the schedule was a documentary movie, *The Last Czar*. It sounded as gloomy as I felt, but I decided to try it, since I had skipped a showing of it yesterday.

In fact, the documentary was well researched and the narrator did a credible job of leading us through the tragic passing of the last of the Romanovs. They were usually portrayed as vain, selfish, stupid, and disease-ridden tyrants, but this film made them seem more human, even slightly attractive.

The final event before dinner was a classical music concert presented by the ship's musicians. As the performance was held in the TV room, there would be no CNN for an hour or so. The audience was sparse. This might have been because it was an afternoon concert, though I suspected many of our passengers might have preferred something other than classical music.

The musicians performed valiantly, but it was a lost cause. The "classical" music turned out to be tunes from former Broadway musicals. I slipped out quietly after the third number.

～

The thought of trying to eat dinner in the dining room while making lively conversation made me profoundly depressed. There was no help for it though. I would have to try.

I climbed slowly to the Sky Bar, and found it full of people already downing before-dinner drinks. I pushed my way to the bar and ordered a glass of Chablis. In my current mood, I was probably better off sticking with white wine.

Taking my glass, I wandered outside and leaned against the rail near the prow of the ship. There was another glorious sunset tonight, but I stared into the water, wondering where Niko was now. I stayed there, trying to imagine what he was doing, until I realized the crowd had thinned and the sun had almost set. There were only a few people in sight. It was time to go to the dining room.

I tossed the last of my wine into the water and straightened my shoulders. As I joined the line of people waiting to be seated, I forced my mouth to smile. I decided to look for new people to sit with tonight.

Halfway down the room, two women were already seated at a table for four. I asked if I could join them, and got a grunt from one and a grateful "Please do." from the other.

I gave my order to the waiter—not Ivan tonight—and glanced at the woman who had grunted. She was small and dark, with a deeply lined face. Not laugh lines, I thought. The other woman was younger, blonde, and sweet-faced.

Unfortunately, my first impressions were correct. Whenever the blonde woman, whose name was Karen, said something positive or complimentary, the other woman, named Edna, answered her with a complaint. Karen was traveling alone with a university group. Her sister had planned to come with her, but became ill just before they were due to leave. Edna told us she was wealthy enough to travel anywhere, and preferred to travel alone. Karen and I exchanged a knowing smile, quickly hidden. We excused ourselves as soon as possible.

I declined an invitation to join Karen in the Panorama Lounge. I thought I should avoid further alcohol until I felt happier. Proud of myself for making such a grown-up and intelligent decision, I returned to my empty cabin.

Niko, of course, was not there—not in person, at least. I tried to read, but gave up when I realized I had turned several pages without comprehending a single word.

Finally, I turned out the cabin lights and sat staring through the porthole window. Running lights lit the water for several feet around the ship, and I could see the whitecaps churned up by our passage through the water of the huge lake. Beyond the lights, all was dark.

CHAPTER 14

Friday, September 3
Day 9

I WOKE up feeling slightly better. After the morning exercise class, I showered and joined a few members of our group for a leisurely breakfast. They had been up on the Sun Deck since six-thirty this morning, birding with Anatoly. Though the morning mist had briefly obscured their view, they had seen a new bird to add to their life lists.

After breakfast, our group was scheduled for a tour of the wheelhouse with our Captain and his senior officers. He bowed and greeted us in his heavily accented English, and then turned us over to his first mate, who gave us a short explanation of what we were seeing. I looked around at the banks of instruments and marveled at the bird's-eye view the Captain and his crew had while steering our ship. The Captain's deep-set blue eyes seemed always to be scanning the horizon. The members of his crew were much younger and clearly held him in awe.

Next on the agenda was Madame Slosky's final lecture, this time on Russian Christianity and the importance of icons. As I listened, I wished we had had this lecture before we had been led through so many Russian churches and cathedrals. I might have viewed the icons with a more appreciative eye.

Then it was time for lunch. Our birdwatching party had disappeared before Madame Slosky's lecture because, at the same time, Anatoly was scheduled to show a video of the singing birds of Siberia and the Far East. It was based on research he was conducting in southeastern Russia, the project he had described to us on the way to the preserve outside Moscow. He told us his research was financed by a combination of government and private funds. Like many scientists, he lived from project to project. He was constantly forced to raise extra money to continue, and hopefully expand his research, by soliciting private contributions and applying for grants from not-for-profit organizations and other institutions.

The birders met me at the door to the dining room, and we entered together. They were obviously very impressed with Anatoly's film. He would likely receive private contributions from several members of our group, many of whom could afford to give him substantial aid.

We spread ourselves over several tables, and I found a seat with Ted and Cindy and three others. We gave our lunch order and they continued to enthuse over the film. I was content to sit and listen.

Finally, Cindy looked at me and said, "Well, Sharon, what have you been up to?"

I felt my cheeks heating, much to my embarrassment. Then, I realized she meant what had I been up to *this morning,* while they were watching the video.

I told them what I had learned about the Russian Orthodox Church and its art. They seemed politely interested, but I kept it brief, and they soon went back to discussing birds.

Suddenly, I felt very lonely.

The next Russian class was in an hour. Back in my cabin, I picked up my book from the bedside table, but again found it impossible to concentrate. Instead, I gazed out my porthole again and watched the sun's rays glint off the ship's wake until it was time for class.

Maddy passed out another of Niko's lists of phrases and helped us learn to pronounce them. The time dragged.

After class, I went to my cabin to put away my word lists and get ready for our visit to Kizhi Island. I packed my tote with camera, binoculars, suntan lotion, and insect spray, and hurried to the Sun Deck. As the *River Sprite* approached the island, the magnificent Transfiguration Cathedral grew larger, its graceful onion-shaped domes dramatically piercing the cloudless blue sky.

Anatoly had promised to lead a special birding tour of the island, and our group waited impatiently to disembark. As we left the ship and began the long uphill walk to the Cathedral, the local guide explained that the tiny island was a

UNESCO World Heritage Site. Only six kilometers long and one kilometer wide, it was being preserved by the Russian government as an open-air museum designed to demonstrate peasant life.

The big Cathedral, with its twenty-two onion domes, was awe inspiring, and very different from any of the other churches we had seen so far. It was built in 1714, entirely of unpainted aspen wood, which sparkled silver in today's bright sunshine. The craftsmen, using only hand tools, had built it without using a single nail. I was disappointed to learn we would not be allowed inside. Problems encountered during a partial restoration in the 1960s forced the authorities to close it to the public.

The much smaller Intercession Church, located nearby, was built to be used only in winter, as it was much easier to heat than its larger neighbor. It was also constructed of weathered aspen wood using the same methods, but only eight onion domes decorated its roof.

Along with a local birder brought to the island for this occasion, Anatoly led our group away on the promised birding hike. I decided to follow them for a little while and then return on my own to visit the other outdoor exhibits.

The hills and meadows of the island were perfectly set off by the beauty of the day, and the sparkling blue waters of the lake. We passed a small cemetery, and climbed a hill overlooking a tiny village huddled at the edge of the water. Further on, we walked through grassy meadows dotted with blooming wildflowers. Butterflies and bees were busily at work, and everywhere there was the buzzing of the insects and the rustling of late summer grasses in the light breeze. We had been warned to use mosquito spray and to watch out for snakes, some of which were poisonous.

Alone, I wandered slowly back to the museum site. At a small cluster of farm buildings, people dressed as peasants did chores and, inside the cottage, two women demonstrated local crafts. Other buildings included a sauna, a picturesque wooden windmill, and a granary.

As I wandered around, I wondered whether Dale had ever visited Kizhi Island. I knew he would have been fascinated by the workmanship and the construction techniques used to build the churches and the other structures here. Remembered love for Dale pierced my heart. I longed for someone with whom I could share this experience.

∞

Back onboard the *River Sprite,* I stood at the rail soaking up the rays of the afternoon sun and watching Kizhi Island recede in the distance. Where was Niko today? Was he thinking of me?

As it was too early for dinner, I headed for the TV room. As usual, it was tuned to CNN International, where the main story was, as it had been since Wednesday morning, the hostage situation in Beslan. The news could hardly be worse. There had been explosions inside the school, and a fire on the roof of the gymnasium had collapsed it onto the hostages inside, killing and injuring many more people. To make matters even more dangerous and chaotic, armed civilians had entered into gun battles with the hostage takers.

Finally, Russian Special Forces, including tanks and armed helicopters, had stormed the school. Unfortunately, their attempt to take over the building and free the remaining hundreds of hostages, ended in stalemate. By mid-afternoon, Russian troops claimed to have taken control of most of the building, but battles were still being fought on the school grounds.

During the confusion, fourteen hostages managed to escape. They were unharmed, but told horrific stories of their ordeal. Several hundred hostages had been shot to death, blown up, in some cases by accident, or killed by the fire on the roof and the resulting cave-in. Hundreds more were wounded or severely maimed by the Army and civilian gun battles. A final body count might not come for several days.

I shuddered, hardly able to imagine what horrors the people of Beslan were going through today. I sent up more silent prayers for a peaceful conclusion as I made my way back to my cabin.

There was a knock on my door almost immediately. Absently, I opened it. Standing there was Niko.

I gasped, and stepped quickly back. Fortunately, there was no one in the corridor as he followed me inside and shut the door. He pulled me into his arms and his lips closed on mine.

Eventually, we broke apart and he took both my hands in his. "I am sorry. I could not wait longer to see you. I returned to the ship an hour ago, while you were still on the island."

I could only make inarticulate sounds as I thrust my fingers into his silken hair and pulled his face back down to mine.

We sat on the edge of my bed to talk.

"Are you well? I have missed you so." He brushed a lock of hair off my cheek and tucked it behind my ear.

I smiled. "Yes, I'm fine. But I missed you too. What was the emergency? Where did you go?"

"It is a long story." He looked down and away from me. "A family matter. Better I keep silent. But everything is fine now, and I am back."

He looked up at me, smiling disarmingly.

I stared at him in disbelief. He really meant not to tell me. Should I be angry, I wondered? I was angry, but also unsure whether our relationship had progressed to the point where I could demand to know the details of "a family matter." I took a deep breath.

"Would you feel better if you talked about it? Maybe it would help you put the problem in perspective."

He was already shaking his head. "No, I promise you, it is nothing for you to worry about. And now, I need not think of it either. The problem is solved." He glanced at his wristwatch. "I must go to the kitchen now and pick up our dinners. I will return in ten minutes."

I nodded, and he was gone. My mind working furiously, I wondered why I was so upset. It was a family matter. It had nothing to do with me. With us. I paused, in disbelief. There was no *us*. This was just a pleasant—no, *fantastic*, was the word—interlude. I was meant to enjoy it and then go home and forget it, right?

After the longest ten minutes I could remember enduring, there was a tap at my door. Niko was back.

We undressed each other quickly. Naked, we stood skin to skin in a silent embrace. In a little while, he picked me up, gently laid me on my back, and then lowered himself onto my body. His mouth found mine and then dipped lower to kiss my breasts. I arched my back and pulled him closer, closer.

At last, when we could breathe again, we lay quietly stroking each other's bodies. But he had only to look into my eyes for our passion to rise again.

CHAPTER 15

Saturday, September 4
Day 10

THE NEXT morning I awoke to a magnificent sunrise. I raced to the Sun Deck to join the aerobics class while the glorious pinks, purples, and oranges still decorated the sky. By the end of the hour, the sun was shining brightly. It would be yet another beautiful day.

I showered quickly and dressed in a casual tee shirt, khakis, and comfortable walking shoes. We were scheduled to arrive at the village of Mandrogi later this morning. A brochure, including a map of the site, had been pushed under our doors last night along with the daily schedule. Unlike the other stops on this cruise, with their ancient origins and many centuries of history, a businessman from St. Petersburg was developing Mandrogi as a theme-park-like village to demonstrate peasant life. He planned to include a collection of typical shops and homes, filled with traditionally costumed artists and craftspeople creating Russian arts and crafts to sell to visiting tourists. Only two buildings were completed and ready for visitors: a vodka "museum" and an artisans' workshop.

After breakfast, I went to the TV room to see the latest news from Beslan. According to the coverage this morning, the standoff at the school had finally come to an end. All the remaining hostages had been freed, but I thought it would be a very long time before they and their families would be able to recover from their terrible physical and psychological wounds.

At last, TV cameras had been allowed inside the school, and the wreckage they showed was devastating. Besides the debris of the caved-in roof, littering the floor were blood, broken window glass, smashed furniture, and wilted bouquets of flowers. It was too much, too sad. I turned away from the set and left the room.

After a few minutes, I visited the Sky Bar where Madame Slosky was scheduled to answer questions on the subjects she had covered in her lectures. I had decided to go mostly to see whether she could be persuaded discuss the tragic situation in Beslan. I hoped she might be willing to share background information not reported by the journalists. Maybe she could help us understand better what had happened and why.

I was disappointed to discover she flatly refused to talk about the Beslan fiasco. She was polite, but adamant. Several passengers were angered by her refusal and left the room. I stayed a little while longer, but her answers to other questions were not very interesting. I slipped away and took a brisk walk on the Promenade Deck until we docked at Mandrogi.

As we had arranged last evening, Niko met me at the bottom of the gangway. He kept his hands in his pockets, and whistled tunelessly as we walked toward the village. He was carrying a backpack over one shoulder.

There was a historic village reconstruction not far from my home in New York State, containing authentic buildings from Britain and Colonial America, painstakingly researched, taken apart, moved to the village, and rebuilt, down to the last handmade shingle and nail. As we came closer, I could see Mandrogi was not like that. The completed buildings were painted in bright, almost garish, colors, and one had crudely carved wooden dragons around its front entrance. I was surprised. We had seen nothing resembling that in Russia so far. I wondered how much of the site would be historically accurate when it was completed.

Following the map I had been given, we wandered around the village. Some of the buildings had been started but not finished, and others were only indicated on the map. I could see this could become an important attraction for the many cruise ships traveling each summer between Moscow and St. Petersburg, but there was a lot to be done before it would be finished.

The vodka "museum" contained scores of different bottles of Russian vodka attractively displayed, but there were no signs and no one available to tell us what we were seeing. Inside the artisan's workshop, the only other building open to the public, brightly costumed craftspeople were at work creating wooden toys, rag dolls, enamel boxes, lace, musical instruments made of painted wood, colorful weavings, leather goods, carved birchbark trinket boxes, and other traditional Russian crafts. There were finished goods for sale, but the prices were higher than I had seen anywhere else. We took a quick look around and went back outside.

A chicken *shashlik* (shish kabob) picnic was to be served at noon at tables set up in the middle of the "village," but we had other plans. Niko had arranged for a picnic lunch of our own from the ship's kitchen. We headed away from the village along a trail through the woods until we arrived at the edge of a sunny clearing carpeted with wildflowers and grasses. Niko opened his backpack and produced a large square of waterproof canvas to sit on, and laid out sandwiches, apples, and bottled water.

There was a slight breeze, but except for the sound of insects, it was very quiet. We sat facing each other while we ate, our knees touching. We were quiet too, speaking instead with our eyes.

When we finished, and had packed away the remnants of our meal, we lay down on the canvas with Niko's arms holding me tightly and my head on his shoulder. It was peaceful in the sunny glade, and I wished I could stay in Niko's arms forever.

Eventually, of course, we had to leave. We retraced our steps to the ship, Niko walking as before with his hands in his pockets.

He went back to my cabin with me. No one was in the corridor, and he quickly followed me inside. Our clothing came off in record time and soon I was in Niko's arms again. We spent the next three hours talking, laughing, and making love as though we had all the time in the world. But I knew we did not.

All too soon, it was time to get ready for Niko's final Russian class. He showered first and dressed while I took my turn in the tiny bathroom. When I was ready, I followed him upstairs. He had planned this session to be more informal. He talked a little about the development of the Russian language, which like English, had incorporated words from many other languages, and answered questions about pronunciation and usage. He also gave us a short written test, and promised a "diploma" to those of us who passed it, to be handed out tomorrow at lunch.

When class was over, I went out onto the Sun Deck, too excited and restless to wait for Niko in my cabin. I saw Barbara's group, clustered as usual around Anatoly, and joined them. I sank onto a deck chair and leaned back, hoping to be distracted.

Niko reappeared at my door at seven bearing our dinners. We made love as though we had been apart for days instead of hours. Eventually, Niko sat up, pulling me up to sit beside him. We ate our cold dinners and then, turning to me, he drew his finger gently down my cheek.

"Soon, early tomorrow morning, in fact, we will dock in St. Petersburg. The voyage is almost over, but we still have a few more days. I wish to spend as much time with you as I can."

I nodded. I was all too aware of how little time remained.

"I will have to travel with the sightseeing bus, but there is much free time in St. Petersburg. I hope you will want to spend it with me." He looked at me anxiously.

I smiled up at him. "I do."

"That is good." He grinned, looking relieved, and brushed his lips over mine. "I have a cousin who owns a flat in the central city. He is also a professor, but this summer he is traveling in France. He has given me the key and wishes me to use it when I am in the city. Will you go there with me?"

"A flat? Are you sure he wouldn't mind your bringing a woman there?"

"He would not mind. The apartment is small, but the furnishings are modern."

"If you're sure it's okay, I'll go with you."

He kissed me, and there was no more conversation. It felt as though time stood still while I was in Niko's arms, but I knew it was only an illusion. Time was moving relentlessly forward, now more quickly than ever.

CHAPTER 16

Sunday, September 5
Day 11

I WOKE up early and ran upstairs to the Sun Deck to catch my first glimpse of St. Petersburg, Niko's hometown. I was excited to be here, but at the same time, our arrival meant that our voyage would soon be over.

I stood at the rail, but instead of seeing St. Petersburg's skyline, my thoughts turned to Niko, and my memories of our days and nights together. I had been reluctant to examine my feelings too closely, but now, I realized, I had been right to wonder whether a light flirtation with Niko would leave my heart untouched. Our physical attraction had become something much deeper, at least on my part, and I was finally ready to acknowledge that fact. I could still refuse to call it *love*, but whatever I called it, it *felt* like love.

In the beginning, I simply could not get enough of him. The sex was marvelous, but I had become fascinated by his mind as well as his body. In each other's arms, we had talked for hours, sharing impressions, asking each other about our lives, and finding we were in agreement on more issues than I ever would have expected.

He was curious about me and my life in America, and in turn, he answered all my questions about himself, and Russia, with patience and pride. Clearly, he had thought deeply about the problems his country faced, and how it was viewed by the world at large. He loved Russia profoundly, but he was sharply critical of her political systems, past and present.

Though he was usually quite serious, Niko had an understated sense of humor very much like my own, and we discovered we could make each other helpless with laughter. I found that extraordinary, since English was not his first language. It was obvious to me that he was very intelligent. And, to my amazement, I found he knew much more about English literature than I did, despite my English Lit. degree from Williams College. His ability to follow whispered Russian endearments with quotes from nineteenth century British poets amazed me.

I had discovered something else. Like Dale's, his birthday was close to mine, only two days earlier, in fact. But to my surprise, Niko was five years younger than I.

Standing there gripping the rail, I was oblivious to all the people around me. Focused intently on my own thoughts, I finally admitted the truth: leaving Niko now would mean leaving behind part of my heart. I still looked forward to returning to Ellen and the firm, but how could I say goodbye to Niko? I wanted to believe he felt as deeply for me as I did for him. He seemed to, and at this point, I could no longer believe he was merely putting on an act. For better or worse, I found it very easy to trust in his love.

Realistically—oh, how I hated that word— what else could I do except love him for as long as we could be together? Our remaining time was desperately short. I had no idea where I would find the strength to leave him, but I had no choice. My visa was valid only for the dates of this cruise. If I tried to stay longer, I might be arrested and deported.

Shivering slightly, I glanced at my watch. It was time to put these thoughts aside for now and get ready for the day's events. When I finally looked up to focus on the city's skyline, the rising sun was sparkling off the water. I blinked, and refocused my gaze. In the distance, the spires and domes of St. Petersburg sparkled and shimmered invitingly. I took a deep breath and went inside for breakfast.

This morning, Barbara's group was scheduled to travel to a sanctuary outside the city for another bird walk with Anatoly. This was the last time the group would be with him, as he would be leaving us to go back to Siberia as soon as the bus returned. I spotted him with Barbara and a few others as soon as I entered the Volga Dining Room. I had decided not to go with them today. I wanted to spend as much of my remaining time with Niko as possible, even though in public we were still pretending there was nothing between us. I shook Anatoly's hand, gave him an envelope containing a small donation, and wished him continued success with his research.

Somehow, Niko had arranged for us to be on the same bus. He was standing by the steps, ready to help me on board, and we exchanged bland smiles and secret squeezes as usual. I took a seat near the back, with Niko sitting directly across the aisle from me.

There were two female guides on our bus, small, blonde, and middle-aged. They looked a little like Irina and Olga, our Moscow tour guides, but I was distracted by Niko's nearness, and never caught their names. Soon our driver pulled away from the dock, heading for the city's center. The guides took turns telling us the history of St. Petersburg, a story both amazing and gruesome.

In 1703, Russia was at war with Sweden. One day, Czar Peter the Great galloped across the marshy land at the mouth of the Neva River, at the edge of the Gulf of Finland. Suddenly he stopped, dismounted, and plunged his sword into the soft soil. Here, he proclaimed, he would build a great city.

It was an unlikely site. It was far to the north of Moscow, swampy, and made up of mosquito-infested islands prone to flooding. Its winters were dark and frigid, its summers hot and humid. But, Peter refused to acknowledge any of those drawbacks. The site was directly across the Gulf and the Baltic Sea from Sweden. He could more easily continue his war from a fortress and navy based there, and after he won the war—he had no doubt he would accomplish that feat—the fortress eventually would evolve into a badly needed commercial port city. He named it St. Petersburg, though it is not known whether he named it in honor of himself or the biblical St. Peter.

On forty-two islands, crisscrossed with canals, Italian architects designed wide boulevards, graceful arched bridges, and ornate palaces to rival Paris and London. German engineers built those marvels—on the backs of tens of thousands of serfs—an army of forced labor.

Over the objections of his nobles, Czar Peter declared St. Petersburg to be Russia's new capital. Though he would have preferred 'Paris of the North,' his city's unofficial nickname became 'The City Built on Bones,' an ironic tribute to the estimated one hundred thousand serfs who died in inhuman conditions in the effort to construct the city.

I was watching the passing scenery during the guides' narrative. Traffic was heavy, but eventually we were driving along a scenic boulevard beside the Neva River. Along the way, we caught glimpses of cathedral domes, palaces, and monuments, including gigantic statues of Czar Peter the Great and other Russian heroes.

After crossing the largest and most beautiful bridge we had seen so far, the buses pulled into the huge courtyard of the Fortress of Peter and Paul. I was the last person off our bus and as Niko helped me down, the warmth of his touch made my skin tingle and ache for more. We moved slowly apart, and I tried to focus on what our guides were saying. This was the first structure built in St. Petersburg, they told us, and Peter the Great himself laid the first stone.

Next, we visited the nearby Peter and Paul Cathedral. To please Czar Peter, who loved everything European and was particularly enamored of Amsterdam, it was built in the Dutch Protestant style. With its tall, golden spire piercing the bright blue sky like a gigantic exclamation point, it made St. Petersburg's skyline different from Moscow's, with its many onion-shaped domes. The Cathedral's plain exterior gave no hint of the opulence inside. In true Russian fashion, every inch of the interior was decorated in an ornate baroque style, with a particularly beautiful mosaic ceiling.

When we returned to the ship for lunch, Niko signaled me to follow him. I hung back until the rest of the passengers had boarded the *River Sprite*, then followed him away from the dock. He was waiting for me around the first corner, just out of sight of the ship. Pulling me into his arms, he kissed me passionately.

When we could breathe again, he took both of my hands in his. "I wish to take you to lunch and then show you a part of St. Petersburg you will not see on this tour. Will you come with me?"

I nodded eagerly.

He hailed a taxi and when we had seated ourselves inside, gave the driver instructions in rapid Russian.

He turned to me then, and placed my hand on his heart. "I wish to show you where I teach, and there is a good café nearby. We will return to the ship in time for the next excursion."

I nodded again, and relaxed as he pulled me more closely against his side. I looked up into his face to find him gazing down at me. He was smiling and my heart lifted. I was happy just to sit quietly with him like this, feeling the steady beat of his heart and only faintly hearing the noise of roaring automobile engines and blaring horns as the taxi driver expertly maneuvered through the heavy mid-day traffic.

At last, we reached our destination, the Café de l'Ouest. The bright sunshine outside made the dim interior even darker, but as my eyes adjusted, I glanced around the room in delighted surprise. Cowboy hats, sombreros, lariats, spurs, and brightly colored serapes decorated the walls, and a sun-bleached skull of a long-dead steer, complete with long, curved horns, hung over the door. Wagon wheels fitted with electric light bulbs hung from the ceiling.

A young waiter directed us to a table for two away from the front window. Three other tables were occupied with diners.

"This is acceptable?"

"Did you bring me here because I'm American?" I was grinning with delight.

"Oh, no!" Niko laughed, shaking his head. "This is my favorite restaurant. It is convenient, very near to my office. Mikhail, the owner and chef, is a great fan of the American West, as you can see, but the food is all Russian."

Just then, the waiter reappeared. Niko spoke to him, and he turned and hurried away.

"What did you say to him?"

"I come here very often and I know Mikhail quite well. The waiter will tell him we are here, and Misha will tell us what he will prepare for us today."

"Misha?"

"Yes, it is a pet name for Mikhail."

Just then, a large man in a white apron and chef's hat came through a swinging door from the kitchen and hurried toward us. Niko stood up, and the two men embraced. There was rapid Russian and laughter, and then Niko introduced me to Misha, who took my hand and kissed it with a courtly gesture. After another minute or two of conversation with Niko, he motioned us back to our seats and pulled up a chair for himself. As he sat down, his expression was sad, and he sighed loudly.

"Niko, is something wrong?"

He smiled ruefully and shook his head. "Misha is sad for two reasons. He knows you will be eating in a tourist restaurant tonight instead of here, and also, he thinks you are too skinny. He wants me to bring you back every day so he can make you fatter." Niko's smile faded. "I have told him why I cannot."

Misha suddenly clapped his hands and spoke excitedly in a torrent of Russian. I assumed he was now telling Niko what he would make for us for lunch.

I was right. In only a few minutes, he re-emerged from the kitchen with the waiter running behind him. They carried trays laden with Russian black bread and butter, small green salads, bowls of cold borscht, and an array of cold meats and cheeses on a huge platter. There was also a small bottle of Russian white wine. The food was served with a flourish and looked fresh and delicious. Misha kissed my hand again and shouted, "*Prijatnogo appetita.*"

"It means 'hearty appetite'," Niko said.

For once, I was ahead of him. The phrase had been on one of his first Russian vocabulary sheets. I was glad I had remembered it.

Smiling proudly, I replied, "*Spasibo.*"

I turned quickly to Niko. "That means thank you, right?"

Niko beamed at me and nodded his approval. "You pronounced it perfectly. I am proud of you."

Misha smiled and bowed, and he and the waiter returned to the kitchen.

Niko poured the wine. When we finished our food, the waiter produced a tray of tea cakes, a platter of fresh fruit, and demitasse coffee.

Eventually, I leaned back in my chair and sighed with pleasure.

"That was marvelous. When you see him next, please tell Misha I feel fatter already." Ruefully, I patted my full stomach.

"You are beautiful, perfect as you are." Niko was serious. He took my hand and laced his fingers with mine.

"You know, I hope, how I wish very much for you to stay. I realize it is impossible at this time. We must talk about the possibilities, but come, I wish to show you my university."

The main campus of St. Petersburg State University was located on Vasilievsky Island, a short walk from the café. The day was much warmer now than when we had left the ship this morning, and I removed the blue cardigan I had worn over a matching sleeveless top. The sun felt good on my bare arms.

We walked the few blocks from the Café to the university. Niko and I were walking apart again, he with his hands in his pockets, as usual. It was important, I knew, for us both to respect his professional environment.

On the way to his office in the Philology Faculty building, Niko pointed out the huge red and white Twelve Colleges building where the administration offices and several other faculties were located.

"Niko, I know you teach English literature, but do many Russian students find that subject interesting?"

"My classes are first and second level, and they are required for aspiring writers and other students in the liberal arts. I am not permitted to diverge from the approved curriculum, which contains nothing modern or controversial. Still, I enjoy it very much, especially the works of Shakespeare, Keats, Tennyson, and Coleridge."

By this time we were inside his building. We walked up the stairs to the second floor and Niko unlocked his office door.

The room was filled with light, books, papers, and comfortable and attractive furniture. There were two black and chrome stackable guest chairs facing a solid, black-painted wooden desk. Its surface held a black desk lamp, a desktop computer, and a digital clock. Shelves overflowing with books ranged behind the desk, where they easily could be reached. Against one side wall, under a wide window, there was a worn, red leather couch, with a modern black floor lamp standing nearby. The walls were painted a light gray, and a large photograph of the city skyline was hanging on the wall opposite the couch.

Niko was watching me expectantly. He was proud of his domain.

"Your office looks very comfortable," I said approvingly. "When will your classes start for the fall semester?"

"The fall term has already begun," he said, "but I have permission from my department head to be away for the first three weeks of the semester. Our cruise is the last one I will travel with this season."

I was surprised. It seemed an unusual arrangement. "What will you do with what's left of your time off, Niko?" I was wishing he could spend it all with me.

"I will rest, read, do errands, and visit on the weekends with my sister, Raisa, and her daughter, Eva. Another professor will take my classes until I return."

"Where do you live? Do you have an apartment near the campus?"

"No, they are too expensive. There is housing for single men in a building a short walk from here. I rent a room there." He frowned. "But, I cannot take you there."

No. I realized there was no way he could take me to his room in a building for single men.

He glanced at the clock on his desk. "There is still time to visit my cousin's flat. Will you go there with me now?"

I nodded in excited expectation.

We left the building and quickly exited the campus. At a nearby taxi stand Niko hailed a cab. He gave the address in Russian and soon we were threading our way through heavy traffic. The driver and Niko kept up a rapid conversation, none of which I could understand. I leaned forward and looked around. Now we were driving through a much more affluent neighborhood than some of the ones we had seen this morning.

In a few minutes, the cab stopped in front of a tall, narrow, red brick building with sturdy but graceful wrought iron railings. An elaborate wrought iron grille protected the front door. In its center, a gilded hummingbird hovered over a large flower enameled in red.

Niko paid the driver and we climbed the marble steps to the entrance. He unlocked the grille and the heavy door beyond. Inside, he gestured toward an old-fashioned ornamental wrought iron cage elevator. Holding my hand and entering first, he helped me into the cage and closed the gate with a clang. The open car rose slowly upward. When it stopped on the top floor, Niko slid back the gate and we stepped out into a bright foyer, lit by sunlight streaming in through large, unadorned windows. There were two flats on this level, one to the right and another to the left.

Niko used another key to open the heavy paneled door on the right, and we entered an attractive apartment. The living area was furnished with dark leather couches and two inviting easy chairs, covered in a paler shade of leather. Bright rugs and pillows were scattered about, and glass and chrome tables held sleek lamps, books, and decorative objects. A large painting of a beautiful woman hung over a white marble fireplace. A small, efficient kitchen held electric appliances and a bistro table with two chairs. There was a luxurious bathroom stocked with fluffy towels and toiletries that smelled of sandalwood, and the bedroom contained a king-sized bed with an ornate dark wood headboard. The apartment was light, comfortable, and beautifully decorated, a place I would be proud to own.

"Your cousin seems quite successful," I said, looking approvingly at the bed. "This place must be expensive to own, right?"

"Yes. I am fortunate he trusts me with it."

Niko moved toward me, and in an instant we were struggling to remove our clothing. Tangled in shirts, tripping over shoes and pants, we were laughing as we fell onto the bed. We stripped off the rest of our clothes and, free at last, we luxuriated in the spaciousness of the huge bed. What ecstasy.

Looking deep into each other's eyes, our laughter stilled for the moment as Niko reached for me, his lovemaking bringing me to new heights of pleasure. Afterwards, we broke apart, and laughing again, lay panting. Like children after a snowstorm, we made angels with our arms and legs, appreciating the width of the bed in contrast to the narrow bunk in my cabin.

Then, it was my turn to make love to him. I straddled his back and kneaded the muscles in his shoulders and upper arms. Trailing my hands up and down his legs, I massaged his calves and feet, his thighs, and buttocks. He groaned in pleasure. Had anyone ever done this for him? I thought perhaps not.

Finally, I nudged him over and straddled him again. This time I bent to rain kisses on his neck, taking possession of his mouth, and brushing my breasts across his chest. When, at last I stroked him, he cried out and, rocking his hips, thrust deep inside me. The rhythm of our love accelerated until I collapsed onto his chest, both of us shuddering in delight. Niko turned on his side and pulled me into his arms, my head against his shoulder. Still trembling with passion, he caressed the back of my neck and wound tresses of my hair around his fingers. Gradually, our breathing quieted.

All too soon, Niko sat up, reached for his watch, and frowned. "We have two more hours." He sighed, any trace of laughter gone. Then, he drew me into his arms once more. "Let us make the most of this."

We made love slowly, tenderly. Soon, memories of our time together would be all I would have of Niko. Afterwards, we held each other tightly.

How could I live without Niko? Yet what possible future did we have? The answers to these questions were too depressing to contemplate and I made an effort to push them from my mind. There would be time enough to examine them in the lonely days ahead.

When our two hours was almost gone, we showered together in the sleek, modern bathroom, straightened the bed, and dressed in silence. Finally we were ready to go, our eyes speaking words we were unable to voice.

It was too much. Tears spilled down my cheeks. Niko cupped my face with his palms and wiped my teardrops away with his thumbs.

"Sharon, you know how I love you, yes? I have made that clear, I hope." He spoke softly, hesitantly, grasping both my hands in his. "I would be with you forever if it were possible. I will try to find a way."

"Please don't make promises you won't be able to keep. I couldn't bear it." I pulled away from him, still crying.

I wiped my eyes with the backs of my hands and took a deep breath. "I have to stop this crying. I want our time together to be happy, not tear-soaked." I made myself look directly at him and tried to smile, my lips trembling. "We'd better go." Yet, how I longed to stay.

The cab dropped him two blocks from the ship. I got out at dockside and made my way on board.

Just as Misha had predicted, my dinner that evening was in a local restaurant apparently reserved for tourists. It was colorful, with an all-male five-piece band in native costumes. They strolled among the tables playing a violin, an oddly shaped guitar-like instrument, and a large bass viol, while a soulful singer with long blond hair and coarse features sang Russian folk songs.

The fifth musician carried a percussion instrument consisting of small, square, quarter-inch-thick pieces of wood strung through their middles on a short rope with knots at each end. He held one end aloft and the blocks clattered together to the other end of the rope. When he raised that end, they all rattled back. It was strangely effective as he twitched the rope back and forth in time to the beat.

The food was far from gourmet, but I was hungry. Apparently, the lavish lunch I had enjoyed with Niko had done nothing to dull my appetite.

Tonight, I was sitting with people I had not met before. Most of them were part of an alumni group from Harvard and they seemed to know each other well. Their jokes were funny and, before long, I began to relax and join in the laughter. As the evening ended and we piled back on our buses—no Niko tonight—I realized I had enjoyed the experience after all.

In my cabin, I slipped off my dinner dress and waited for the familiar knock at my door. It came within minutes, and I was back in Niko's arms again, where I dared to believe I belonged.

CHAPTER 17

Monday, September 6
Day 12

TODAY AND tomorrow were the last two days Niko and I would have together. I begrudged every moment we had to spend apart. At least, here in St. Petersburg, he no longer had to hold Russian classes for the passengers.

This morning's tours, first to the ornate Catherine Palace in the village of Pushkin, a short drive out of the city, and later to the world-famous Hermitage Museum and the imposing St. Isaac's Cathedral, both in the heart of St. Petersburg, were interesting, but their over-the-top displays of opulence were mind-boggling. Yet again, I was uneasily aware of the enormous chasm between the wealth of the Czars and the nobility and the poverty of the ordinary Russian people whose unending toil had made such luxurious lifestyles possible.

In the Hermitage Museum, thousands of items of furniture and accessories were on display, yet we were told they were only a small fraction of the numbers of items in the museum's collections. More than the fabulous furniture and decorative items on display, I found myself admiring the simple, yet beautiful, geometry of the inlaid wooden floors, each enormous room done in a different pattern.

After we toured St. Isaac's Cathedral, we crossed the street for luncheon at the famous Astoria Hotel. Acording to one of our guides, "Adolf Hitler planned to hold a victory banquet in the hotel's Winter Garden after his army conquered Russia. He was so certain of success, he ordered the banquet invitations printed in advance. Instead of the expected victory, however, the invading German army was brutally beaten. Ironically, Soviet soldiers found the unused invitations in an abandoned office when they occupied East Berlin in 1945."

The hotel's dining room was quietly elegant and the food was excellent. When dessert was served, a waiter brought an interesting assortment of teas to try. I discovered a new (to me) and delicious one—chocolate! I saved the foil packet the tea bag came in, hoping I would be able to buy it at home, or perhaps online.

Back on the bus, I turned to Niko, who was sitting across from me near the rear.

Niko," I called softly.

Frowning slightly, he was staring out his window. I wondered what he was seeing in place of the heavy traffic flowing by.

"Niko?"

He started, and turned to me, his expression softening.

"I want **to** tell you my impressions of St. Petersburg. I need to do it now, because I'm sure I'll be distracted later."

He grinned and nodded. "Tell me."

"I hope you won't be disappointed or offended." I looked at him hopefully. He nodded again, waiting for me to continue."Okay, so at first glance, and especially from a distance, St. Petersburg is beautiful. But, after seeing more of it, I find it striking how complete a contrast it is to Moscow. It seems to have very little of Moscow's energy, where so many people seem to be working hard for success. St. Petersburg seems stuck in the past, looking backward to previous glory. There is so much poverty here. I'm sure there are many poor people in Moscow too, but they weren't as visible."

"Ah, well, what you say is true. Moscow sends money to update systems, restore buildings, and construct new ones, but the money seems to vanish into the air. Or, maybe, it vanishes into the politicians' pockets. It's possible."

"Every country has politicians like that, mine too." I leaned slightly closer and whispered, "I *am* enjoying seeing St. Petersburg. I just wish we were alone together and you were my guide."

He sighed. "I, too, wish that."

∞

Back on the ship, I changed clothes and hurried to the taxi stand where Niko was waiting. In the cab, as the driver fought the early afternoon traffic, he took my hand, kissed its palm, and again held it against his heart.

At last, we reached our destination. Niko counted out rubles for the fare and unlocked the two outer doors. In silence, Niko's hand clasping mine tightly, we took the elevator up to the beautiful top-floor apartment. It felt like coming home, a realization that saddened and frightened me. I must not think of this place as home, though now, I knew wherever we were, if Niko and I were together, it would feel like home.

As soon as we were inside, Niko pulled me into his arms and kissed my forehead and each eyelid before claiming my mouth. Pulling slightly apart, our arms entwined, we made our way to the bedroom. Slowly we undressed each other, carefully folding our clothes and laying them aside. We sat cross-legged on the wide bed facing each other, as if to memorize each feature, curve, and muscle.

After a few moments, Niko reached over and gently stroked my cheek with his fingertips. It was too much. I could do nothing to prevent our separation, and I was beginning to understand the absolute finality of our relationship. Crying was no solution. Acknowledging this to myself, I collapsed into his arms. Only then did we lie down and gently begin to caress each other's bodies.

We had done this so often in recent days, and yet, it always felt as if we were doing it for the first time. Now our shuddering passion brought sadness as well as joy. How many more times would we be able to do this simple thing? We would never have the chance to take this extraordinary act for granted.

During a pause to catch our breath, I said, "Niko, remember the famous tenor we heard during the concert we attended in Yaroslavl?"

He nodded.

"I was so moved by his performance of that poem by Pushkin. I could feel the emotions he expressed, but the words were in Russian. At the time, you promised to tell me the story behind the song, but I forgot to ask you about it until now."

Pushing pillows against the headboard and pulling me up to sit beside him, Niko smiled down at me. He wrapped me in his arms, and I leaned my head against his shoulder. He thought for a moment and then he began, his bass voice soft and expressive.

"The words are from a poem called, in English, 'Winter Evening.' It is one of those poems Russian schoolchildren learn by heart to recite for prizes. I once won a prize for reciting a similar poem."

"Really?" I was proud of him.

He smiled. "Yes. It was a long time ago."

I reached up to kiss his lips.

"Stop." He laughed. "You will distract me." He kissed me back before turning serious again. "The poem tells of a man sitting in his room during a winter storm. It is late in the night. It is snowing, and windy, and the wind sounds almost like a wolf howling, or as if a child, lost in the night, is crying. His thatched roof is rotting and the wind blowing through it makes a sound as if someone is knocking against his window. While the soft snow drifts down and the wind shrieks, the man raises his cup of vodka and drinks to his poor, wasted youth. Yet, somehow, his heart is lifted."

"How sad," I said.

"Yes, but it is very Russian. My poor translation does little justice to the beauty and truth of the poem."

He hugged me tightly as we lay down again in the immense bed.

Determined to make the most of our last few hours, we broke apart only briefly to unpack the food Niko had brought for a quick supper. I sat on his lap as we ate, feeding each other between caresses. We hurried back to bed as soon as we finished our meal.

It was late when we left the apartment. On the drive back to our ship we were quiet, Niko holding me firmly at his side, his fingers laced with mine. Repeating the charade of last evening, he got out two blocks from the ship, while the taxi took me directly to the dock.

Niko came almost immediately to my cabin and stayed with me for two more hours. We could look forward to only one more afternoon and evening together.

CHAPTER 18

Tuesday, September 7
Day 13

OUR LAST day of tours began early. I dashed upstairs for one last morning workout, showered quickly, and dressed for yet another warm and sunny day.

I sat alone in the dining room until Joan, Marcia and Sara appeared. We exchanged addresses and telephone numbers and promised to keep in touch. We said our goodbyes, and left for our separate buses.

Niko waited as usual to escort Barbara's group on our final tour, which was to Peterhof, Czar Peter the Great's summer residence, set in a three hundred-acre pleasure park on the edge of the Gulf of Finland. We were to tour the Grand Palace, admire the magnificent grounds, and return to the city via a ride on a hydrofoil, a first for me.

Niko sat directly behind me on the bus. I had grown used to his protective presence as we traveled. Though it was comforting to have him near, I wanted to be able to ask questions about what I was seeing, exchange smiles, share a joke, lace my fingers with his, and press my body against his warmth. Impossible, as long as we were with Barbara and her group.

Czar Peter's Grand Palace was long and narrow, its exterior elegant and surprisingly restrained, especially in contrast to the excessively ornate Catherine Palace we had toured on Monday. There were luxuriously appointed rooms within the Palace, but I was most intrigued by Peter's simple study. Paneled in oak, it was smaller than most of the other rooms, almost cozy. Some of the instruments, tools, and books he had treasured were displayed around the room, on his desk, and on bookshelves and tables, evidence of his sharp intelligence and far-ranging interests.

After the Palace tour, our guide released us into the gardens, but with only thirty minutes to enjoy them before we had to be at the dock to board the hydrofoil. I had read about the remarkable fountains, statuary, and picturesque buildings in the gardens, said to rival those in the gardens at Versailles.

Niko was waiting by the Palace's exit door and drew me away from the group. He had decided to stop wasting our precious time together pretending we were casual strangers.

With relief, I agreed. Nevertheless, as we strolled away from the palace, he kept his hands in his pockets.

Directly in front of Peterhof, was a marble terrace with a view down the huge park toward the Gulf of Finland. Below the terrace was the fabulous Cascade Fountain, made up, according to my guidebook, of seventeen waterfalls, sixty-six fountains, and thirty-nine gilded statues, all of which had symbolic meaning. One of the more striking examples was the huge gilded statue of Samson subduing the Lion, which symbolized Russia's effort to conquer Sweden. We joined the hundreds of tourists admiring how it shimmered in the sun, dazzling our eyes. After a moment, Niko took my hand, drew me closer, and led me away to the lower gardens.

Even more beautiful than the ones above, the lower gardens contained other interesting fountains, each one of a different design: long rows of trees; wide green lawns; and colorful flowers, both in containers and in the now familiar geometric flowerbeds that reminded me so much of oriental carpets. At first, I had found those flowerbeds odd, but I had soon grown to admire them.

In one secluded glade, we found a delightful wrought iron fountain in the form of a small tree dripping "rainwater" on spouting iron tulips below. We took advantage of its isolation for a scorching kiss that left us longing for more.

All too soon, it was time to leave. At the dock, there were two hydrofoils waiting to take us back to St. Petersburg. I had looked forward to this ride, assuming we would glide smoothly above the surface of the water. Niko knew better. He led me to a partially protected part of the deck where we could sit together more or less unobserved. He put his jacket around my shoulders and pulled me onto his lap, holding me tightly.

I soon found out why. The ride was uncomfortably cold and bumpy. The cushion of air on which we rode was affected by the action of the waves, which were white capped today.

The trip took a very long forty-five minutes. Even with Niko sheltering me, I was shivering and very relieved when we finally reached the hydrofoil dock in St. Petersburg.

∽

Back on our bus, we returned to the *River Sprite* for lunch. I hung back when we arrived and hurried to the taxi stand to meet Niko.

He pulled me into a waiting cab and kissed me fiercely. Enfolded in Niko's strong arms, I closed my eyes. This would be our last afternoon together making love in his cousin's wide bed in his beautiful apartment.

Finally, we arrived. Niko paid the driver and unlocked the doors. Impatiently we waited for the elevator to descend. A short, heavy-set man, dressed in a military uniform, exited and held the gate for us. The two men stared at each other for a long moment, and then the other man bowed slightly, clicked his heels Prussian-style, and left the building. At last the elevator rose and Niko unlocked the door of the flat.

"Niko, who was that man? Do you know him?"

"He is no one important," he replied, shaking his head. He was already pulling me back into his arms.

Strewing clothing along the way, we dashed to the bedroom. Fueled by the knowledge of the shortness of our time, we were desperate to waste none of it, our lovemaking more passionate than ever.

Reluctantly, at eleven o'clock, we realized we had to leave. Every sense aware we would never share this beautiful apartment again, we showered together and tidied the room. We were silent on the drive back to our ship, Niko holding me tightly, with my head on his shoulder and our fingers entwined.

Immediately, Niko came to me in my cabin. We made love and talked softly, murmuring words of love and promise until almost two a.m. Niko finally tore himself away, dressed, and went to the door. One last embrace, one final whispered endearment, and he disappeared down the corridor.

I turned back to my lonely bunk and wept. In less an two hours, I would have to say goodbye to my new friends and the members of our group, and let no one see how upset and unhappy I was. Thankfully, Niko would not be there for that scene. I was too much of a coward to attempt to say goodbye to him in front of other people.

CHAPTER 19

Wednesday, September 8
Day 14

MY SUITCASES were ready. I had packed them after Niko left my cabin Monday night. Wiping away my tears, I showered and dressed. With the last few items stowed, I put my bags outside my cabin door. In about an hour, at four o'clock, they would go with me on the bus to the airport. Now, it was time to meet our group, one last time, in the Volga dining room.

I looked around my cabin, reluctant to leave. I had experienced so much in this tiny room. From now on, I would have only my memories.

The dining room was filled with sleepy passengers drinking coffee and filling their plates with the continental breakfast provided for us.

I sipped coffee and nibbled a blueberry muffin. Across the room, I waved goodbye to Joan, Marcia, and Sara, thanked Ivan for his excellent service, and, finally, went to the reception desk to turn in my key and my envelope containing tips for the crew.

Barbara was there before me, saying grateful goodbyes to Maddy, and her staff, and finishing the last bit of paperwork. All things considered, the voyage had gone very well for her group, thanks in large part to Maddy and her staff's helpful and efficient coordination.

Barbara signed the last document and turned to me with a smile. "Whew! I'm finally off duty. What a relief. If you asked me right now if I'd ever do this again, I'd probably say no way! Lucky for my boss, my negative feelings go away pretty quickly. He'll probably be able to persuade me to lead another tour some day."

I shook my head. She had done an excellent job on this trip, and it sounded as though her boss appreciated her abilities. Nevertheless, she was probably being paid less than she was really worth.

"So, how do you feel," she asked. Shouldering the awkward spotting scope, she led the way off the ship toward the waiting bus.

"I'm sorry to see the cruise end," I said, quite truthfully. "I'm going home to an empty house. But, I do look forward to getting back to the office. It's been my refuge since Dale …"

"Maybe you need to do what I need to do: find a new man. Ellen will be graduating soon, right?"

"Yes, next spring, and then she'll start her graduate program in September. It'll be awhile before she can take over the office. Even then, I'll want to keep working, I think. Unless she has other ideas."

"Not if she's smart." Barbara grinned at me, and looked around for the bus driver. He spotted us, and hurried over to open the door. "But you really should take more vacation time for yourself. Go traveling. Take up a hobby. Find a new interest—and a new man."

"Sure, easy for you to say. But look, you need to take your own advice." A strange man—not Niko—helped us climb on board the bus.

Barbara settled into a pair of seats with the big scope next to her. I sat in the row behind her and closed my eyes, missing Niko desperately.

How did I really feel? It was taking all my energy to appear calm and happy. I had always laughed at the cliché, but today I was experiencing what I imagined must be the actual physical symptoms of a broken heart. Now, when I needed these minutes before we reached the airport to relax and take a deep breath, I found it impossible to breathe normally, and there was a terrible ache in my chest. For now, I had to choke back my tears. I was finding that extremely hard to do, but there would be plenty of time for them later, at home.

∽

The bus arrived at the airport in good time. We waited as our luggage was unloaded and then we headed inside. The security line was mercifully short this morning, our papers were checked and rechecked, and finally we were cleared to board our plane for the flight to Frankfurt.

As before, Barbara donned headphones and pretended to listen, but I thought she was probably sleeping. I leaned back and closed my eyes as well, but despite my sleepless night, sleeping now was the last thing on my mind.

Behind my eyelids, there was Niko. Snapshots of our time together flashed by—Niko handing me the book I had dropped, leading me through Uglich's back streets, knocking at my cabin door, showing me his cousin's apartment, and most of all, Niko making love to me. I shivered.

Could I ever again find a love like his? I had been doubly lucky, first to find Dale, and then Niko. His love had been an improbable surprise, all the sweeter for its unexpectedness.

I must have slept after all. The pilot's announcement of our approach to the Frankfurt airport startled me awake. Barbara had not stirred, so I touched her arm. As we sat up and gathered our possessions, I was astonished to find I was hungry.

In my experience—limited though it was— airport food was neither delicious nor nutritious. A few concessions might offer something resembling the local cuisine, but American style fast foods seemed to be the norm. At least we knew what to expect.

We opted for the easiest and fastest: burgers, fries (we shared those), and cokes. We still had forty-five minutes before we needed to board our plane to New York City, so we visited the duty-free shops again. I already had chosen presents for everyone on my gift list, so I followed Barbara around and nodded my approval when she treated herself to an unusual pink-gold Tissot dress watch with a mother-of-pearl dial.

Soon we heard the call to board the plane for the final part of our journey. This time Barbara stayed awake, reading and listening to her music. I opened a book and pretended to read, but my mind was picturing Niko.

∽

Our landing at JFK airport was, thankfully, uneventful. We hurried to retrieve our luggage and struggled through customs. At last, it was time to say goodbye.

"Barbara, I'm so grateful you invited me on this trip. I had an amazing time. I can't thank you enough!"

Barbara laughed. "I was delighted you could come. I hope you'll consider doing it again some time in the future, if I ever in a weak moment agree to lead another trip. I'm so glad you enjoyed yourself. Sorry I couldn't spend more time with you, but my donors had to come first."

"Don't you mean Anatoly came first?" I teased, with a smile.

"Ah, well. Our relationship was the definition of 'platonic.' He never even *tried* to get to first base, but I definitely enjoyed meeting him. He did a great job for us, and I wish him well."

"Good," I replied. She had all my sympathy if she was disappointed. "Listen, be careful going home and keep in touch. It was much too long since we'd last seen each other."

"Yes, it was," she said, as we touched cheeks. She beckoned to a porter to help her with the spotting scope and her luggage. "I'll call you soon. Stay well!"

She walked away with the porter and his baggage cart in tow. I watched her for a moment and then rolled my bags to the exit. I had to wait only a short while before the shuttle bus appeared to take me to my car in the long-term parking lot. I considered checking into a nearby hotel and driving home tomorrow. I was unsure how long I could keep my sadness at bay. It would not be wise to drive while blinded by tears.

By the time I reached my car, I had decided to risk the drive home. It was early afternoon. Driving through New York City's snarling traffic would take all my concentration. Once I got away from the city, there would be fewer cars on the road, and I would soon be home.

Then, I could cry.

Two hours later, I pulled into the driveway and clicked the garage door opener. To my relief, the house looked fine, at least from the outside, the garage just as usual. I had arranged for the house sitter to be gone when I arrived, so I came inside to an empty house.

I checked my messages. There were calls from Ellen, the office, and a few friends, and a note from the house sitter. She had had an uneventful two weeks, I was relieved to learn.

I dragged my bags up to my bedroom and sorted through their contents. I emptied the outside pockets last and, to my surprise, I found a small envelope tucked beneath my bedroom slippers.

I sat down on the bed and examined it closely. My name was scrawled on the outside in large, black letters. I recognized the handwriting immediately. Niko!

At last, the tears of unbearable sadness I had held back for so many hours poured down my cheeks. I hugged the envelope to my breast and sobbed.

Finally, I wiped my eyes and blew my nose. Carefully, I pulled the note out of the envelope and opened it.

My darling Sharon,

I cannot believe I will not see you after tonight. I do not know how I can say goodbye. I would go with you if I could. I do not know how I will pass the next two weeks without you. However, after these weeks are passed, I must report to my university, and prepare to meet my students.

There will be an intersession break between terms from mid-December to mid-January. If I can arrange a visa to visit America at that time, would it be possible to see you? I also would like very much to meet your Ellen, if you would agree to this.

Please tell me you still wish to see me, and where we could meet. I would not intrude upon your home if you do not wish it.

I look forward to your letters. It is best to use the address below.

I love you, my Sharon. Please write soon.

His name was scrawled at the bottom, and under it a St. Petersburg address.

My heart was bursting. Did I still wish to see him? Yes, more than I could express. Tears threatened again, and I let them come. This time they were tears of hope.

CHAPTER 20

September to December 2004

THE TIME passed slowly. I wrote to Niko every week. I had been puzzled, at first, why we were exchanging handwritten letters instead of sending email. He did not have a personal computer, he explained, and he was not allowed to use his office computer for personal business. I understood, but it seemed awkward. It had been a very long time since I had routinely put pen to paper in this way.

Niko was a good correspondent. He told funny and touching stories about his colleagues, students, his sister, and niece, and shared intimate details about his daily life. He also wrote passionately about his feelings for me and his hopes for some kind of future for us. He told me over and over how much he loved and missed me.

In early November, I received an excited letter telling me he had been given permission to visit the United States. I was thrilled. I immediately wrote back, inviting him to stay here with Ellen and me.

As the days passed, I became more and more impatient. I tried to keep busy. I went to work, visited the gym, and kept in touch via email with Barbara and the three women I met on the river cruise. I had prints made of the digital photos I had taken during our cruise and arranged them in two albums, one for me and one for Niko.

At night I dreamed. Often they were snippets of my former life with Dale and Ellen, on some trip to the city perhaps, or just sitting together in the family room, enjoying the fire. Sometimes, they were jumbled. I still had nightmares of car crashes, and of hearing strange doctors telling me Dale was dead. Sometimes, I would wake up in the middle of the night in a panic. That had happened often until I went to Russia. Now, it was happening less frequently, but the nightmares still came.

As for Niko, I longed for him. I ached for his touch, just as I had for Dale's after his death. My memories of Niko—how we met, how we both felt the electricity between us even before we became intimate, and how my feelings had turned so quickly to love afterward—helped comfort me. My dreams of our love making were filled with vivid pictures of tenderness and delight. He made me feel beloved, cherished. Many people might find it strange that I believed this strongly in his love after so short an intimacy, passionate though it had been. Naïvely or not, when he declared his love for me in St. Petersburg, I believed him. I still did.

Thanksgiving came, and Ellen arrived home from college for the long weekend. She was alone this time. Suzi was spending the holiday with her family in Texas. Ellen and I walked, talked, and baked holiday cookies together as we had done since she was little. I had told her about Niko in October when she came home for the Columbus Day weekend.

She had been shocked and angry that I could fall in love with a man other than her father. It was difficult for her to accept, as it had been at first for me. Her reaction was understandable. But, I told her, what Niko and I had experienced was so much more than just a passionate interlude.

I tried my best to explain how we had fallen in love, and more importantly, how the fact of my loving Niko took nothing away from my love for her father. Dale and Niko were very different men, I told her. I loved them both deeply, but differently.

She was too upset to listen. At last, I held my tongue and let her anger and disbelief wash over me like a flood tide. It was a very uncomfortable weekend. For the first time—and, I fervently hoped, the last—I was relieved when she went back to school.

Since then, her anger and hurt had gradually lessened. Now, we could talk about Niko on our twice-a-week phone calls and, during this Thanksgiving holiday, she even admitted to being curious about him. She told me she was actually looking forward to meeting the man who had taken the place of her father in my heart. Again, I tried to reassure her that each man had a unique and special place in my heart.

Did she understand? Perhaps not yet, though I hoped she would in time. But for now, she had decided to forgive me. That was the most important thing. The closeness between us, on which I depended so heavily, had been restored.

One morning, about two weeks before Christmas, I received a letter from Niko. As always, I opened it with anticipation, but unlike his previous letters, this one brought devastating news. Niko had told me he was in the Army Reserve and spent a few weeks each year in special training with his unit. Now, he wrote, his trip to visit me had been canceled. He and his unit had been ordered to report to Moscow in mid-December. They were to be posted to Chechnya for special duty lasting one year.

I was bitterly disappointed, but as I read his impassioned words, I understood how much he, himself, had been counting on his visit to America. His writing was disjointed, with several cross-outs, but his meaning was plain. He was frustrated, angry with fate and, especially, with his Army's commanders. He implored me not to forget him while he was away. This was extremely important, because he would not be allowed to write to me, or receive my letters, while he was in Chechnya.

I was shocked. I simply could not believe we would not be able to write to each other for an entire year. How could I wait so long to hear from him? How could I know whether he was thinking of me, and if he was well—and uninjured—in such a dangerous part of the world?

Now, I cried bitter tears of anger and frustration. At last, still clutching my sodden tissues, I opened my cellphone and called Ellen at school. It was the last weekend before finals, and she had been planning to come home.

"Hi, Mom, I'm just putting some stuff into my suitcase. Suzi and I are planning to leave here in about an hour and I should be home by dark. Do you want me to pick anything up for you?"

"No, darling. I just wanted to hear your voice. Drive carefully. I'll be waiting here for you. Niko won't be coming to visit with us after all. Something has come up. I'll tell you about it later."

After we hung up, I sat holding Niko's letter, unable to find the strength to do anything else. Finally, with resignation, I went slowly upstairs to add it to my collection of Niko's letters, and to put clean sheets on Ellen's bed and the trundle bed that Suzi slept in when she was here.

When finals were over, the girls came home loaded with Christmas presents for me, each other, and for their boyfriends. I tried to respond positively to their good cheer, but it was a struggle. My disappointment was too deep.

Two days after Christmas, they left for Colorado. They were to meet their boyfriends at a resort in Aspen for a few days of skiing. Next, the girls would travel to Texas to visit Suzi's brother and his family, and her grandmother. Though there was still hope, Mrs. Smith's cancer was worse, and Suzi was determined to spend as much time with her as she could before returning to Williams for the spring semester. Ellen was going with her for moral support.

After they left, the house fell silent again. I was unbearably lonely.

CHAPTER 21

December 2004

TWO DAYS before New Year's Eve, I realized, with sudden panic, I had skipped several cycles of my period. For a long time after Ellen was born, Dale and I had tried to give her a brother or sister. It had not happened, and after several years, we had stopped consciously trying. Niko and I had never used protection. I had told him I was unable to conceive a child, and I had believed him when he told me he was healthy.

Now, I counted on my fingers the weeks since my last period. I was due for my yearly gynecological checkup in mid-January. There was no way I could be pregnant. Surely not.

⌘

January 2005

I was still using the same Manhattan-based gynecologist who had guided me through my pregnancy with Ellen. On Monday morning, my fingers shaking, I dialed his office for an appointment. I had resisted rushing to the nearest pharmacy for a pregnancy test. It was possible I was ill with some terrible disease, or maybe I had suddenly entered menopause. I wanted to hear the doctor tell me... whatever he had to tell me.

I had to wait a week for an appointment. Meanwhile, my period still had not come. The nurse checked me in, noted my weight, and took my blood pressure. By the time I undressed and sat on the examining room table waiting for the doctor, I was in a state of nervous anxiety bordering on panic.

Though I still worried I might be in menopause, or dying of some dreadful disease, at this moment a possible pregnancy seemed far worse. I was in my mid-forties. Surely a pregnancy would be dangerous, both for me and for the baby. I would need to be tested, but what if the result indicated the possibility of a serious problem? Would I go ahead with the pregnancy? And, how would I break the news of my condition to my daughter and my staff? It would be shocking, and embarrassing too. How could they ever understand?

Dr. Foster examined me and, without speaking, bent over my chart and began writing. After what seemed like ages, he turned and looked at me.

"Well, I have what I hope is good news for you." He smiled slightly. "You are approximately nineteen weeks pregnant. Everything seems normal and you can probably expect a healthy outcome. I assume you have remarried?"

I felt like an idiot. This diagnosis was, of course, not news. Somewhere in the back of my mind, I had known it all along. I simply had refused to accept it, despite symptoms I never would have ignored had I been younger and still married to Dale.

I had been tired all the time recently and a week ago I had begun feeling a fluttering sensation in my stomach. That, I had assumed, was caused by panic. My clothes had become tight in the waist, and my breasts were swollen and tender. The tiredness I had put down to depression over leaving Niko in Russia, Niko's cancelled visit, and now, our inability to communicate. In my grief, I had ignored all the other symptoms.

Now, with my pregnancy confirmed, I would have to brazen it out to all the people who would wonder where—and who—the father was.

Suddenly, my doubts and fears melted away. With one hand cradling my belly protectively, I smiled.

"No, Dr. Foster. I haven't remarried, but I intend to have this child."

He gave me a long, considering look. Finally, he nodded.

"Okay. Get dressed and meet me in my office. I want to go over a few things with you."

Dr. Foster, who had delivered Ellen when both of us were twenty years younger, gave me advice on how to handle pregnancy at my advanced age, as well as some precautions. We discussed genetic testing, and he scheduled me for amniocentesis and a sonogram at New York-Presbyterian Hospital. He outlined possible outcomes, and suggested I consider carefully what I would do if the baby tested positive for Down syndrome or some other abnormality.

At the end of my visit, he smiled and wished me well. I was to come back to see him monthly until closer to term, and then more often.

I took the prescription for prenatal vitamins to my pharmacy and drove home in a daze.

Ellen's schedule was packed this semester. She was beginning an internship with a large Manhattan-based architectural firm and would be graduating in May. Then, unless she accepted another offer, she would work in our office this summer as she had done most years since entering high school.

I needed to tell her about this, but she would not be coming home until the Easter break. Dr. Foster had given me an approximate due date in early June, about two weeks after her graduation day. I was hardly showing now, but by Easter, I would be quite obviously pregnant. I decided to call her and ask her to come home as soon as possible.

She sounded distracted when I finally got her on the phone.

"Darling, I'm so sorry to ask this, but could you possibly come home this weekend? I have something important to tell you and it really can't wait."

"Oh, Mom, now?" She sounded annoyed. She wanted me to know what an enormous sacrifice I was asking of her.

Reluctantly, to humor me, she agreed.

By the time she arrived home, she had stopped being annoyed. Instead she was curious, and a little afraid. When I told her I was pregnant, she reacted with amazement and fury. I watched with dismay as she stalked away. I heard her door slam shut when she reached her bedroom.

I was heart-sick. Her reaction was even worse than I had feared.

The next morning, she joined me for breakfast in her robe and slippers. She was somewhat calmer, but still angry. She could scarcely believe I had let something like this happen. After all, I was her mother, not some young girl who was ignorant of the facts of life.

I tried again to explain what had happened between Niko and me, my fears when I noticed I had missed several periods, and how as the days passed since the confirmation, I had begun more and more to welcome the idea of having Niko's baby. Though he himself was absent, he had given me a precious gift. I intended to cherish this baby, no matter the consequences.

Gradually, she began to listen, trying to understand. We took turns airing our views, sharing tears, and some chuckles as well.

"Mom, you really scared me. I was positive you were going to give me bad news—either you were ill, or you were going to sell the house and move. I couldn't imagine either of those things. They were just too awful."

"Oh, Ellen. You know, I hope, I would never sell your father's house. But I'm glad to assure you I'm not ill. I guess some people might consider being pregnant an illness, but at least it's temporary."

"No, not an illness, but your being pregnant definitely will be embarrassing. I don't know what I'll tell my friends, but that's not really important. The cool thing is that I'll finally get the little brother or sister I'd wanted so badly when I was younger. I think I'll really enjoy that. Better late than never, right?"

I smiled. Her enthusiasm was another precious gift.

"I can see how much you want this baby. I was kind of jealous at first, but I'm over that now. I just want you to be happy. I don't think I could stand to watch you be unhappy again. It was really awful after Dad died."

"I know, honey." We hugged, and shed a few tears together.

Finally she straightened, and blew her nose. "So Mom, how are you feeling physically? I guess you're pretty old to be having a baby. Are you doing okay?"

"Yes, the doctor is pleased with our progress. I was pretty tired until recently, but now I seem to have more energy than I know what to do with. The public library is offering a quilting workshop. I think I'm going to sign up for that. It might be fun, and I'll have a new skill."

"Good for you. That sounds great."

"I'm also starting to think about decorating a nursery. Maybe you'd like to help me pick out colors and furniture?"

"Sure, I'd love that! Let's go the the paint store now."

"Okay, let's get dressed and go."

An hour later, we were in the car. "Mom, I'm thinking about colors for the nursery. Do you want a girl or a boy? And, don't you want to find out which before you give birth?"

"Honey, I want what most expectant mothers want: a healthy baby. Its sex is irrelevant. Don't worry. We can still pick out great colors without going overboard on pink or blue."

To my profound relief, the results of the amnio test were negative. My sonograms showed the steady growth of the baby, and the little one kicked vigorously. I considered baby names, but there was really no doubt. Depending on its sex, my baby would be either Nicholas or Nicole. As my belly swelled, I continued to feel amazingly well.

I called Barbara to tell her my news. Predictably, she shrieked her approval.

"Wow! I'm shocked, but I'm so happy *you're* happy. How are you feeling? Wow! That's amazing! Who could have predicted that would happen?"

We talked several times over the next several weeks while I was waiting for the baby's arrival.

Since I had returned from Russia, I had received and responded to several emails from the three women I met on our river cruise. I decided not to tell them about my pregnancy, since I had never told them about Niko. I felt it would be too much of a shock for them to learn about it now. I would let our tentative friendship lapse gradually.

I hired a workman to paint the nursery with the colors Ellen and I had chosen—medium teal and a pale, rosy peach—and at last, the baby furniture we had picked out was delivered. Meanwhile, I continued to go to work each day, and learned to deal with the stares of colleagues and acquaintances.

The months passed slowly. Then one morning, time accelerated dramatically. Nicholas Grant was born on May 20, two weeks before my due date. We missed Ellen's graduation ceremony, but she forgave us. In fact, she came home as soon as I called to tell her that Nicholas was here. She returned to Williams only to pick up her diploma and pack her belongings.

Barbara visited us in the hospital and remarked on how beautiful Nicholas was. He was as red-faced and bald as most other newborns, but she insisted he looked just like Niko. My favorite comment of hers was: "Well, I guess you got a new man after all."

Summer 2005

It was hectic that summer, but we made it. After three months at home, I hired a nurse/housekeeper and returned to work part-time. Ellen interned in our offices as usual and spent most weekends at home. Nicholas thrived with three doting women to care for him, and when Suzi visited on the occasional weekend, there were four.

Life was messy, but since I could now focus most of my attention on my son instead of his absent father, it was infinitely better than I could have imagined.

CHAPTER 22

January 2006 to July 2008

ONE DAY in mid-January, the doorbell rang, but when I opened the door no one was there. A large, square white envelope lay on the doormat.

When I opened it, there were two letters inside. One was from Niko. I trembled with joy and anticipation. I had agonized all these many months over whether I would ever hear from him again.

I barely glanced at the other letter, but the first sentence caught and held my attention. The writer claimed to be a friend of Niko's, someone I could trust to be a go-between.

Niko was no longer allowed to send letters to me openly, the letter said, or to receive mine. However, he had recruited a friend who would smuggle his letters to me into the diplomatic pouch delivered from St. Petersburg directly to Dept. N in the Russian Consulate in New York City. My letters to Niko, addressed to Dept. N at the Consulate, would go back to Russia in the pouch, and be retrieved and delivered to Niko by the same friend. I was not to put Niko's name on my envelopes to Dept. N.

Oddly, it never occurred to me to question whether this elaborate scheme was a trap to catch Niko in an illegal correspondence. Naïvely, or not, I simply accepted it. I did worry, though. We were taking an enormous risk. I could only imagine the consequences to Niko and his co-conspirators if we were found out, but I was profoundly grateful for those nameless people who were willing to take the gamble.

Enclosed was Niko's letter.

4 January 2006
My darling Sharon,

I have returned to Russia. I thought my time in Chechnya would never end. You were in my thoughts at every moment. I worried you might be ill, and I not know, or perhaps you had forgotten me after so long a time. I wondered continually if you still loved me as I love you. I hope so, very much.

It will be impossible for me to come to America in the foreseeable future. I seem to have made my superiors suspicious. I can only hope they will someday relent.

I was slightly wounded in fighting in Chechnya—nothing to worry about, I am now recovered—and was sent back to Moscow for physical therapy in early December. It was then I learned I can no longer write directly to you. My friend in the Consulate has agreed to be our go-between. Do not fear. He can be trusted.

I have now returned to St. Petersburg. You may imagine me there, back in my classroom at the university. I wish you were my student. I would give you private tutelage, and very high marks.

I love you, my darling. Never forget how I love you. Please write soon to the address of the Consulate.

We exchanged letters as often as possible, given the logistics involved. We were lucky. As far as I knew, Niko was under no further suspicion, and though frustrated by his continued inability to come to America to see me, he at least was able once again to communicate with me.

Early in our secret correspondence, I made the decision not to tell Niko that I had given birth to his son. Niko's spirits seemed very low, though he tried to disguise his anger and frustration. I was worried he might put himself in danger by trying to come to America to see him if he knew of Nicholas's existence. I was afraid to take the chance.

Of course I *wanted* to tell him. But the longer I delayed, the more awkward my confession would be. I realized it was too late. I would have to keep that secret from him, at least for a while, possibly a long while.

Time flew by and Nicholas thrived. From a fat and happy infant he turned almost overnight into an active toddler. He was tall for his age and very bright. He walked and talked early and had a cheerful, even-tempered disposition. He was mischievous, but he was rarely spiteful. With his brown eyes focused intently on us, he would pay close attention whenever Ellen, or I, or his nurse explained something to him, and he never forgot anything he heard.

My heart swelled with pride at Nicholas's every achievement while it ached with loneliness for Niko. Nicholas looked so much like his father. How I longed to show Niko his beautiful son.

❧

In May, 2008, Nicholas turned three. Ellen and I hosted a birthday party for him and invited all his play-date friends. I treasured the photos we took that day of Nicholas with his little friends, opening his presents, and eating his birthday cake and ice cream, chocolate smeared from ear to ear.

Niko and I had been exchanging letters approximately every two weeks. Suddenly, in late May, he stopped writing. There was no warning. I reread his last few letters carefully, but could find no hint that he planned to end our correspondence.

I waited two more weeks before writing directly to Dept. N at the Consulate. There was no reply. I was devastated. I could not believe Niko had tired of me. Yet the only other explanation filled me with dread. Had we been found out? Was Niko being punished? Had something else happened to him? Was he hurt? Ill? I was frantic, but there was only silence from Russia.

❧

One evening in late July, my doorbell rang soon after I had returned home from work. I was alone in the kitchen warming leftovers for my supper. Nicholas was staying overnight with Ellen after she had spent a precious day off entertaining him at the Bronx Zoo. It was just after sunset, but when I opened the door, it was still light enough to see. There was no one there. I glanced down and there, on the doormat, lay a large white envelope, identical to the ones I was used to receiving from Dept. N.

I snatched it up, rushed back inside, and sat down in the family room to open it. Inside the envelope was another, addressed to me in Niko's familiar scrawl. With shaking hands I drew out the letter and began to read.

26 May 2008
My Darling Sharon,
I am writing this letter in haste. I am to undertake a mission for my government early tomorrow morning. It is a simple task, with little danger. However, it involves a certain amount of subterfuge, and it is always possible something will go wrong.

If you are reading this letter, it means the mission did not go well. There are things I must tell you. I would have told you these things in person, if it had been possible. They have been weighing heavily on my conscience, and I have decided I must tell you now.

Before I write anything more, I want you to understand that I have loved you for a very long time, even before we met in Moscow. As always, I yearn to be with you, to hold you and love you as I did when we were together in my country.

You will, perhaps, find my story strange, even unbelievable, and you may react with anger and despair. I would never hurt you if I could avoid it, but I must tell you the truth. Do not, I beg of you, judge me, or Dale, too harshly.

I was born and raised, as I told you, in St. Petersburg. I did well in my studies, grew physically strong, and was encouraged to become a good Soviet comrade. I was singled out for KGB training in spy-craft and I did well in this too. I succeeded in many missions, at first small, but later bigger assignments. After the USSR fell and the KGB was disbanded, I transitioned into the FSB, Russia's new domestic intelligence service. Soon after, I met your husband.

Dale was my colleague and I dare to call him my friend. We worked together several times when our two governments found it useful to cooperate. Dale did not tell you he was a CIA agent, recruited in graduate school. It was his most closely guarded secret. He believed only your ignorance of his activities could keep you and Ellen safe from harm.

One evening, after a particularly difficult joint mission, we got drunk together and he told me of you. I think I began to fall in love with you that night. He showed me your picture and described the woman of my dreams—you, my Sharon.

Dale was a good man, a fine architect, and I treasured our friendship. Please do not hate him or be angry with him because of his secret.

There are always enemies in this business. When Dale died, my government sent me to investigate whether his death was truly accidental, especially since he had been involved in another automobile accident only days before his fatal one. I wish I could tell you they were indeed accidents. However, when I arrived, sufficient time had passed for Dale's enemies to have concealed any evidence of foul play beyond my limited ability to discover it. In your shock and grief, you did not see me at his funeral, but I was there, though I could not approach you at that difficult time.

When my superiors discovered you were to visit Russia on the river cruise, I was ordered to travel with the ship as its Russian teacher. I was overjoyed. I would again see you in person, and this time we might be able to speak to each other. Perhaps you would smile at me.

You were everything I had dreamed of, and so much more. I love you. I will always love you. If you believe in God, perhaps you can believe we will be together again some day. I put no faith in gods, but I do believe, somehow, we will be together again one day. You are my beloved.

Niko

I stood, dropping the letter unheeded to the floor, and stumbled to the window. I stared blindly outside. How could this be? Dale? A spy? I cast my mind back over our marriage. Was it a sham, entirely based on a lie? How could I have lived with him so long and not known, or at least, suspected?

And Niko? Also a spy?

Tears came, first of shock, then of rage, and finally, grief. I struggled to understand. How could I accept what Niko had written? How could it possibly be true?

After my tears ran their course, I began to calm myself. Taking deep breaths, I realized, to my amazement, I believed every word of Niko's story. I trusted him completely, just as Dale had so many years ago when he showed Niko my picture.

I bent to pick up the pages I had dropped. Folding them over in my hands, I noticed there was a postscript, written on the back of the last page.

⚭

Please do not endanger yourself by trying to contact anyone in the CIA. The person who delivered this letter will watch over you. He will stay in the background. You will not see him, but do not fear, he is a friend.

⚭

I began to read Niko's letter again, more slowly this time. In my initial haste, I had skipped over the first sentence of his second paragraph: *If you are reading this letter, it means the mission did not go well.*

I stared at it in disbelief. I had overlooked the most crucial part of the letter. What had happened to Niko? My frantic mind pictured his two most likely fates. Had his government, or some other entity, thrown him in prison? Or, was he already dead? Either possibility shattered any fragile hope we might be able to build a future together.

I paced as my mind whirled. These last two months, as I went about my daily tasks—taking care of Nicholas and looking forward to Ellen's visits, working in the office, chatting with friends, and loving and worrying about Niko—he was already beyond my reach.

What was I going to do? To lose both men so suddenly—how could that be? How was I going to survive this second blow?

Finally, I sat down, still holding Niko's precious letter. After what might have been a few minutes or a few hours, I refolded the pages and returned them to their envelopes. I would keep Niko's letter safe, and someday, after his words had become a part of me, I would burn it.

∞

That night, I lay sleepless in bed, my mind reeling with my newfound knowledge. I would need time to come to terms with Dale's and Niko's secret lives and Niko's sudden disappearance. I would have to deal in private with my grief for the two men I loved, and with the fact I knew so little about them after all. I was unsure, right now, whether I would grieve more for the sham of my idyllic marriage—in which I believed Dale and I had shared everything, or for the near certainty I could never again hope to see Niko.

I was finding it particularly hard to believe Dale had managed to keep his CIA activities secret during all the years of our marriage. Granted, he had been away from home quite often, sometimes for several weeks, even months, at a time. It was just possible he could have trained at CIA headquarters in Virginia, while I believed he was overseeing some architectural project in another part of the world. Once his training was completed, he could have been sent on any number of dangerous missions, and I never would have known.

Now, finally, the long silences with no contact between us were explained. I thought back to his first project in the Ukraine, so many years ago. He must have been acting for the CIA then, and so many other times as well. All those trips through the years to Russia and other countries around the globe, what dangers, what ordeals, had he survived? And, when he checked out his car— every time—before getting in and starting the engine? It was because he truly *was* a spy! The "joke" was on me.

And, had there been other signs I had overlooked? If so, how could I have been so blind? How could I have spent so many years blithely leading my seemingly charmed life, never suspecting things were not as they seemed?

On one hand, I was proud he had served our country in this way. At the same time, I was furious with him for not trusting me with this knowledge, so central to his life. Was it really true Ellen and I might have been endangered if he had told me?

I would never know. I had loved Dale unconditionally, with all my heart, and also our life together. I could never wish it had not happened. Without Dale, there would be no Ellen, and what would my life be without her?

Something—coincidence?—had brought Dale and Niko together. Or, perhaps it was simply an inevitable consequence of their undercover activities.

I can never tell Dale's secret to anyone, not even his daughter. It is simply not my secret to tell. Niko's continued silence easily can be explained, should anyone ask. I will say he has changed his mind about me and has decided to end our correspondence. His secrets, as well, are not mine to tell.

I longed for someone with whom I could share my confused feelings about the odd intertwining of our three lives.

I briefly considered finding a counselor, but I knew I could never tell my story to a stranger. It would be impossible. I would have to be the keeper of all of our secrets.

CHAPTER 23

August 28, 2009

NICHOLAS'S DAY camp was finishing for the summer. The camp bus had picked him up for the last time at eight this morning, and would bring him home this afternoon soon after three. I had taken the day off from work because we were going on a special outing to a local ice cream parlor to celebrate this milestone. He was four years old now, and would be starting pre-school in a little over a week. He was growing up too fast.

When the doorbell rang later that morning, my first thought was something must have happened to him. I was upstairs putting away laundry, fresh from the dryer. I looked out the front window, but there was no camp bus in sight. I sighed in relief.

A moment later the doorbell rang again, more insistently. I ducked into the hall bathroom to check my hair in the mirror. I decided there was no time to fuss, and ran down the stairs.

In the front hall, I peeked through the side windows.

There was no one in sight.

Puzzled, I unlocked the door and opened it just far enough to see a white envelope lying on the doormat. I scooped it up and ran back inside, relocking the door securely. I examined the envelope as I walked down the hall into the kitchen. After all this time, could it be a letter from Niko?

I continued into the family room and sat in my favorite chair near the wood stove. My fingers shaking, I drew out a single handwritten page. Disappointment crushed me. The handwriting was not Niko's.

I cannot come openly to your front door, but I have news of a mutual friend I believe you will wish to hear. Please do me the favor of meeting me on the patio near your pond. I am waiting there now.

There is no reason to fear me. I bring good news.

It was unsigned.

I stared at the paper. What could this mean? Every instinct told me to stay inside, to call the police, to protect myself.

And yet…

Should I go? Stay? If I called the police, what would I say? Would they take me seriously? I was hesitant to make a fuss over nothing, but what if it was something…

I stood at my terrace door, straining to see the patio. It was, of course, out of sight. It was at the bottom of the garden near the pond. Dale and I had designed it specifically to be *secluded*. It was not large, but it contained a rectangular, wrought iron umbrella table with eight chairs. Our entire property was fenced and hidden by trees and shrubbery from the casual view of our neighbors. If someone were waiting for me on our patio, how had he gotten there?

Slipping my cellphone into my pocket, and leaving the terrace door slightly ajar, I went outside. Carefully, I tiptoed down the steps to the first of the garden's tiers, where newly planted lavender asters and white mums bloomed among small Japanese ferns, and the branches of large purple-leafed shrubs swayed gently in the breeze. Though the day was cool for the end of August, the sun felt warm on my shoulders. I paused. The only sounds were the splash of the brook feeding the pond, and muted birdsong.

Slowly, I continued down from tier to tier, moving in and out of the shade cast by the shrubs, and passing wooden half-barrels filled with more early fall flowers.

As I approached the patio, I slipped off the path and stopped behind one of the purple shrubs. Carefully, I moved a branch so I could see part of the scene. Standing in profile was a tall man carrying a khaki trench coat. He stood motionless, staring out over the pond. There was something familiar about him, striking a chord in my memory. I was sure I had seen him before.

Forgetting my uneasiness, I stepped onto the patio. He turned, and I gasped. It had been five years since I had last seen this man. Then, he had been serving coffee in the Volga Dining Room aboard the *River Sprite*, in the pre-dawn of my final morning in St. Petersburg.

It was Ivan, the nice waiter with the polite smile and fluent English. I had never expected to see him again.

What on earth was he doing here? And why now, after all this time?

My mouth agape, I shook my head and stammered, "I-Ivan? What…"

"Hello, Mrs. Grant. Please forgive me for coming here without notice. I have news I think you will wish to hear." He nodded toward the table. "May we sit?"

My heart was pounding. Yet, despite Ivan's unexpected arrival and the fact that I was alone with him, I was not afraid. My heart was racing because he was a possible link, however tenuous it might prove to be, to Niko.

Clearing my throat, I found my voice. "How did you get in here?"

He made a wry face and shrugged his shoulders. "As you will hear, there are reasons I cannot come openly to your door. I have been careful. No one has seen me arrive."

Though he had avoided answering my question, I came forward to sit at the table and gestured for him to join me. He looked capable of anything, but foolishly or not, I felt completely safe with him. Ivan laid his coat on one of the other chairs drawn up to the table and took a seat next to me.

We sat for a moment in silence. An egret glided down onto the far bank of the pond and began stalking long-limbed through the shallows, no doubt in search of an early lunch. The sun glinted off the water. The splashing of the brook seemed hushed and even the birdsong had stopped.

"It is beautiful here. Peaceful." Ivan leaned forward, his elbows on the table. "You must spend much time here." He indicated the table and chairs with a strong-looking, long-fingered hand.

It was a question, rather than a statement. I hesitated, looking down at my own hands, now clenched in my lap, my fingernails digging painfully into my palms. I made a conscious effort to relax. At last I looked up, and took a deep breath.

"Yes. Sometimes I bring a book, but often I just come and sit. It's very quiet most of the time."

Ivan nodded without speaking. He seemed comfortable with silence. He was going to take his time, despite my growing impatience to hear his news.

After a long pause, he turned his head to look closely at me. Funny, I had taken little notice of him while he was serving us on the ship. He was just a pleasantly polite waiter. Now, I realized with surprise how handsome he was. Not classically handsome, perhaps, but with strong features, well proportioned. His nose was straight, and not too long. His wide mouth was nicely shaped, indented in the middle of the upper lip. Broad cheekbones and large, blue-grey eyes were balanced by a firm, square chin. He was closely shaven, I was pleased to see—I had been waiting years for the stubbled look to lose its cool. His straight, white-blond hair was cut short on the sides, and neatly brushed, though one lock fell forward over his brow. He looked to be in his early forties, or maybe a few years older.

He was gazing again at the pond. I wondered what he saw besides the picture book view. I had an idea he was seeing a much different scene.

I waited, expecting… I had no clear idea what. Beyond all the obvious questions, what was he doing here in the United States? Like the rest of the crew of the *River Sprite*, he was a Russian citizen. I looked more closely at his clothes. He was dressed in a summer-weight suit, dark grey, single breasted. Ordinary, except the fabric was good and it fit his broad shoulders and trim waist as though custom tailored. His shoes were polished black wingtips, of decent quality. A grey and blue striped tie over a pale blue shirt brought out the color of his eyes. He looked more like a successful businessman than a Russian tourist on vacation. *Was* he on vacation? What was he doing on my patio?

"You must be wondering why I have come all this way."

I nodded.

"My superiors in Moscow believe I requested permission to visit our consulate in New York City to clear unfinished business related to our most recent operation. It is true, but only part of the truth. Though indeed, I am meeting with a highranking official who is stationed in the consulate, I have not told them of my plan to visit you. But, I must tell you before I proceed further, my name is not Ivan."

He scanned my face, making sure I understood what he was saying. Not Ivan?

"My name is Vladimir Ivanovich Morozov. I am a Major in the Russian FSB, our state security service. I am sure you have heard of it."

I nodded again.

Like most Americans of at least middle age, I had seen many stories in the news media about Russian espionage, and Russian spies were the featured villians in countless movies, TV programs, and novels. The FSB had partially replaced the KGB, I had read. Everyone knew about the KGB, or at least thought they did. In his last letter, Niko had confessed to having worked for both organizations.

Watching me intently, he went on.

"Please call me Vladi. My friends call me by that name.

"Five years ago," he said, "I was a Captain, second in command to Nikolai Petrovich Novikov, the man you knew as the Russian teacher aboard the *River Sprite*. He held the rank of Lieutenant Colonel and was leader of his own team of agents. You would call us spies.

"Niko and I were on the riverboat because of you. When our superiors learned you had applied for a Russian entrance visa, they became suspicious that you were either working for the CIA, or were being used by them to deliver something, perhaps a package or a message. They sent us to spy on you. Niko was ordered to seduce you and find out why you had come to Russia. They did not believe your husband would have kept his CIA involvement a secret from you. It never occurred to them you might be simply a tourist."

I was having trouble believing my ears. Niko *ordered...* to *seduce* me? I felt lightheaded with shock.

"I'm sorry." Vladi lightly touched my arm.

"Of course, they had no way of knowing that Niko was already half in love with you. He took the assignment with much excitement and anticipation. He tried to hide his feelings from me, but I knew him too well by then. I was relieved when he arranged for me to be on board too, as I thought I could keep an eye on him. A few years ago, he had a very bad experience with a female agent, a beautiful Israeli. She seduced him, made him believe she was in love with him, and then played him for a fool. Niko almost lost his life, as well as his career. I was determined to prevent something similar from happening to him again. Niko is not easily seduced, nor is he a womanizer. He is a good man who has much love to share.

"Niko worked with Dale several times on joint missions and counted him a friend. It is rare for the agents of two adversarial nations to become friendly, but Dale was a special person, as is Niko. I believe Niko wrote to you of the circumstances under which Dale showed your photo to him."

I gasped. How could he know the contents of Niko's letter to me?

"Please forgive me. Niko trusted me to deliver a letter to you if something bad happened to him. When his last mission went wrong and he disappeared, I opened the letter and read it. I had to know what he meant to do about you."

In the space of a few minutes, I had moved from surprise to shock to dismay and finally, to fury. Unfortunately, when I am very angry I cry, my face turns red, and my nose runs. Vladi removed a freshly laundered handkerchief from his breast pocket and pressed it into my hand. I mopped my face as well as I could and raised my swollen and furious eyes to his.

"How *could* you? That letter was *private*."

Vladi shook his head. "I will not apologize for wanting to help Niko. It is the only reason I read the letter. I am, first of all, Niko's friend. I would be yours too, as I believe you still care for him."

"*Care* for him?" I took a deep breath in an effort to calm myself. "Yes, I do, more than I can say."

"I was sure of it." He nodded briskly. "That is why I am here."

I stared at him, shaking my head in confusion.

"What do you mean?"

Vladi looked intently at me, willing me to understand. "Niko's last mission ended in disaster. It was routine, or so Niko was told. He was to proceed to an FSB safe house in a suburb of St. Petersburg, deliver a package, and escort a young woman waiting for him there back to headquarters. Nothing could be simpler.

"However, when he and the young woman failed to return on schedule, a search was made at the address. Inside, the woman was found in the hallway—strangled—with no trace either of Niko or the package he was supposed to deliver. The man who was to receive the package was upstairs, shot execution style, one bullet to the back of his head.

"It was assumed that Niko murdered them both and ran away with the package, which as it turned out, contained gem quality diamonds worth a total of several million dollars. There was a broad and intensive search for him, but Niko could not be found."

I stared blankly at Vladi, stunned by this story. After a few seconds, my mind began to function again. Niko could never have murdered two people and run away with a fortune in diamonds. He was devoted to his country, and intensely proud of the work he did at his university and for the FSB. Besides, he never would have left his sister and niece without his help and protection.

Vladi paused, taking a deep breath to calm himself. "Of course, Niko could never have done those things! There was an official inquiry, but with the lack of evidence in his favor, he was found guilty *in absentia*. Soon afterwards, he was declared officially dead."

One large hand raked through his hair in an unsuccessful attempt to tame the fallen lock. "Naturally, Niko's team was broken up. We were each questioned relentlessly, though as his second in command, I was singled out for more intense interrogations. Finally, I was able to convince our superiors I knew nothing. I had suspicions, however. Niko told me that on the last day you and he went to the apartment in St. Petersburg, an old enemy of his was stepping out of the elevator as the two of you arrived."

"Yes," I said, nodding. "There was a man. I remember him. He was about Niko's age, but heavy set and very unpleasant looking. He was wearing some sort of military uniform, and I thought he looked like a movie villain."

"That is a good description. He is Grigor Smetlov. He and Niko were in KGB training together. Grigor was abnormally jealous of Niko and did everything he could to get him into trouble. Since then, Grigor has become even more of a troublemaker. He is a braggart, a cheat, and a liar. His career has stalled and I doubt he will rise higher in rank. But as he watched Niko's career flourish, he became more and more desperately jealous and resentful. He has tried several times over the years to cast suspicion on Niko. I believe he has now gone completely crazy, driven to extreme and terrible actions by his insane jealousy."

Vladi shook his head in disgust. "I immediately suspected Grigor had something to do with the murders in the safe house, the theft of the diamonds, and Niko's disappearance, though he must have had help. Grigor would know how to blackmail people to find out information and to make them do what he wanted.

"After my interrogations were over, I was transferred to Moscow and assigned to another FSB team. Eventually, I was promoted to become their leader. We often performed surveillance, or tracked enemy agents, and sometimes the tasks were dangerous. I learned much from Niko, and my team has been lucky so far. But, I am telling you this because I never stopped looking for clues to what had happened.

"Whenever I was in St. Petersburg, I followed Grigor as often and as closely as possible. Perhaps, if I could have spent all my time searching for Niko, so many months would not have passed. I want you to understand. I had to go very slowly and carefully, and make sure no one knew what I was doing, especially Grigor Smetlov.

"Finally, just two weeks ago, I found Niko. He is alive."

"Alive! Where? Is he hurt?" My indignation and anger vanished in a tide of happy excitement. Jumping to my feet, I grasped Vladi's upper arms and attempted to shake him.

Vladi pushed back his chair and stood as well. He took my hands in his and held them tightly. He looked as though he were as overcome with gladness as I was, but it lasted only a moment.

"Please understand, my news is not all good. Niko is being held in the basement of an abandoned factory in a suburb of St. Petersburg. I was right about Grigor. And, this is not Niko's only prison. Grigor had him moved several times, always at night. At first, Grigor came often to gloat and torture Niko, but recently, he has been coming less frequently."

"How did you find out all this? When will he be released? When can I see him? Can I go there?" I was breathless, shaking with tension.

Vladi held up his hands to stop me.

"Please. One question at a time."

He gently pushed me back into my chair and took his own.

"I followed Grigor and watched his house whenever I could, and began to recognize his associates. One night a little more than a month ago, I followed Grigor and one of his men to a dacha in the countryside. It was quite late, and no one was around. It was very quiet. When Grigor got out of the car he seemed drunk, and he was holding a gun on the other man, who had been driving. The driver was pleading for his life, but Grigor kept pushing him toward a small shed behind the dacha. He fumbled a key out of his pocket, tossed it to the driver, and told him to unlock the door. When he did so, Grigor made him kneel inside the doorway, and then shot him twice from behind. He kicked the man into the shed and slammed the door, never bothering to lock it. Then he stumbled back to his car and drove away.

"I waited until I could no longer hear the car's engine, and then ran to the shed. Luckily, the man was still alive. Instead of shooting him cleanly in the head, Grigor had grazed him above the right ear and also hit him in his back, below his right shoulder. He was bleeding heavily from the head wound.

"I dragged him out of the shed, and ran to get my car, which I had left hidden a short distance away. I used the man's shirt to fashion a bandage for his head and wrapped him in a blanket from my trunk. He was conscious long enough to tell me his name was Andrei. I drove him back to the city, and brought him to a medic I know who can be counted on to keep quiet. He was able to remove the bullet in Andrei's back, which had almost punctured his lung. The man is alive and is slowly recovering.

"Andrei, who was once Grigor's closest friend, has no love for Grigor now, as you can imagine. He is very grateful to me for saving his life, and after the first week, when he was mostly unconscious, he has been filling my ears with stories of Grigor's misdeeds. Among them, was how Grigor loved to visit a man he had hated for many years. Grigor had found a way to disgrace the man, which was good, but even better, he had kidnapped and imprisoned him. Andrei was happy to tell me where this man was being held, and who his jailors were. The prisoner he described was Niko."

I shook my head. "But Vladi, why didn't Grigor kill Niko at the beginning? Why did he keep him alive all this time?" I shivered. "How bizarre. He *must* be crazy!"

Vladi nodded his head. "As I said before, I believe Grigor *has* gone completely crazy. He has always been jealous of Niko, not just because Niko was bigger, stronger, smarter, and more successful than Grigor at almost everything. Grigor believed Niko received special privileges and promotions because of his great uncle, a famous KGB General, who oversaw Niko's training and career. So I think, in Grigor's twisted mind, he was finally defeating Niko each time he watched him being tortured. He apparently enjoyed it too much to end it by killing Niko."

I shivered again, and Vladi placed his hand gently on my arm.

"I watched the factory as often as I could and observed Niko's jailors' routines. I recognized two of them—they are criminals from St. Petersburg's underworld—but there are six men altogether sharing guard duties. They rotate in shifts. While two rest inside, the other four patrol the property. Once a week, supplies are delivered from St. Petersburg: food, vodka, cigarettes, clean clothes, etc., which the driver exchanges for bundles of dirty laundry, garbage, and whatever else the men need to dispose of.

"I am working on a plan to rescue him, but I needed to see you before I go further. There are problems. Niko was viciously beaten multiple times over the many months of his captivity. Most of his beatings left scars but no permanent damage. However, there were some more serious effects. He may be at least partially blind in one eye, and his left leg was broken in several places and not set properly. He is sure to be in some degree of chronic pain.

"Unfortunately, I have no idea of his mental state. He has been kept in total darkness, except when he is being tortured, and he is not being given enough food. The guards told Andrei that Niko is silent most of the time. This concerns me. I would rather that he was making a lot of noise. I cannot believe Niko has given up completely. He used to be quite strong, but fifteen months is a very long time to live in pain, hunger, and darkness."

I was sobbing again, this time in shock, horror, and anguish. I could imagine now what Niko was suffering, but I was powerless to help him.

Vladi took one of my hands in his and waited for my tears to stop.

"I must be sure. Do you wish to be with Niko again, even if his mind is as damaged as his body?"

"Yes, yes, of course. There are doctors, psychiatrists, physical therapists... Surely, he can be helped. I could never abandon him. Vladi, I have his son. Now that we know Niko is alive, Nicholas must be given the chance to know his father."

I gazed eagerly into Vladi's face.

"You must understand. This is not the first time Niko has been captured and tortured."

I looked at him in stunned silence.

"Yes, while we were in Chechnya, rebels captured him and beat him severely. We were able to rescue him before they could kill him, but it was months before he was well enough to return to St. Petersburg."

"Oh, Vladi! He wrote that he had been only slightly wounded and had undergone physical therapy in Moscow. I guess he didn't want to upset me."

"He would make light of his injuries for your sake. It is like him. I only mention it because the remembrance of that time may make his recovery now more difficult."

"Yes, I see. But Vladi, I love Niko. I want the chance to be with him, to help him recover, and to make a future with him. If he agrees to come here, this will be his home. But, he will have to defect, won't he?"

"Ah." Vladi sighed. "Yes. Niko cannot stay in Russia. His career is over, and he would be in too much danger from Grigor and his friends to stay. Even after Grigor is stopped, it would be too dangerous. Niko has other enemies as well. You and Nicholas are his best hope for the future."

Vladi paused and looked at me closely.

"Here is another thing you need to understand. If Niko defects, there will be increased surveillance around you and this house, not only by us, but also by the CIA and, very possibly, other foreign and domestic agencies. You will be watched, your privacy will be disrupted, and you, Ellen, and Nicholas may even be in danger."

I gasped.

"And there is another consideration. It is likely the U.S. government would decide to put you into some sort of witness protection program. If that is the case, you, Niko, and Nicholas would be relocated to some other place with new identities. I do not mention Ellen, as she is an adult pursuing her own career. But, these are possibilities you will have to accept if we succeed in freeing Niko."

It took me only a moment to process this. It would be difficult to leave this house, and possibly, lose day-to-day contact with Ellen, but weighed against a life with Niko and Nicholas? My heart filled with hope.

"Vladi, I will do whatever is necessary. Gladly."

"Good. I will arrange the delivery to you of a secure cellphone. When Niko has been extracted and I have a better idea of his condition and how we will need to proceed, I will call you on that phone. You must answer it outside, not inside your home. Do you understand?"

I nodded.

"I will wait anxiously for your call. Thank you, Vladi, for what you are doing for Niko."

"I do this for me as well as for him. I love him too."

We sat quietly for a little while, each of us busy with our private thoughts. I watched a pair of ducks waddle into the water and swim away across the pond. At the same time, I was envisioning a happy homecoming for my Niko.

Homecoming? In my excitement, I was making a huge assumption. He was Russian, a patriot. Could this physically damaged and probably mentally disturbed man be reconciled to life in the United States, his career gone forever, and with it his sense of self? Would the memory of our brief time together, passionate though it had been, be enough to help us recapture the magic of our love?

At last, I raised my head and looked directly into the future. I vowed I would do whatever it took to help Niko achieve contentment, peace of mind, and the strength to be the father our son needed.

CHAPTER 24

Afternoon, the Same Day

VLADI STAYED for lunch. In the kitchen, I piled sandwiches, fruit, and bottles of sparkling water on a tray, and brought it back to the patio. While we ate, he warned me never to speak of Niko, or of anything to do with his planned rescue, while inside the house. He thought it was probable the CIA, and possibly, some Russian and other US government agencies, had planted bugs. The thought of all those ears listening to us talking about the events of our everyday lives probably should have shocked me, but somehow it did not. I agreed to be very careful.

Vladi asked me about Nicholas and Ellen. I told him about Nicholas's accomplishments, and my pride in him. "Vladi, Nicholas is so much like Niko, in looks, intelligence, and temperament. I can't wait for them to meet each other. I hope it won't be too long until Niko is ready."

He nodded. "I hope so too."

"Ellen has her own place now, shared with a fellow architect, near our offices. He says he loves her, and I think she loves him too. Young as Ellen is, she's closely following in her father's footsteps, and is beginning to make a name for herself in international architecture. I have no doubt the firm will continue to be successful with her in charge. But, Vladi, I've often wondered whether she's been approached to serve her country like Dale did. Because I haven't told her about her father's CIA involvement, it's a question I will never—can't ever—ask."

"I understand."

As Vladi talked candidly about Niko, it was obvious how much he admired Niko. Finally, he spoke of the night he met my husband. "I was very impressed with Dale's coolness under extreme danger. I believe it was inevitable two such talented men as Dale and Niko would become friends."

I nodded. Dale's prominence in his field had given him the perfect cover for CIA activities, and his long trips to oversee architectural projects gave him sufficient opportunity. He had been extremely intelligent and physically strong. He would have been fearless and cool headed in almost any situation.

Since Vladi had mentioned Dale, I remembered my two unanswered questions. I had tried to forget them, since I never expected to learn the answers. Now was my chance.

"Vladi, when Dale was brought to the hospital after the second accident, he was still alive. The surgeon told my doctor that Dale was semiconscious and mumbling. He said Dale kept asking for 'Vladimir.' Could he have been asking for you?"

He reacted with shock. "Ah. Perhaps so. We— Niko's team, Dale, and a few other CIA agents— had performed a joint operation just weeks before Dale died. It had been mostly successful, but there were a few details yet to be completed. It is possible Dale had just uncovered some information he wanted to pass on to us. I was in charge of communications for our team."

He sat in silence for a moment, deep in thought. He finally looked up at me, an unhappy expression on his face. "You must have been wondering all this time to whom he was referring. It should have been your name on his lips, not mine. I am very sorry."

"At least, now I know. But, I have another question. Niko's superiors, he wrote, sent him to find out whether Dale's death was accidental or not. Why?"

"I cannot tell you about the operation, but it was sensitive, and the timing of Dale's death was odd. We thought there might have been a connection. Now that I know he spoke my name before he died, I am sure of it."

Vladi looked miserable. "Niko was distraught over Dale's passing, and he was unhappily aware he could do nothing to console you. He wanted badly to speak to you at Dale's funeral, but he knew he could not. So, he stayed in the background and tried to find conclusive evidence whether either or both accidents were the result of foul play. He was frustrated that so many days had passed. If there ever had been any real evidence, it had already been destroyed."

I nodded. I had the answers to my questions, but I was unsure whether I was better off now than before.

After a long silence, Vladi made an effort to lighten the atmosphere.

"I have begun spending time with Niko's sister, Raisa, and her daughter, Eva. Whenever I am in St. Petersburg, I bring them gifts of food, toys for Eva, or music CDs. I know Niko is worried about them. I am hoping to reassure him. I will continue to watch over them."

"Oh, Vladi. That's wonderful. Do you enjoy their company?"

"They have been very lonely and worried about him, though I cannot tell them anything until he is safely away from Russia. Even then, I will have to swear them to silence." He shrugged. "Of course, that conversation will depend on our success."

"Are you afraid they might tell someone they shouldn't about him?"

He nodded. "Yes. Not on purpose, of course, but it is difficult to keep a happy secret. I will have to be very careful what I say, but it would be cruel not to let them know he is safe."

As he spoke warmly of their growing friendship, I understood more completely what a kind and generous man Vladi was. He would be a formidable enemy, but he was much more than just someone's idea of a hero. If a romance developed between Vladi and Raisa, I thought she would be a very lucky woman.

When we finished our lunch, Vladi rose and helped me put our leftovers back on the tray.

"Vladi, thank you for coming today. I'm so excited. But, please, take care."

Tears were threatening again, as I took his hands in mine. He leaned down and kissed me on both cheeks.

"Don't worry, Mrs. Grant. I will be careful. I am very sorry I cannot stay to meet Nicholas, but I hope to have an opportunity to do so one day."

He touched his forehead in a mock salute and melted into the shrubbery. I wondered if I would ever see him again.

My eyes filled with tears, but this time, they were tears of joy and hope. I knew Niko was alive now, and I could begin to breathe freely again. A part of me had been clenched in fear while his fate was unknown. I was filled with hatred for the evil Grigor, appalled at the way Niko had been betrayed, imprisoned, beaten, tortured, starved, and left alone in the dark. I agreed with Vladi. Niko had been a very strong man, but I had no idea how anyone could withstand all he had endured without his body and his spirit shattering. I ached to hold him in my arms. and to begin trying to help him heal.

I was ready to give up everything I had for Niko. Some might find that surprising, but it would not be the first time. I had already turned my back on my privileged former life when I married Dale against my parents' wishes. I had never been sorry. Our lives together had been rich, first in love and later in material wealth— and we had Ellen.

Now I had Nicholas, but the future was unclear. It was far from certain Vladi would succeed in freeing Niko. And, if he was successful, could Niko be healed in body and mind? Would he and I be allowed to make a life together with Nicholas?

I paced as second thoughts flew through my head. What was I letting myself in for? And how about Nicholas? How could I expose him to a man who might be unable to bear the responsibilities of fatherhood?

Finally, I stopped and stood looking out over the pond. Gradually, I was flooded with a sense of calm and the rightness of what I proposed to do. I believed I knew Niko's heart, and I was certain Nicholas and I would be safe within his love.

At last, I realized Nicholas would soon be home from camp. Back inside, I put away the remnants of our lunch, washed my face, and tried to repair my looks. The last thing I wanted now was to frighten Nicholas. He would notice I had been crying and would want to know why.

A few minutes after three o'clock, I heard the bus stop in the street at the foot of our driveway. Nicholas. I ran outside and waited on the front stoop to greet him. Now he was big enough to ride on a "school" bus, I was no longer allowed to hug him in public. I would have to wait until we were inside.

CHAPTER 25

September 18, 2009

THE SECURE phone Vladi sent me rang this afternoon. I ran outside to take the call, quickly calculating the time difference.

"Vladi, what's happened? Are you all right? Do you have some news for me?"

"I have had a long and busy day, but the news is good. We have been successful! Niko is free at last. He is now on his way to a safe house in Cornwall, England. A team of top doctors are waiting there to evaluate his physical and mental injuries and prescribe treatments. Soon, he will begin the healing process."

He sounded tired, but triumphant. "Oh, Vladi. I can't even begin to thank you. But, I want to hear everything that happened. Please tell me."

"Some of it will be hard to hear."

"Yes, Vladi, I know. I'm prepared for that. Please tell me exactly as it happened."

"I had the help of many people. Niko's great uncle, who is now retired but was once a very powerful KGB General, arranged the cooperation of agents from the CIA and Britain's MI-6 by calling in old favors. Thanks to him, I had a CIA agent who had been a friend of Dale's, as well as a member of Niko's old team with me. We overpowered the guards and found Niko in a locked room in the basement.

"The room was dark, and unbelievably dirty. Unfortunately, before we could take him out of that terrible place, Grigor Smetlov and two of his associates arrived. They knew something was wrong when they saw there were no guards outside. They burst through the door shouting curses and waving their guns. We were waiting for them, and after we had them cornered, one of his men ran away in fright. There was a short gun battle, and the other man was killed. I killed Grigor myself."

"Vladi! How? Were you or your friends hurt? Tell me everything."

"We were lucky. Smetlov took a bullet in his shoulder, and when I shouted at him to surrender, he threw down his handgun. He appeared to realize he was trapped with no help in sight, but I was skeptical. I was sure he had no intention of surrendering. He had to know what we would do to him once we had him in our hands."

"But, he did surrender, right?"

"No. It was not that easy. When I ordered him to lie face down on the floor with his hands on his head, he crouched as though he would obey. But suddenly, with his good hand he pulled a small gun from his boot. He stood, stumbled slightly, fired, and I felt a burning sensation in my left arm."

"Oh no, Vladi! Are you badly hurt?"

"It is nothing—only a small flesh wound. But, I had no choice then. I put a bullet into his heart."

I imagined blood everywhere. I wanted to believe him, but I wished I could see for myself exactly how badly he was hurt. "I never thought I would ever say this about another human being, but I'm so glad that man is dead. Vladi, thank you. He was evil."

"Yes."

I shuddered. There was a pause while we tried to stop thinking about the terrible things people can do to each other. I took a deep breath. "What happened next?"

"The CIA agent had chartered a fast boat. We drove Niko immediately to the docks where the boat was waiting to ferry us across the Gulf of Finland to a spot on the Finnish coast. A British MI-6 agent met us there with a plane to fly Niko to Cornwall. In spite of the gun battle, the operation went very smoothly. It is extremely rare for our three clandestine agencies to cooperate so successfully. It may never happen again!"

"Vladi, what about Niko? Tell me how he looked. Was he aware of what was happening to him? How badly had he been hurt?"

Despite a fragile long distance phone connection, often interrupted with static, I sensed Vladi's strong reluctance to describe Niko's injuries and state of mind. But, I realized, Vladi's silence was mostly due to his efforts to contain his emotions. I understood how difficult it must have been for him to see how badly Niko had suffered.

Vladi cleared his throat and began again. "Niko was barely conscious when we found him. At first, he seemed not to believe I was actually there, as if my appearing to be there was just another form of torture. When he finally realized it was really me, he wept."

Vladi's voice broke. I gave him time to recover, especially as I was struggling to hold back my own tears. Finally, Vladi spoke again.

"Niko's body is crisscrossed with scars, some were made by canes and whips, others are cigarette burns. His face is also scarred, but his facial bones, including his nose, surprisingly, seem intact. He was filthy, of course. We had to shave his beard and hair, but I was shocked to see they are both more silver now than black. He is very thin and has almost no muscle tone. We knew his leg was bad. It is *very* bad. In fact, he cannot walk. He also has lost several teeth, and one eyelid droops. That eye may be completely blind. I do not know how much he sees with the other."

His voice broke again. I had been sobbing during his description of Niko's injuries. I was trying to do it silently, but Vladi must have heard me. It was a long moment before he was able to speak again.

"Niko's mental state is questionable. He spoke little, though he seemed to follow our conversation when we spoke directly to him. He is very weak, even after we fed him some soup and bread. He seems to have lost some of his English, but it soon will come back, I believe, in England. You should be prepared for anger, frustration, and bitterness. He has lost so much." His voice trailed away again.

"Vladi, I know you didn't want to tell me all of this, but I'm so grateful you have. I realize there is probably a lot you haven't told me, but now I have a better idea of how he actually is and my imagination won't paint an even darker picture. Of course, there are no words to express my gratitude for all you've risked to help Niko. I know you love him like a brother, and I understand the sacrifice you have made. Will you ever be able to see him again?"

"I'm no hero! But, I do love him. Yes, even more than I love my own older brother. Perhaps one day, far in the future, Niko and I will be able to embrace again, and talk over old times. I will hope for that day to happen."

He paused again. I waited. I wished I knew of some way to console him.

At last, he was able to continue. "It is late, and I have returned to St. Petersburg. By now, Niko will be in Cornwall being examined by the doctors. I will know more in a few days. As soon as I can, I will call you again."

He broke the connection and I slowly walked back inside. Vladi *was* a hero, whether he was willing to acknowledge it, or not.

After our conversation, I felt almost as drained as I knew Vladi must feel. My emotions were bouncing back and forth between exultation that Niko was free, anger and revulsion at Grigor Smetlov and his sick actions, fear for Niko and the painful treatments he would have to undergo, and sadness for Vladi's selfless sacrifice, not to mention his wound. That would heal in time. He might never recover from the loss of Niko, his idol, mentor, and brother in arms.

I was having trouble calming down, though I would have to find a way soon. Nicholas was due home from pre-school in less than an hour. I walked down to our little patio near the pond. Maybe the peaceful setting would help me to relax.

I had so many unanswered questions. I wished I knew more about the safe house in Cornwall. What was it like? Would he feel welcomed there? And most importantly, would the doctors be able to heal all his wounds?

How long would it take for his mental state to be evaluated? I was more worried about that than about his physical problems. Those could probably be fixed, I fervently hoped, though recovery would be painful and might take longer than I hoped it would.

But how could he put his fear, anger, frustration, and depression behind him and begin a new life? Even with the help of a skilled psychiatrist, he might need a very long time, though Vladi had assured me Niko's Dr. Kennedy was both highly qualified and experienced in cases such as Niko's.

In my own fear and frustration, I longed to be with him to help him recover. How long would I have to wait to be with him again?

CHAPTER 26

September to Late December 2009

VLADI KEPT in constant contact with Niko's doctors, and called me often to give me progress reports. His first call came six days after Niko arrived at the Cornish safe house:

"Mrs. Grant, a team of respected doctors in various fields have finished evaluating Niko's physical injuries. He needs three separate surgeries, first for his leg, and later for his left eye, and his teeth. They believe most of his vision can be restored. A dental surgeon will repair his teeth and replace missing ones. Luckily, Niko has no internal injuries that require surgery."

"Oh, Vladi… When are they going to start? He's still very weak, right?"

"Yes, but he is being fed a 'super' diet high in protein and other nutrients. So, though he is still weak, he is somewhat stronger than when we found him. The team of doctors who evaluated Niko have gone back to their practices, and a highly regarded English orthopedic surgeon came two days ago to review Niko's case and prepare to operate. The proceedure was done yesterday. I do not fully understand all the details, but I believe it involved inserting assorted metal rods and pins to hold the bones together. The good news is, Niko came through the surgery better than any of the doctors thought he would, and he will start therapy almost immediately. He may need another operation at a later date, but perhaps not."

"I'm so glad it went well, but he must be in so much pain."

"Yes, no doubt, once the anesthesia wore off. Pain medication never seems to help as much as one hopes. However, his psychiatrist, Dr. Kennedy, will begin working with him early next week. At first, she will use an interpreter, but she thinks his English will soon return to fluency."

The second call came a week later:

"A few days after Niko's leg was repaired, a dental surgeon came. He has begun work to install two bridges, and after that, he will prepare Niko's gums for three new teeth to be implanted. Dr. Kennedy said Niko was amazed by all that. He had not known such things could be done."

"Really? He didn't know?"

"Yes, until now, his teeth have been perfect. No cavities or other problems. He has been lucky."

"Wow! There is one possible good thing, Vladi. Maybe work on his teeth will distract him from from the pain in his leg. You think?"

"No. It is most likely, he is suffering from both. However bad, though, the pain is only temporary, though the leg will take much longer to heal."

Several weeks later:

"I have good news! Niko's leg has responded well to rehabilitation, though it is painful. The orthopedic surgeon and physical therapist are both quite pleased with his progress. They have told him he might always walk with a slight limp, but he will be walking."

"That's wonderful!"

"Yes! Dr. Kennedy told me that bit of news was worth all the pain he has suffered so far. During their sessions, she said, Niko repeatedly told her about his dread of being left unable to walk again—if, by some miracle, he was extracted from his prison. And, in fact, by the time we succeeded in freeing him, he had lost all hope he would have any future at all."

"Oh, Vladi." I was having trouble keeping my tears in check.

"Well, I do have some other good news. Last week, Niko's left eye was partially corrected with a cornea transplant, and the drooping muscle in his eyelid was surgically repaired. In just one week, enough sight in his left eye has returned for most tasks, and the sight in his right eye has improved dramatically with no special treatment."

"Really? Because of his super diet?"

"It probably helped. It is also helping him regain the weight he lost. But, now he will be able to see well enough to do many things, such as driving a car, though he needs to wear glasses for reading and other close work. He may need cataract surgery in the future, but not yet."

"Thanks, Vladi. I'm so relieved."

"According to Dr. Kennedy, Niko is as well. He had been almost as worried about his eyesight as he was about his leg."

One week later:

"Mrs. Grant, not all of my news today is good. Niko's hair has grown back since we shaved it off on the day of his extraction, and he has decided to keep a short beard and mustache. But, he is having trouble accepting the change in the color of his hair. It was once so dark, and now it is more white than black."

"I guess that's not so suprising, under the circumstances. But, it must have been a big shock to him."

"Yes, shock is the right word. Dr. Kennedy said they had kept him away from mirrors for the first few weeks while he began to heal. But, finally, he asked to see his reflection. His reaction was bad. He was almost unable to recognize the man who stared back at him. It was not simply the scars—he knew there would be scars. He ran his hand over his hair and face, and wept."

"Oh, Vladi, no!"

Vladi sighed. "When you left Russia, Mrs. Grant, Niko was forty-one, not young, but still youthful. He is now forty-six, but he believes he looks as though he has aged at least twenty years."

One week later:

"Dr. Kennedy tells me Niko has regained almost all of the weight he had lost and has grown much stronger. Of course, the muscle tone and flexibility he once depended on has not yet completely returned. That worries him, though his physical therapist tells him he will regain all of his strength in time. Niko is still finding that difficult to believe."

"Vladi, how about his English?"

"His fluency has returned, since he must speak English all the time now. In fact, a speech therapist is working with him daily, both to make his English more idiomatic, and to remove his Russian accent. They believe whatever happens after he leaves Cornwall, it will be better if he is not immediately recognized as a Russian."

Vladi paused for a moment. I could hear kitchen sounds in the background. He was probably heating something to eat. He had told me his housekeeper kept his freezer stocked with microwaveable meals. Soon, he was back.

"Physically, Niko is greatly improved. What concerns me more now is his mental state. Dr. Kennedy tells me he has suffered terrible nightmares almost every night since he arrived. And, he is very angry. At first, he behaved quite unpleasantly. He is sorry for that now, but every day he shouts furiously against fate and his enemies, particularly Grigor Smetlov and the men who were ordered to torture him. Dr. Kennedy says such anger now is only to be expected, but he is ashamed of himself, and cannot understand why he cannot overcome it. To recover fully, the doctor says, he must learn to refocus his anger, and eventually to move beyond it. He does not know if he can."

"Vladi, what do you think? Can he?"

"I hope so. And yes, the man I knew would eventually be able to. But, he has much work to do with Dr. Kennedy. He is deeply grateful to all who played a part in his extraction and rehabilitation. But, he is desperately homesick. He is lost without his comrades, his sister and niece, and he mourns the loss of his career. His identity has been taken from him, along with the last of his youth.

"He does have one thing he can look forward to. His long-time friend, Leo Sokolov, visited him briefly at the very beginning of his stay in Cornwall, and promised he would come again before Niko leaves the safe house. But, leaving is a huge question mark for him. He does not know where he can go. He knows, of course, he cannot return to Russia, but the future he faces is unknown."

"How I wish I could be with him. I guess I would just be in the way, now though. He hasn't asked about me, has he?"

"No, not yet."

One week later:

"Niko has discovered the library in the safe house, which is filled with books of all kinds. He has found several of his favorite novels and poetry collections from his days as professor of English literature at the university in St. Petersburg. When he is not in therapy or outside limping along the path on the bluff above Whitsand Bay, he sits in the library and reads. Dr. Kennedy believes it is good for him to read the classics. In them, he will be reminded of some important truths. First, he is not the only man whose daily routine has been unexpectedly destroyed. Second, he is certainly not the only man to have suffered a defeat at the hands of his enemies. She believes Niko will find hope as well as despair within those pages. Even laughter."

I remembered how much I had loved the musical sound of Niko's laughter. It was infectious. I yearned to laugh with him again one day.

With every phone call, I was more grateful to Vladi for keeping me so well informed. My heart ached for Niko, but also for me. I went to work as usual, and was even able to concentrate once I was there. I increased my visits to the gym, emailed friends, met Barbara occasionally for lunch in New York City, saw Ellen and Suzi on most weekends, and planned special outings with Nicholas. But, with Ellen living with her boyfriend in their own apartment, Nicholas and I were alone in our big house. He was a beloved distraction when we were together. But, after he was in bed for the night, I was alone with my fears for Niko. I prayed constantly for him to be able to respond completely and successfully to the care he was receiving.

My emotional state was chaotic. I was extremely impatient to see Niko, but I knew I might have to wait a very long time. I tried to keep in mind the progress he was making. It was agonizingly slow, but he *was* improving.

More time passed, but Niko still had not mentioned me to anyone. I tried not to panic over that. Though I could think of none, there might be good reasons for his silence. I wondered constantly if he had forgotten me. Had his long ordeal wiped the love we had shared from his memory? How I could bear it if, when reminded of my existence, he refused to see me.

He had not forgotten his sister, Raisa, and his niece, Eva. Niko never deliberately would have left them defenseless and alone. Instead, he would have tried to bring them with him, if he had ever intended to leave Russia for good. Under the present circumstances, he could not even contact them, let alone provide for them, and it was preying on his mind. As soon as Vladi learned that from Dr. Kennedy, he told Niko about his visits to Raisa and Eva's apartment, and how much he enjoyed being with them, bringing them treats, and helping them when they needed it. I hoped Vladi's care of them would help to ease Niko's mind.

I was delighted to hear that Niko was reading again. If he could find stories that made him laugh, I would be much more hopeful of his eventual recovery.

CHAPTER 27

Early January 2010

FINALLY, VLADI called me with the news I had longed to hear.

"Mrs. Grant, Niko's doctors agree. They want you to come to England now to see him."

"Vladi! That's wonderful. Has he asked about me? Did he ask for me to come?"

"No, I'm sorry. He has not yet spoken of you."

"Oh!"

"But, Dr. Kennedy believes it might be because he is afraid. He may think, after so long a time, you will have forgotten him. He has, of course, no way of knowing you are anxious to see him. In fact, she and the other doctors have agreed it would be best to keep your visit a secret. They think it might put too much pressure on him if they told him in advance of your visit."

"But Vladi, is that wise?"

"They think so, yes. They believe it is important for him to see you now, and to be reminded he has not lost everything."

I decided to leave Nicholas at home with Ellen, at first. I wanted to be alone with Niko for a bit, to see if the magical love we once shared was still alive. If my visit went well, Ellen could bring Nicholas later for a short visit.

I booked a flight leaving for England the next evening. I also arranged for a car to meet me the next morning at London's Heathrow airport. According to the car service, the driver should deliver me to the Cornish safe house in mid-to-late afternoon.

I had waited so long for this, yet naturally, I was nervous. There was no guarantee Niko would welcome my visit.

⚬⚬⚬

Two Days Later, in England

My flight was uneventful, despite the weather. England was experiencing the coldest and snowiest winter in many years. Luckily, though it had snowed heavily the day before I landed, and more was expected, the airport was open. It was crowded with passengers whose flights had been canceled because of the previous snowfall, but I was able to clear Customs and find my driver easily. I checked briefly into a London hotel to bathe, change clothes, and eat a light breakfast before going on to Cornwall.

I was too nervous at first to pay much attention to our route. I did notice traffic was lighter than I expected as we exited the city limits, but that may have been because of the predicted storm. I was busy imagining how well, or not, my surprise visit with Niko might go.

Finally, when we left the main highways and drove along secondary roads, I began to pay closer attention to the snow-covered scenery. It had begun to snow again, light, fluffy, flakes that gave my driver little trouble on the the winding, hilly road.

It was a relief to concentrate, for a few minutes at least, on something other than Niko's reaction to my sudden appearance. I found myself fascinated by the stark beauty of the English countryside. I tried to imagine how the neat fields and hedgerows we were passing would look painted in springtime green. I wondered if I would still be here to see an English spring.

By the time we reached Devon, the snow had begun to taper off. Further on, in Cornwall, it stopped. Only an inch or two had fallen. I looked around with interest as we drove through picturesque towns and villages with narrow winding streets. In some of the villages, quaint shops and houses opened directly onto the road. Even on this bleak winter day, the scenery was charming.

Finally we turned into a lane that led— eventually—to an imposing electronic gate. My nervousness returned as I watched the driver punch a code into a keypad. A moment later, the gate swung slowly open. We continued down a long drive and, in the fading light of late afternoon, at last I could see the safe house, perched close to the top of a bluff that overlooked Whitsand Bay. It was a large, grey stone mansion in a neo-classical style, with a pale slate roof and several ornate chimneys puffing smoke toward the darkening sky. The house was grand, but to my eyes at least, it appeared welcoming. I relaxed slightly. I had been afraid it would seem cold and forbidding.

At the front of the house was a circular gravel drive. We stopped under the portico and my driver helped me out of the car. A white-coated doctor stood waiting in the open doorway. She was younger than I expected, and pretty.

"Mrs. Grant? I'm Dr. Janet Kennedy, Niko's psychiatrist."

"Yes. Hello, Dr. Kennedy. Where is Niko?" We shook hands, but I was too impatient for anything but the briefest of greetings.

"Come with me, please. We have been looking forward to your visit." Her smile was warm.

"We?"

"Yes, Dr. George Watkins, who has overseen all of Niko's treatments, and Martin Stanley, his physical therapist. You will meet them later, at dinner."

She led me inside and directly up a grand staircase to the room I would be occupying during my stay.

"Niko is walking on the bluff path. You can join him now, or if you wish to rest a bit, you could wait until he returns. In this weather, he won't be out much longer."

"I'll join him now. I've waited a long time for this."

"I understand. Your luggage will be here when you return."

I dropped my pocketbook on the bed and looked around. The room was spacious and comfortable, with wide windows overlooking the bay. There was a writing desk and padded chair under the windows next to the door. On one side wall there was an enormous armoire, while on the opposite wall, an easy chair and a floor lamp were positioned next to the double bed, which faced the door. The bed was covered with what looked like a hand-sewed blue and white quilt.

Dr. Kennedy said, "Come. I'll show you to the path. You will find Niko somewhere nearby."

She led me back downstairs and along a broad, red-carpeted hallway to a side door. I thanked her and stepped outside into a large, formal walled garden. It was barren now, but I imagined it would be lovely in the spring. A gate at one end of the garden opened onto a path leading away from the house and slightly uphill toward the bluff.

Once through the gate, I ran as quickly as I could. The path along the bluff was not very steep, but it was wet and slightly slippery with patches of melting snow.

As I rounded the last bend, I saw him, silhouetted against the grey sky. He was standing with his back to me, looking down at the crashing waves far below.

I stopped a few feet behind him. Despite the cold wind, I untied the scarf I wore over my head so he could see and touch my hair. "Niko." I called his name softly, fighting to catch my breath.

He raised his head and awkwardly turned toward me, leaning on his cane.

"Niko." Tears filled my eyes. I wiped them away impatiently. Vladi had prepared me for his scars and graying hair, and had warned me Niko might not react as I hoped he would. But, I had envisioned impassioned meetings in a hundred different settings. In all of them, he had opened his arms and welcomed me home to his heart.

I waited, hardly daring to breathe.

"Sharon?" He limped closer. "Is it really you?"

At arms-length, he reached out and touched my hair.

"Sharon!" His lined, still-thin face registered wonder.

Then, just as I had imagined, he opened his arms, and I went home. I could hear the thud of his heart as he held me close and then, his lips found mine.

CHAPTER 28

Next Day

NIKO WAS still sleeping when I awoke this morning. I lay on my side, facing him, watching him breathe. It was amazing. After all this time, I had finally slept for an entire night with the man I loved. Such a simple thing, yet we had never before had the chance to wake up beside each other.

Yesterday, when I found him on the cliff path, I thought nothing could ever make me happier than I was at the moment he opened his arms to me. We finally turned to walk back to the house with his free arm holding me tightly to his side, and both of mine hugging his waist. We could not bear to release each other.

Dr. Kennedy was waiting for us when we reached the house. It was long past lunchtime, but she had ordered pots of tea and coffee, sandwiches, fruit, and cookies. She led us to the library, where the food was waiting.

"I'll leave you now," she said. "I know you have much to say to each other. Dinner will be served buffet style at seven o'clock. Niko will show you to the dining room."

We had not stopped for lunch on the drive to Cornwall and the light breakfast I had eaten in the hotel in London had long since worn off. The coffee smelled wonderful, but the last thing I wanted right now was food. I wanted only Niko.

As soon as the doctor disappeared around the door, we threw off our heavy outerwear and Niko led me toward the big hearth where a fire burned brightly. Seating himself on the sofa facing the fire, he leaned his cane against the upholstered arm and drew me down next to him. Turning toward me, he traced my face with his long, sensitive fingers, relearning my features. He tilted his head so he could peer closely into my eyes. He must have read the love shining there, because with a groan, his gaze dropped to my lips for an instant before he recaptured them with his own.

After a long moment, he suddenly pulled back. He straightened, and turned away from me. Picking up his cane again, he sat twirling it between his hands.

I was bewildered. Why had he pulled away so abruptly?

"Do you want to eat? How about some coffee?" He indicated the tea tray.

Taking my cue from him, I said, "Yes, some coffee would be nice."

He leaned his cane back against the arm of the couch and picked up the coffee pot. His hand was trembling slightly. I reached for a cup and saucer and moved to help him pour. He held up his other hand to stop me, and concentrating intently, he slowly filled my cup and, then, his own.

I handed him the cream. He passed me the sugar.

What was going through his mind, I wondered? His face was carefully blank.

We each took a small sandwich and a cookie. I was silent, waiting for him.

We ate.

When his coffee cup was empty, he finally turned back to me.

"Tell me of your journey."

I took a deep breath. I was enormously disappointed. I had envisioned us making passionate love by now. I was beginning to realize how utterly changed the Niko I had met today— with so much love in my heart and the need for his touch drumming in my blood—was from the Niko I had once known.

This man had withstood a year of fighting in Chechnya, ending with his capture and torture by Chechen rebels; difficult rehabilitation and physical therapy in Moscow; sudden imprisonment with fifteen months of terrible torture and near starvation in St. Petersburg at the hands of a bitter enemy; and finally, in England, many weeks of painful recovery from major and minor surgeries, as well as from his other physical and mental challenges.

I was ashamed of myself. My expectations were far too high. I would have to wait for him. But, I was used to waiting. I had done it for years. A little more time would be difficult but, surely, not impossible.

Giving myself a mental shake, I told him about my uneventful flight, the crowded airport, the hotel in London, and my impressions of the countryside on the drive to Cornwall. He nodded whenever I paused, seemingly genuinely interested. I wondered again what was really going on in his mind.

I looked around the room. "Niko, I've seen only a little bit of the house so far, but it seems very comfortable, and this room is lovely. Can you tell me more about who it belonged to and how it became an MI-6 safe house?"

"Dr. Kennedy has done extensive research on the history of the house and its contents. She will be able to tell you more at dinner, and answer your questions." He smiled. "My favorite room is this one. I've spent many hours in here, thinking about how certain characters have handled their problems—or not—in the books I've been reading, mostly classical literature, but also some more modern fiction."

I glanced around at the tall book cases that ringed the room. "It's certainly well-stocked. I'm glad you've been able to spend some quality time in here."

"Yes, but the house is quite large, and there are other rooms to see. I'll take you on a guided tour tomorrow."

Our conversation turned to other topics. He told me about his treatments since he had arrived in Cornwall and outlined his daily routine. From there we moved on to recent news stories and finally to the specific books he had been reading."

I was amazed to hear almost no traces of his Russian accent. Gradually, my uneasy feelings gave way to excitement as I began to catch fleeting glimpses of the old Niko. At one point, he took my hand in his, and again I felt the electricity between us flare. It was still there, even after all this time.

Anticipating a kiss at the very least, I turned to him, but he dropped my hand and looked away, gesturing toward a painting on the wall. Disappointment almost overwhelmed me. We had not been talking about art.

I sighed. "Perhaps you can show me to my room now. I'd like to freshen up before dinner."

Niko picked up his cane and rose stiffly.

"Come with me," he said.

He led me down the hall to a small elevator, our fingers entwined. As the car slowly rose, he kissed the hand he held.

When the elevator arrived at the second floor and we stepped out into the hallway, Niko pointed toward a door a little way down the hall.

"That's my room. Now I'll show you to yours, okay?"

"Okay."

I shook my head in wonder. Niko's American-English lessons were making a huge difference. The old Niko never would have used the word "okay." Not in any context.

He limped down the hall past several doors until he came to mine. He had kept my hand in his. Now, he kissed it again, dropped it, and turned away.

"Won't you come in?"

"Thank you, no. Not now. I'll come for you in twenty minutes to take you to dinner."

I glanced at my wristwatch. It was twenty-five minutes to seven. Surely there was time enough to kiss me and hold me tight. Just for a few minutes.

But, Niko was limping back toward his room.

It was exactly seven o'clock when we entered the dining room. Dr. Kennedy greeted us, and introduced me to the others at the table: Niko's physical therapist, the medical doctor who was overseeing all his various treatments, and two MI-6 agents staying at the house for a few days.

Vladi had explained how the costs of Niko's extraction, medical and psychiatric treatments, and physical rehabilitation were being shared between the British and American governments. I knew they must be quite high. Niko was privileged to be here, though I realized both governments were expecting him to provide important information when he formally defected.

We helped ourselves to the buffet and tried to find topics of general interest to discuss. I felt a little self-conscious. I knew the others were assessing me and wondering whether my visit would have a positive effect on Niko.

"I understand this is an MI-6 safe house now, Dr. Kennedy, but who owned the mansion before?"

"Yes, MI-6 personnel staff the house now, but it was once a country estate belonging to a member of the English House of Lords. The mansion was built in the late 1600s, but I can only tell you a little about the family. The first Earl of

Whitsand was a close associate of Prince Charles, the eldest son of King Charles I. The king was deposed by Oliver Cromwell during the English Civil War, and ultimately beheaded. When, after years of exile in Europe, the Prince was restored to the English throne in 1660 and became King Charles II, he rewarded his supporters with lands and titles. Unfortunately, by 1978, when the last Earl came into his inheritance, the family was bankrupt and the mansion had fallen into disrepair. He had no heirs, and when he died, only a few years after he inherited, the government took it over. It was later refurbished for use, as needed, by MI-6." She smiled. "Niko may be able to give you more details."

"Thanks, Dr. Kennedy." I smiled, and glanced at Niko. "He's promised to give me a guided tour of the mansion tomorrow."

When we finally finished our dinner, Dr. Kennedy invited us to join them in the library for coffee and dessert. I looked at Niko, hoping he would refuse and go upstairs with me.

Again, I was disappointed. He took my arm and escorted me to the library. We sat before the fire, drank coffee, and made stilted conversation with the others until I thought I would scream.

Finally, pleading fatigue, I asked to be excused.

Niko gallantly rose, and led me again to the elevator. When we stepped out into the upstairs hallway, I stopped and faced him.

"Will you come to my room tonight? I've missed you so much." I was trying to hold back tears, though they threatened to come no matter what he did next.

Niko's face turned white. He was afraid, I suddenly realized. Of me? Of what might happen—or not—between us?

I reached up and touched his cheek. With my other hand, I ran my fingers up through the silky hair at the back of his head, and pulled his face down to mine.

I kissed him with tenderness and passion. To my profound relief, he responded. Against his lips, I whispered, "I love you, Niko. Ever since we first made love, I have been longing for us to share the same bed, sleeping side by side, for an entire night. Please. Couldn't we start tonight?"

Niko had tears in his eyes. He nodded. "I will come to you. Give me five minutes."

He limped back down the hall to his room.

My heart pounding, I watched him go. Inside my room, I turned down the bed covers, and changed into a lacy nightgown. Then, I lay down to wait.

Five minutes passed, and then ten. At last, there was a faint knock at my door.

"Come in."

Niko opened the door, stepped inside, and stopped. He seemed unable to move forward. He was holding a robe and slippers and a few toiletries, and was still dressed as he had been at dinner.

I slipped out of bed, and took his belongings from him, laying them on the desk under the window. When I turned back to him, he was staring at the floor. He looked frightened and miserable.

My heart aching, I stood in front of him.

"Niko. I love you with all my heart. Please, don't worry. I'll be so happy just to have you lie next to me. We'll go slowly, just as slowly as you need to go."

I took his hand, and gently tugged him toward the bed.

He took two steps and stopped again. "Sharon, I do love you, you know I do, but I need to be able to love you completely. I don't know if I can. It's been so long. So much has happened to me. I thought… No… I'm afraid."

I opened my mouth to speak, but he raised his hand to stop me. "No, please. I must say this. Sharon, it may not be possible for me to feel desire. Without that, I will have lost my ability to make love to you as you deserve."

"I do understand why you're so nervous. But Niko, we're here, together, at last. I have waited so long to be with you, but I can wait as long as you need me to, if you are lying next to me."

His arms came around me in a long embrace. When he finally dropped his arms, I helped him take off his jacket and tie.

"Sharon, before I remove the rest of my clothing, I want you to know…" He hesitated, then said in a rush, "There are scars on my body. Please do not be frightened or..."

He looked down, unable to continue. He was afraid I would be disgusted.

"Hush." Reaching up, I laid my finger against his lips. Having a baby at the advanced age of forty-six had changed my body more than mere age could have done, but Nicholas was still a secret. I longed to tell Niko about his son, but now was not the time.

"My body has changed too. I'm five years older. It makes a difference."

"Not to me, Sharon. You are as beautiful as I remember."

"And you, Niko, are beautiful to me."

With a brave half-smile, he began to undo his shirt buttons. My hands trembled as I pulled out his shirttail and began to unbuckle his belt. Eventually, we both stood naked in the light. If he found my body less than perfect—and indeed it was, despite regular visits to the gym—he pretended it was exactly as before.

For me, hearing about his scars was vastly different than seeing them for myself. I burned with hatred for the evil Grigor. I gladly would have killed him myself, with my bare hands, if I had had the chance. I was grateful I had not. Vladi had taken care of Grigor for all of us.

I hid my dismay and anger. Niko was trusting in my love. There was no way I could let him down.

He limped toward the bed and waited. I hugged him tightly from behind, slipped around him and lay down. When he joined me, he lay rigid, as if afraid to move.

As promised, I lay quietly next to him, curled against his side, but not otherwise touching him. I waited as long moments passed. Finally, he shifted and tentatively touched my breasts. Desire building within me, I began to stroke his chest and abdomen. Gradually I reached lower until, at last, I found what I had longed to find.

It was awkward at first. His leg was still mending and we had to be careful. It would, I knew, be easier as he healed.

Afterward, as we lay panting, I heard Russian love words once again. He gathered me into his arms, and rocked me gently, just as he had on the *River Sprite*. I made a fervent vow: somehow we would build a future together, no matter how long it might take or what we might need to do to make it happen.

We fell asleep with Niko's arm across my body and his good leg over mine.

As I lay remembering, Niko sighed, stretched, and regarded me with his bird-wing eyebrows raised.

"So, my pretty, you are under my spell."

He grinned, chuckled wickedly, and twirled his mustache, playfully acting the part of the heartless pirate who had stolen my virtue during a night of passion.

I played along, sighing deeply and batting my eyelashes.

"Yes, master. You have captured my heart. I am yours to command. And, if I may say so, the rumors of your loss of strength have been greatly exaggerated."

With a growl of triumph, the golden flecks dancing in his eyes, he grabbed me and began raining kisses along my throat, dipping lower to caress a nipple. I arched my back and we were swept away.

Eventually, we had to stop. Niko was scheduled for a physical therapy session in an hour. He showered, dressed, and left for the dining room. He had just enough time for coffee and a light breakfast.

I watched him get ready, and when he left the room—after a long goodbye kiss—it was my turn in the shower. I dressed warmly. We had agreed to meet in the dining room after his physical therapy session to share a more filling breakfast. Then we were going to walk the bluff path until it was time for his late morning psychotherapy session with Dr. Kennedy.

I was under no illusion our lovemaking could "cure" him. But, guided by Dr. Kennedy, maybe I could help him put his past life into some sort of perspective. I was prepared to do everything I could to accelerate his recovery.

⚬⚬

I dressed quickly, and knocked on Dr. Kennedy's door.

"Come in. Oh, good morning, Mrs. Grant. How is Niko this morning? The housekeeper tells me you and he shared your room last night. He has made good progress in conquering, or at least, dealing with his depression and anger. His other pressing worry was whether or not he still had the physical ability to make love. That is why we asked you to come now, rather than waiting a few more weeks."

"It was difficult, of course, because we had to be careful with his leg, but we found ways to cope. He has no need to worry about his capabilities. He is *very* capable."

"That is good to hear!"

"I've come to see you now because I need your advice. I'm not sure when I should tell Niko about his son. I'd like to do it soon, but I'm afraid. What if he refuses to believe Nicholas is his?"

"Mrs. Grant, I would counsel caution. He is still fragile. I believe you should wait until he is stronger. Why don't we talk again in a few days? Do you agree?"

I nodded. "Yes. Thank you."

Selfishly, I was glad to postpone that conversation with Niko. I wanted more time alone with him, without distractions. Plus, I dreaded his reaction to the stunning news that he was the father of an active four-year-old.

Before I met Niko in the dinning room, I made two quick calls. The first was to Ellen, to let her know I had arrived safely and to tell her that things were going well with Niko. I was missing Ellen and Nicholas badly. It was the first time I had been away from Nicholas since he was born.

The second call was to Vladi. He was anxious to hear my impressions of Niko's health. I was able to reassure him.

"Vladi, Niko seems to be eating well, and his sleep—last night, at least—was free of nightmares. Physically, Niko and I are together at last."

"That is good! How are his spirits?"

"Very good now, after a slow start yesterday. I'll need to see how things go over the coming days."

"You haven't told him about Nicholas yet?"

"No, not yet. I'll need to pick the right time. Dr. Kennedy believes I should wait until he's stronger, but I know I can't put it off for very long. If all goes well, I'd like Ellen to bring Nicholas to England to meet Niko. Then we can begin to make decisions about our future."

CHAPTER 29

One week later

EXCEPT WHEN Niko was in physical therapy, having American lessons, or meeting with Dr. Kennedy, Niko and I spent all our time together eating, walking, talking, and making love as often as we could. It was a blissful time, better in many ways than our days—and nights—on the *River Sprite*.

Niko never failed to amaze me with his linguistic skill. His English was becoming much less formal, and though he was not yet using all the latest slang phrases, his vocabulary was growing.

At first, we kept our conversations light, with no mention of the future. We read to each other and reminisced about our voyage to St. Petersburg. He wanted to know every detail of my life since then. I told him about Dale's firm and my work there, as well as Ellen's dreams and accomplishments. In turn, I learned how his great uncle, the famous General Novikov, had guided his education, his training, and later, his career.

One question had puzzled me for a long time. "Niko, how could you work for the FSB and still be an English literature professor?"

"The university was a good cover for my FSB activities. In fact, the university president was one of my FSB superiors, so when I was ordered to travel outside St. Petersburg, I could leave the classroom to accomplish the missions assigned to me without having to worry whether I would be fired. Another professor would take my place for as long as necessary. Usually, it was only for a few days, or maybe a week or two."

Though he tried to keep his tone light, I began to catch signs of a lingering depression. He told me about the deep bonds he shared with the men who had been part of his team, especially Vladi and Ilya Popov, the man who had helped Vladi and the CIA agent extract him from his warehouse prison. He knew he would probably never see these men again.

Gradually, we raised more serious topics. One day, I described the television coverage of the Beslan disaster, and how I had prayed for the victims and their families. Niko nodded wryly and confessed the "family problem" he had left the ship to handle had not been personal at all.

"An Army helicopter lifted me to a MIG fighter plane waiting for me at a military airport about an hour away. The MIG flew me to an Army base near Beslan. My orders were to interrogate two Chechen men who might have given us information about the terrorists involved in the hostage situation. I had successfully questioned one of them—without resorting to violence—during an earlier posting to Chechnya, and my superiors believed he might be willing to talk to me again. But, by the time I arrived, both men had been tortured to death by cruelly inept Army interrogators."

"Tortured?"

"Yes, unfortunately. There was no reason to have done that, and nothing was gained. I was disgusted with the Army's incompetence. The whole operation at the school had been badly mismanaged and too many innocent victims had been killed or injured. I yelled at the officer in charge, sent a very critical report of his handling of the situation to both his and my own superiors, and demanded immediate transportation back to the *River Sprite*. Even so, I had to spend a miserable night there!"

"I was miserable, too, without you. But Niko, it's strange. I thought I heard a helicopter lifting off the morning you left. But, I had been asleep, and I just assumed I had dreamed it. I was so angry with you for leaving me with just a note, and then, when you came back, you refused to tell me why you had to leave."

He shook his head and kissed the hand he held, our fingers entwined. "I apologize for misleading you. I couldn't tell you where I'd been, and all I wanted was to forget it and return to your arms. I was ordered to go there. Otherwise, I never would have left you."

❧

I had believed Niko when he claimed Dale had been a CIA agent, but I was having a hard time imagining exactly what that meant.

"Niko, what did Dale do for the CIA while he was in Russia? Was he ever in danger while he was there?"

"I can't tell you about specific operations. I'm sure you can understand why. But, I can tell you how we met, and that might help you understand it better. It's a long story, but I'm happy to tell you. Does Ellen know her father was a CIA agent?"

"No. I want her to remember him the only way she knew him, as her beloved father, and a famous and talented architect."

"Ah. That's wise. He was all of that, but he was also very brave as well as an excellent agent. I met Dale for the first time in 1996, at the Grand Hotel Europa on Nevsky Prospekt in the heart of St. Petersburg. Besides coming to oversee the progress of a new office building he'd designed, he was in the hotel to attend a three-day conference on designing and building ecologically sustainable projects. There had been two other such meetings that year, but this was the only one in Eastern Europe. We wanted to show the world how forward-looking we could be." Niko smiled, and shrugged his shoulders at the irony.

"Yes," I said. "I remember Dale telling me about that conference. He was excited about it." We were sitting side-by-side on the couch in the library. Niko's arms were around me, my head on his shoulder as we gazed into the fire.

"He was very interested in the subject matter, and so was I. Since I was a child, I've been fascinated by the way buildings are designed and built. I studied the various styles and looked for examples in my city whenever I had the opportunity."

Now that I had Nicholas, I could imagine Niko as a child. I looked up at him. "Niko, did you want to be an architect when you grew up?"

He nodded his head. "Yes, but it was not to be. Anyway, though I was intrigued by the conference agenda, I was there to work. I needed to find out quickly what Dale was supposed to be doing for the CIA during his visit, because he would be leaving St. Petersburg as soon as the conference was over. I was posing as Mikhail Kuznetsky, a fictional architect from Vladivostok, which is a port city in southeastern Siberia on the Sea of Japan. The city is heavily industrialized and notoriously polluted, so it was a good cover."

He paused to kiss my cheek.

"I wasted no time introducing myself and talking with Dale between conference sessions, as if we were really colleagues meeting for the first time. We hit it off, as you Americans say, immediately. On the second day of the conference, he invited me to go with him to check on the progress of the office building he had designed for one of our new oil billionaires. It was located in a suburban office park. There had been the inevitable delays in the delivery of building supplies, and enormous bribes had to be paid, but the project was moving slowly forward. Overall, he was pleased with what he saw."

"Dale never told me about his overseas projects in detail. Now I wish he had."

"Well, this one was very interesting. Where possible, he had used recycled materials and low cost, high efficiency electric and water systems. These materials and systems were difficult to obtain in Russia, and I was impressed with what had been accomplished so far. In turn, I talked about the many innovations I was planning to bring to my work in Vladivostok. If only that were possible, I thought to myself. By the time we returned to the city, it was dusk. We agreed to meet for drinks in the hotel bar before going to dinner at a restaurant I had recommended, followed by a visit to a nightclub."

I pulled away and turned to face him. "A nightclub? You took him to a *nightclub*?"

"Shhh. It was nothing. We weren't there to pick up girls!"

I was skeptical, but I let him pull me back into his arms.

"The evening began quietly in the bar, but in the restaurant it became more exciting. Between the main course and dessert, Dale left our table to visit the men's room. I followed. If there was going to be a meeting or exchange of some kind, that would be a good time for it to happen. Dale went in, and the door closed behind him. It was quiet for a moment, and then another man entered. I counted slowly to ten, and tensed, ready to burst into the room. Just as I was about to hit the door, I heard a muffled gunshot."

I gasped. Niko's arms tightened around me.

"Inside, I found the man who had just entered on the floor, unconscious, and bleeding from a wound in his shoulder. Dale stood over him with a gun."

"A gun?" I pulled away again to stare at Niko.

"Yes, but it wasn't his."

I relaxed slightly, and he pulled me back against him.

"Dale handed me the gun and told me the man had threatened him with it. He said he'd never seen the man before, but that we should get him out of there. I nodded and pointed to the window, which overlooked the back alley, and began trying to remove the flimsy metal grille covering it. Finally, I smashed it with a hard kick and knocked out the remaining pieces of window glass. Dale shimmied through and I shoved our unconscious friend over the sill. A minute later, I followed. By lucky chance, no one had interrupted us."

I was stunned. "No one else heard the gunshot?"

Niko shrugged. "I considered whether to tell Dale I had recognized his attacker. It was possible the man had been hired by an enemy of the owner of the new office building Dale had designed. However, I thought it was more likely he was working for the owner himself. Until I knew what Dale was in Russia to accomplish, it would be difficult to know for sure who had hired the gunman.

"I looked closely at Dale. In the dim light from the restroom window, I could see he was pale, but he didn't seem to be nervous. I pointed toward the entrance to the alley. Dale nodded, and together we lifted the man between us and propped him against the alley wall near the street entrance. I told him someone would find the man and take him to the hospital. We left the alley, came out onto the sidewalk, and quickly walked away."

I pulled away and turned so I could watch Niko's face. "Wait! You left the restaurant without paying for your meals?"

"Yes. The proprietor knew who I was. There was never going to be a bill. So, anyway, I suggested we continue to the nightclub. It wasn't far, and by then it was eleven-thirty, and the club was beginning to fill up. We pushed our way to the bar and ordered vodka. Five bored musicians were playing something, but it was unrecognizable since it was amplified to a deafening rumble. Scantily clad women were dancing on the bar.

"We found a table in a corner, as far away from the band as possible. Dale put his back to one of the walls and I took the other, both of us facing the room. He searched the crowd, probably either looking for someone specific, or memorizing faces. I did the same.

"Finally, I looked at him, smiled, and told him it would save a lot of time and effort if he'd tell me the other reason he was in St. Petersburg. He thought for a minute and said, 'You realize, don't you, I'd have to kill you then?' He watched me closely to make sure I understood he was joking. I smiled and he laughed, but not because he having a good time. He glanced away, frowned, and looked back at me. He asked me if I was an

FSB agent. When I said yes, he asked me how I knew about him.

"At that point, I decided to be frank. I told him we kept a list of known CIA agents, and a few years earlier, his name had appeared on it. He was famous, and since, so far, he hadn't done much to annoy us, we let him come and go unmolested. I told him it was my job to keep an eye on him.

"Dale shook his head and said normally, he'd have made me work a lot harder than this to get answers. But, he decided to be frank too. In this case, he said, telling me might be the only thing that could stop a small arms dealer from becoming a bigger one. He said a deal was about to go down between rebel leaders in a troubled mid-eastern nation and one of my countrymen. The deal was big enough to take him to the next level.

"I could think of several possible suspects, all of whom wanted to get to the next level. I asked him who he meant. That's when he told me it was his current client, Sergei Tronsky.

"I knew Tronsky had already made fortunes in oil, money laundering, and prostitution, but it was a nasty surprise to get this confirmation that he was branching out into arms dealing. Dale told me the CIA wanted to stop Tronsky, and designing his shiny new office building had allowed Dale to get close to him.

"I decided to tell Dale I had recognized the man he'd wounded, and that I suspected the man was probably working for Tronsky. He was a Mafia hit man who also did free-lance work, and of course, I knew Tonsky was a big man in the

Russian Mafia. Somehow, Dale must have made him suspicious. We needed to work very quickly to get him to safety, because as soon as Tronsky knew his man had failed, he would hire someone else to try again.

"In many ways, the nightclub was as safe as anywhere in St. Petersburg. We needed to stay out of dark hallways, men's rooms, taxis, and our hotel. No problem."

Niko chuckled. He probably expected me to laugh too, but I was too shocked by this evidence of Dale's double life to appreciate his joke. I had been watching Niko in silent amazement. Now, he pulled me back into his arms, and I relaxed against him.

"I took out my new mobile phone and dialed Vladi. I had ordered my team to stay close in case of trouble. Vladi picked up immediately and listened carefully as I spoke a few coded words into the phone. When I hung up I told Dale to wait quietly, and to follow my lead. He wanted to know what was going to happen next, but I said everything was under control, and all he had to do was watch me and do what I did.

"We waited, sipping our drinks and trying to look interested in the dancing girls. Then, about twenty minutes later, police dressed in SWAT clothing and armed with heavy artillery burst into the club. Panicked patrons rushed for the nearest exits. We sat. It was all over in a few minutes. Soon we were alone with my team and several other FSB operatives, dressed for the occasion as police officers and medics. Vladi approached and motioned us to follow him.

"The phony medics carried us out of the club on stretchers, bandaged and smeared with fake blood to hide our identities and suggest we'd been injured during the panic. They loaded us into a van with false ambulance insignia and drove away.

"Inside the van, we removed the bandages and wiped off the fake blood. Vladi handed us heavy, dark colored garments to wear over our street clothes. Soon, the van stopped in a deserted parking area. Two of my men jumped out to remove the ambulance signs from the van, and a short time later, we arrived at the docks.

"We had an hour to kill before a boat would come to ferry Dale to a village across the Gulf of Finland, where friends of his would be waiting. In the meantime, Dale and I hurried into a dockside hut. We sat at a wooden table, surrounded by boat gear and life jackets, nursing black coffee laced with a shot or two of vodka. He thanked me for helping him. I shrugged. He might have done the same for me had our positions been reversed.

"He wanted to know how we would deal with Tronsky. He thought maybe he could help. I told him the problem was no longer his, the FSB would deal with Tronsky and it would be a very long time before he would be making deals with anyone. He seemed to accept that."

I reached for Niko's hands, and held them in both of mine. "Niko, when Vladi visited me in New York to tell me he'd found your prison, he said he had met Dale that night for the first time. He was very complimentary about Dale's intelligence and bravery, but he didn't give me any details about what happened. Thank you, Niko. Now I have a slightly better idea of his CIA life, but I guess I'll never truly understand what it was like for him."

"It's probably better you don't. But, anyway, that was the first of several times we worked together. Usually, it was accidental, but twice it was a planned joint venture. One night, in June, 2002, after a particularly difficult job, we got drunk together. That was, of course, against regulations as well as common sense, but we felt we deserved to celebrate a bit."

I was shocked. "Niko, I never ever saw Dale drink too much!"

"It was mostly the let-down after the adrenaline. We were buzzed, but not falling down drunk. So, anyway, after a few minutes, Dale relaxed and began talking about his 'real' life. He planned to retire soon from the 'spook' business, he said, so he could spend more time with his wife and young daughter. From a hidden pocket in his belt, he pulled out a small photo of you, Sharon, taken during your college days. Taking that photo with him on CIA business was extremely foolhardy, but he said it was his 'good luck charm.'

"Maybe you remember the photo, Sharon. You were turned partially away from the camera and were looking over your right shoulder. A breeze had lifted your hair. Your dark eyes gazed into mine and your lips seemed to be smiling at something I had just said."

I nodded. "It was Dale's favorite picture of me."

"To my surprise and, at that time, my dismay, I wanted you," Niko said, kissing my cheek before possessing my mouth.

After a long moment, he went on. "My physical reaction shocked me. It was unacceptable, though I have to admit, not so surprising. FSB agents in my division were prohibited from marrying and fathering children. Our entire energies were supposed to be devoted to the State, and families were considered to be distractions. Also, loved ones could be used as hostages. It made sense, but it was very difficult.

"That night was the last time I saw Dale. Five months later, he was dead. His team and mine worked together again a few weeks before he died, but Dale did not come to Russia then."

I began to cry. Niko held me tightly and tried to kiss away my tears.

At last, I found my voice again. "Niko, when Dale was brought to the hospital after his accident, he was still alive, but only semi-conscious. My doctor told me he was mumbling something about someone named Vladimir. It meant nothing to me then, but when Vladi came to visit me, he said Dale had been working with you and your team just before the accident, and that he, Vladi, had been in charge of communications. He thought Dale might have uncovered something he wanted to pass on to you."

"Ah, well. We'll never know, now. The operation was not completed to my satisfaction, though we did get some answers."

We sat looking into the flames. I was thinking about Dale, thankful he had survived his secret life for as long as he had. I was thankful for so many things, especially for the love of the man who now held me in his strong arms. Niko. I looked up at him, only to find him looking down at me. Our eyes met, full of love, and held for a long moment.

Suddenly he stood up, pulling me with him. Grinning, he tugged me into his arms again, and walked me toward the elevator. "Speaking of physical reactions, I'm having one right now. Want to help me with it?"

I laughed. "Sure, but you'll have to help me with mine, too."

"Yes ma'am." He bowed, and pushed the button to summon the elevator. "I'll be very happy to help!"

We made love each time with tenderness and insatiable passion, the electricity between us continuously flaring. At the beginning of our relationship on board the *River Sprite*, when he had claimed there was a connection between us, Niko had been right. It had existed then, and since then, it had stretched far across time and space. Though initially, the connection had been our separate relationships with Dale, Niko and I had forged our own connection. We were finely attuned to each other's needs.

I had been careful not to mention the evil Grigor in my conversations with Niko, and neither had he. One afternoon after lunch, we lingered on the bluff path. The view was spectacular. For the first time in weeks, the sun was shining, sparkling on the water and highlighting the whitecaps dancing in the stiff breeze. The water was a brilliant shade of blue, a welcome contrast to the more usual gray seas produced by overcast and snowy skies. We were hatted, coated, gloved, and muffled warmly enough to be comfortable. Though the wind was as sharp as ever, the temperature was a little less bone-chilling than it had been.

We sat together on a stone bench sheltered from the wind by a large boulder. Niko had one arm around my shoulders and his free hand held one of mine. He kissed my lips, then pulled me more tightly against his side as he began to speak.

"You're aware, I know, that I was ordered to find out why you were visiting Russia. Vladi phoned me and explained about his visit to you, and how he kept you updated of my progress here. I am very grateful to him for all he has done."

I nodded. "I am too."

"Now, I need to tell you about my enemy, Grigor Smetlov. Beginning in the early days of our training, Grigor created problems for everyone, but especially for me. He was a bully and a liar. He was expert at twisting the facts so he could put the blame on others for his own mistakes. He seemed to dislike everyone, but he focused most of his hatefulness on me. I believe he was jealous of my connection to my great-uncle. Apparently he felt I received advantages not available to him. I tried to keep out of his way, but he seemed always to be behind me, waiting in the background to pounce."

I squeezed his hand, and opened my mouth to speak, but Niko shook his head to stop me.

"As the years passed, his jealousy and hatred turned more vicious. Several times, he tried unsuccessfully to get me into real trouble. As Vladi told you, the man we saw getting out of the elevator when we arrived at the apartment building on our last afternoon in St. Petersburg, was Grigor. I think I was able to hide it from you at the time, but I was very worried. I thought he'd probably followed us there the day before, though I hadn't spotted a tail. I should have paid closer attention to that possibility, but I was too preoccupied with you, Sharon. It was an inexcusable lapse, though maybe an understandable one. I was so in love with you, I had almost forgotten I was supposed to be questioning you.

"The idea that Grigor might have been snooping around, fingering upholstery, and sniffing sheets, was disgusting. The next day, after your plane left for America, I went back to the apartment. I was afraid he might have bribed or blackmailed someone to get the key. But despite his sudden appearance, I couldn't find any evidence he'd actually been inside the apartment. Perhaps his presence there was just to intimate me.

"And, now, I have another apology to make to you. One of many, I am afraid."

"Niko, you don't have to apologize for any of this. You were doing a job, performing a mission for your government. I understand that now."

He stopped my lips with a long kiss. "Okay, but please listen, Sharon. I need to tell you this. That beautiful apartment we used doesn't belong to my cousin. I have no cousin." He paused, looking unseeingly out over the bay.

He turned back to me, frowning in apology. "It was once a KGB safe house. In recent years, its use has been reserved for representatives of foreign governments engaged in high-level talks with our leaders. I was granted permission to borrow it, but I didn't want you to see it looking like an impersonal hotel suite. I asked that it be made to look as though my fictitious cousin actually lived there."

I squeezed his hand. "Whoever did that, did a great job! The apartment looked as though someone with excellent taste lived there, and I had no trouble believing it belonged to your cousin."

"Well, the apartment was bugged, of course, but whatever the listeners picked up would sound as if I were succeeding in my mission to seduce you and find out your secrets. I thought it would be difficult for Grigor to point a finger of suspicion at me for that. I would receive praise from my superiors, not censure."

He held my gaze, one gloved finger tracing my cheek. "But, they didn't understand how my mission had become reality. I had fallen deeply in love with you, Sharon. There have been other women—I am not a monk—but no one has ever made me feel the way you do. With every moment we spend together, I love you more."

All conversation stopped as we clung to each other.

Niko drew back, finally, and stared back out over the water. A few minutes later, he began to speak again. His voice was low and halting, and the color had drained from his troubled face.

"Do you know what Grigor used to say to me before he ordered his 'friends' to torture me? He would say, 'I just wanted to be your friend. Why wouldn't you like me? Why wouldn't you be my friend?' He kept repeating that over and over, louder and louder, as I was beaten." Niko shook his head, his face registering expressions of shock, amazement, and sadness.

Hours later, I realized that while he had spoken of Grigor without prompting from me, and had repeated Grigor's own anguished words, Niko had told me nothing else about his long, terrible ordeal at Grigor's hands. I wondered if he would ever be able to do so.

CHAPTER 30

Late January

AS THE days turned into weeks, I began to worry more and more about how to tell Niko about Nicholas. Since my conversation with Dr. Kennedy, I had been watching for signs of Niko's fragile mental state. Beyond glimpses of his profound sadness at the loss of his family, friends, and career, I had seen no direct evidence of mental frailty. I was particularly glad to see he had not lost his dry sense of humor, in spite of everything he had suffered. We could still make each other helpless with laughter.

Was Niko hiding his fears and insecurities for my benefit? What if I told him about Nicholas's existence and he became angry? Or worse, what if he refused to believe Nicholas was his son? These questions were becoming ever more pressing. I was finding it harder every day to be so far away from Ellen and Nicholas.

One day, while Niko was in his afternoon physical therapy session, I called Ellen as I did almost every day. She told me about Nicholas's latest doings in his pre-school class, and told me again how much he was missing me. Then, she put Nicholas on the phone.

Talking with him was wrenching. I wanted our little family to be together. I felt terribly guilty keeping Nicholas's existence secret from Niko.

In my wallet, besides my driver's license, library card, and credit cards, there were three photos: one of Ellen, one of Nicholas, and one of the two of them together. I took them out when I was on the phone with them, so I could see their faces.

I was still on the phone when Niko returned to our room. I said a hurried goodbye to Ellen and gathered up my photos to put them away.

"Wait," said Niko, limping closer. "May I see those?"

I froze. What was I to do? Then, with a silent prayer for guidance, I held them out for him to see.

"Is this Ellen?"

I nodded.

"She is beautiful, like her mother. But I see Dale in her too." He went to the next photo.

"But who is this handsome boy? He can't be Ellen's son. She isn't married, is she?"

My heart lurched.

"Niko, this is Nicholas. He's *your* son."

"My *son*? *My* son? You are mistaken. I have no son."

Niko sat down suddenly in the bedside chair.

"What are you saying?" His voice was harsh, grating. There was anger and disbelief in his expression. He turned aside, muttering in Russian.

I knelt at his feet and reached for his hands, clasping them tightly.

"Niko, please listen to me. I will explain."

I took a steadying breath.

"Niko, for so many years, Dale and I tried without success to give Ellen a brother or sister. When I met you, I was convinced it was not possible for me to conceive a child. When I returned home, I was busy trying to catch up with the work of our office, and trying to convince Ellen I hadn't lost my mind. That even though I had fallen in love with you, I hadn't completely forgotten her father. I was longing to see you again. You were in my every thought.

"Then, one day around the New Year, I suddenly realized I hadn't had a menstral period in several months. At first, I thought I was must be ill, maybe with cancer or some other disease. If I had been paying closer attention to my body's signals, I would have realized I was pregnant right away. Nicholas was born nine months after I met you. He is four years old now.

"He is yours, Niko. All yours. He is like you in so many ways."

Niko was trying to control his emotions, one hand covering his eyes, the other gripping mine. I slid into his lap and held him tightly.

"Why? Why did you not tell me of this?" His old, formal speech patterns resurfaced.

He pushed me off his lap and stood, angry, hands curled into fists.

"Why did you not write to me of this? And now? Do not!" He was trembling, hands held out to keep me from trying to embrace him again. "Do not tell me the doctors here have told you to keep this secret from me," he shouted. "Have we not had enough of secrets?"

"Niko, please listen to me. I'm so sorry I kept this from you, but I felt I *had* to. I was afraid to tell you in a letter. You were so disappointed and angry when your trip to see me was canceled and you were being sent to Chechnya. How could I tell you I was pregnant then? What would you have done? And after that? When could I have told you? Even Vladi agreed. He knew what you would have tried to do if I had told you."

"As for now, Dr. Kennedy did tell me to wait awhile, until you were stronger. She was wrong. I should have told you as soon as I arrived. But, don't you see, I was selfish. I wanted you to myself. I wanted time to be alone with you—just the two of us alone together."

I was crying now, sobbing into my hands.

For a long moment, there was silence. Suddenly, Niko's arms came around me, almost crushing me, his face against my hair.

He was trembling now with emotion. "You have given me a son?"

I nodded, my face mashed against his shoulder. He held me away, and wiped my tears with his thumbs. There was wonder in his face.

"A son? Called Nicholas?"

"Yes," I smiled proudly. "Oh, Niko, wait until you meet him. He is so much like you, what you

must have been like as a child. He is all I have
had of you all these years."

"When can I see him?" Now, he was as eager
as a child himself.

"Well, let me think... Ah, school will be
closed soon for our Presidents' Week holiday.
Maybe Ellen can bring him then. But wait, don't
we have to get permission from someone here?"

"Yes, at dinner we will raise the subject. I
don't see how they can object."

◈

Niko was right. After a moment of thought, Dr.
Kennedy nodded her approval. I mentioned the
possibility of Presidents' Week, when schools
were closed to commemorate George
Washington's and Abraham Lincoln's February
birthdays. She agreed that would be a good time.
The visit would be for only a few days, but if all
went well, a future visit could be longer.

◈

That night, Niko had a nightmare for the first
time since I arrived. It was terrible to watch. I was
unsure what to do. He never actually woke up, but
I tried to hold him, whispering words of love to
him until he was finally calm.

What had made him suffer such a horrible
nightmare, and how often could I expect him to
have them in the future, I wondered? Should I
have tried to wake him?

The next morning, I went to see Dr. Kennedy
with my questions.

"Mrs. Grant," she shook her head ruefully. "I
apologize. I should have discussed Niko's
nightmares with you as soon as you arrived here.

At first, his sleep was disturbed every night, sometimes more than once. He is having them less often now," she said, "but he may experience them off and on for the rest of his life. It's difficult to know what might trigger them as time goes on."

"What can I do to help him?"

"I would advise you simply to call his name until he wakes. I am concerned he might hurt you if you touch him or attempt to hold him. Often, people will fight the loved one who is trying to calm them."

"I'm not sure Niko would do that. He seemed terrified. He was actually cowering, and it sounded to me as if he were begging for something—mercy, I thought—in Russian."

"Nevertheless," she said, shaking her head. "I still feel you should not try to touch him until he is awake. He would be devastated if he inadvertently hurt you."

I had to acknowledge the truth of that.

Even after all our conversations, I still found it difficult to imagine the life Niko had led. I was overwhelmed with thankfulness he had survived it all. Scarred, and still mentally fragile he might be, but he was alive, and we were together.

CHAPTER 31

Presidents' Week, February 2010

ELLEN AND Nicholas were due to arrive on the Sunday before President's Day and stay until the following Wednesday. I could hardly wait to see them.

Niko spent the last few days before their arrival alternating between excited anticipation and panic. I tried to reassure him when his anxiety became too much for him, but I understood his feelings. We had decided not, at this time, to tell Nicholas that Niko was his father. Then, over the precious days of their visit, the four of us could interact naturally, without pressure. At least, we hoped so.

For Niko, there was nothing but pressure. He studied Ellen's and Nicholas's photographs until they began to fray around the edges. I promised him we would take new photos of all four of us.

On the day of their arrival, it snowed during the morning, but by lunchtime the sky had cleared. After we ended our futile attempt to eat the delicious lunch set out for us, Niko and I walked on the bluff, Niko clutching his cane in one hand and my hand in his other. He stopped at one point and pulled me into his arms.

"Have I thanked you yet for saving my sanity? For bringing me your love? And now, for bringing my son and your beautiful daughter to meet me? What have I done to deserve all this?" Trembling with both fear and excitement, he kissed me with tenderness.

Just then, we heard a child's voice calling "Mama? Mama!"

We turned. Running toward us was our little boy.

"Nicholas!"

He ran to me and threw himself against my legs. I scooped him up and hugged him tightly. Then I turned to Niko.

"Nicholas, this is my very good friend, Niko. Say hello to him. Niko is hoping to be your very good friend too."

"'lo," he mumbled, shyly. Then, as I had taught him, Nicholas held out his right hand for Niko to shake.

Gravely, Niko took it in his large one and shook it firmly.

"Nicholas, I'm very pleased to meet you. I've heard a lot about you." There was an expression of joy and wonder on Niko's face.

Meanwhile, Ellen was coming toward us. Nicholas wriggled out of my arms and ran back to her.

Niko whispered, "She is even more beautiful than her picture. And Nicholas, he is… perfect."

His eyes filled with tears. I gave him a reassuring squeeze and went to greet Ellen.

"You're here at last!" We hugged, holding each other for a long moment. "I've missed you both so much."

My own tears were threatening. But not for long.

"I'm hungry!" Nicholas announced loudly. And then, in an urgent whisper, he added, "And I need to go to the bathroom."

We laughed. As we followed the path back to the house, I introduced Ellen to Niko. They shook hands warily, looking closely at each other. Finally, Ellen smiled. "I've been waiting a long time to meet you. Let's get Nicholas taken care of, and start getting to know each other. You knew my father, I understand."

Niko, who had been holding his breath, let it out in relief.

"Yes, your father was a true friend. I am very lucky to have known him."

Once again, Dr. Kennedy had provided a substantial tea in the library. At last, the three people I loved most in the world were here together in this beautiful room. I sent up a silent prayer of thanksgiving.

The time passed all too quickly. Nicholas and Niko formed a solemn male bond, finding common ground in sports. Niko was thrilled to learn of Nicholas's prowess, even at his young age, on the soccer field. He would have to stop calling soccer *futbal*, Nicholas warned. American football was a completely different sport.

Nicholas was also a baseball fan, a sport Niko knew very little about. He nodded in happy confusion as Nicholas chattered on about his experiences playing T-ball with his friends.

Ellen discovered Niko's interest in architecture, and found he was not only knowledgeable, but also as intrigued by new techniques and sustainable materials as she was. She hugged him when he explained how their mutual interest led him to meet Dale at the conference in St. Petersburg. He did not explain the real reason why he, himself, had been there, nor did he mention Dale's CIA mission. He was honoring my decision not to tell Ellen of her father's secret career.

All in all, it was a very successful visit. I was unwilling to return home without Niko, and I was not yet sure how long it would be until he was well enough to leave. It was very difficult to say goodbye to Ellen and Nicholas, though I promised to continue phoning them as often as possible. As for Niko, saying goodbye to Nicholas was heartbreaking.

He had a nightmare again that night, a disappointing setback. I called his name until he woke, and held him as he quieted. We fell asleep again with my head cradled on his shoulder.

CHAPTER 32

March 2010

THREE WEEKS after Ellen's and Nicholas's visit, Niko's long-time friend and FSB colleague, Leo Sokolov, came to see him again, as he had promised. Leo closeted himself with Dr. Kennedy first, then joined us in the library. Niko and Leo embraced and held each other off, each inspecting the other for changes.

Niko had regained the weight, strength, and flexibility he had lost during his ordeal, and his clothing emphasized his strong physique. His hair was more salt than pepper, but it made him look distinguished. His face had filled out and was no longer so obviously lined. His facial scars, partially hidden by a closely trimmed beard and mustache, made him look slightly dangerous, but they enhanced rather than detracted from his looks.

We knew Niko would need to leave Cornwall soon. Despite the occasional nightmare, his mental state was much improved, and Dr. Kennedy was ready to discharge him from her care. Leo was here to speak with Niko about his future.

Leo left after two days of talk and reminiscences lasting far into the night, aided by significant quantities of vodka. It was wonderful to see them together. Much as Niko loved Vladi, Niko was always the superior. With Leo, it was different. They were equals, with a shared history, both vivid and dangerous.

Before Leo arrived, Niko explained how their relationship had begun with rivalry, but later, changed to something close to the love of brothers as they were forced to rely on each other in battle. Now, Leo told me how Niko had saved his life during a particularly dangerous mission early in their careers. And, I learned the role Leo had played in our correspondence. It was he who facilitated the exchange of our letters when Niko came back from Chechnya. Leo was Dept. N at the Russian Consulate in New York City!

"And, Leo did much more," Niko explained. "He was the man I asked to watch over you and Ellen if anything happened to me. As it did." He stopped, frowning. Then he shook his head, as if to put aside his anger. "He let me know when you arrived home safely from Russia, and kept a general eye on you."

I looked at Leo in shock and the beginnings of anger. "Were you spying on me?"

Leo shook his head, throwing a quick glance at Niko for help. "No, not really. I was concerned only for your security. I sent no reports of your movements or conversations."

"You must have known I was pregnant, Leo, and had given birth to Niko's son. And you kept that a secret from Niko?"

"Yes, I knew what he might try to do if I told him. And, you had the right to privacy. I respected that."

I stared at Leo, wondering whether to believe him. Niko turned to face me. He reached for my hand and laced his fingers with mine, his eyes pleading with me to forgive anything Leo might have seen or heard. I sighed in reluctant acceptance. I understood how important it was to Niko for me to think well of Leo.

"It's thanks to Leo that I am here now, and have been given this chance to recover my health. He coordinated my extraction, the journey to this beautiful safe house, and all my medical treatments. My great uncle set the operation in motion by calling on former colleagues in the CIA and MI-6 for help, but it was Leo who negotiated with them to devise a workable plan. Then, Vladi did the rest, with the help of Ilya Popov, one of my former team, as well as CIA and MI-6 agents. Vladi told me one of the CIA men had been a friend of Dale's."

He smiled at Leo. "Without Leo, I would still be imprisoned, or dead. Eventually, I would have starved to death. Vladi is brave and a very good agent, but he never could have achieved all this," Niko spread his hands to indicate the safe house and the treatments he had received, "without Leo working in the background to arrange it."

I looked at Leo with tears in my eyes, my anger of a few moments ago replaced with overwhelming gratitude. I had believed he was simply a close friend from Niko's youth. This man had risked his own career—had something gone wrong—to do whatever he could to help Niko, and ultimately, to bring us together again.

I was very sorry to see Leo leave, but he and Niko had come to an agreement over Niko's future. His next visitor would be from MI-6, followed by someone from the CIA, the first steps in Niko's ultimate defection to the United States.

CHAPTER 33

April 2010 to September, 2012

THE FALL term is underway. Niko is adjunct professor of English literature at a small midwestern college. He is mostly content, I believe, though underlying his acceptance of his new life there remains a degree of sadness. I am in awe of him. He is very brave.

As I had anticipated, Niko's defection was extremely difficult for him. He is practical, however, and just as everyone expected, he did what was necessary. He knew very well what was required if he were to survive and have any kind of future.

Through it all, there were compensations. We were together, and we finally could envision a future in which we could *remain* together. In his lowest moments, I was there for him. And, for one perfect four-day weekend toward the end of our time in Washington, we were able to see Ellen and Nicholas. Their visit was arranged at a safe house in Virginia.

During those magical days, Niko and Nicholas, then five years old, became fast friends. We still had not told Nicholas who his father was, but I was confident Niko would know when and how to tell him. Ellen and I watched them together with delight. For the first time in his short life, Nicholas had undivided adult male attention and companionship, and Niko—Niko had his son. His joy and pride were profound.

They went exploring together in the woods, returning muddy but happy, bringing back treasures to be admired: sparkling rocks, a dead but still beautiful butterfly, a partial snakeskin, and a hummingbird's nest. Ellen and I did admire them, but we were intent on spending as much time together as possible. Ellen was soon to be married, and it was deeply satisfying to know she and her husband would make their home in the beautiful house Dale had built for us.

We discussed what she would tell our staff and any acquaintances who might ask about my continued absence. We finally agreed she would say I had decided to move to Europe with Nicholas. Later, if anyone still asked about me, she could say Nicholas was attending school in Europe and I had decided to continue living there indefinitely. No further details were necessary.

Niko and I were married while we were still in Washington. With Nicholas, we are a family now in every sense of the word.

Thanks to the preparation the CIA gave us, along with our new identities, we have settled into the university community without much difficulty. They arranged Niko's professorship, our transportation, housing, basic wardrobes, and the money to furnish our new home, a rented house within walking distance of the campus. Eventually, we hope to buy something of our own, though it will take time. Niko is proud. He is reluctant to accept more financial help from the CIA.

Niko has refused to accept my financial help as well. The money Dale set aside for me is held in trust for Nicholas. I have never wanted to live an extravagant life, and we have everything we need, Niko and I, now that we have each other and Nicholas.

Early in Niko's defection process, his handlers decided Nicholas could keep his first name, though his new surname would be the same as the one Niko and I had been given. They thought Nicholas might have an easier transition if he could keep a part of his identity. His school friends call him Nick.

Though Niko and I have to be careful to call each other by our new names when we are in public, I am finding contentment in the everyday routines of our new life. Each morning during the week, after Nicholas has gone to school, I volunteer a few hours in the campus day-care center. Working there gives shape to my days, and I love being with the children.

We have made new friends and, now and then, we give and attend dinner parties and other celebrations. Niko and I are planning, as we did for the first time last December, to host a Sunday afternoon tea for his students. Our living room was filled with young people last year. I was thrilled to watch Niko talking with them, and to see how highly they regarded him. I am looking forward to that again this year.

I have always enjoyed cooking and baking. Now that I have a family to cook for again, I am trying new recipes and updating old favorites with fresh enthusiasm. In the evenings, Niko, Nicholas, and I eat the dinner I have prepared, and Niko and I wash the dishes while Nicholas does his homework at the kitchen table.

After we put Nicholas to bed, we have the rest of the evening and the night to ourselves. We make the most of every moment. Niko's nightmares come very rarely now. Most nights, we sleep entangled together, reluctant to stop touching even in slumber.

Over the past year, we have been spending time exploring our town and the surrounding countryside in our "new" second-hand car. We have grown to love the rolling hills, the neat farms, and the sleepy villages we see in our travels. When the weather is good, we pack a picnic lunch to eat by the roadside, next to a small spring we recently discovered. It is beautiful there, and peaceful, with the happy sound of dancing water.

Sitting on a blanket with our picnic spread out before us and the sun shining though the tree branches overhead, I find it easy to forget we have anything to worry about. If the weather is bad, we go to the movies, or stay home and read or watch television. It matters little *what* we do. It matters that we are together.

Of course, we have no illusions about what might happen if any of Niko's former enemies succeed in locating him. In this age of swiftly moving technology, anything is possible, although we do not go around peering over our shoulders, expecting the worst. But, of course, I do worry about our security. I feel as though we have stepped out of the pages of a spy novel, but this is real life. It will be up to us to survive—or not—if the worst were to occur.

Nicholas has weathered the changes in his young life more smoothly than I could have imagined. He is now in the second grade and is popular with his classmates. He does well academically and enjoys playing Little League soccer and baseball. Though Niko is still mystified by American football, and was never a fan of basketball, he loves watching Nicholas play soccer and baseball. He is looking forward to the spring, so he can learn more about baseball. He would love to be able to coach his son in both sports one day.

Nicholas knows now that Niko is his biological father. Niko picks Nicholas up after school each day, and they spend the next hour alone together, a time sacred to both of them. Sometimes they read aloud to each other. At other times, they play board, card, or word games. Niko is teaching Nicholas to play chess and is finding his son an apt pupil. Always, they have much to talk about. To me, the sound of their voices—Niko's musical bass in counterpoint to Nicholas's piping treble— is more beautiful than the finest operatic duet.

Even now, after more than a year, Niko almost bursts with pride when Nicholas calls him Dad.

Nicholas's one sorrow is how much he misses Ellen. She helped take care of him from his babyhood, and they became even closer while I was with Niko in England. He had never known life without her, but he is being very brave and grown up about it. It is strange that such a little boy should be able to understand why he can no longer be with her. He knows her absence is due to circumstance, not because he or anyone else has done anything wrong.

⧉

While we were together in Washington, Ellen showed me photos of her wedding dress and accessories. Her friend Suzi, who served as Ellen's matron of honor, played a large part in the wedding preparations. Suzi had been briefly married two years after she and Ellen graduated from Williams College, though the marriage failed. She now works in a public relations firm in Manhattan and she and Ellen see each other as often as Ellen's travel schedule allows.

As Ellen told me about all their plans, I was saddened to realize Niko, Nicholas, and I would not be able to be there with her on her special day. She would have moved the date forward for us if it could have been arranged, but it was not to be.

And so, Ellen's wedding day came last year without us. I shed more than a few tears, wishing things were different. To miss her wedding day, of all days, was hard to bear. While I fully understand the need for our government's protection—and am more than grateful for it—I am lonely for her daily presence in my life. And though it is a constant heartache not to be able to hug and kiss her, it is our casual phone conversations I miss most, sharing all the little details of our daily lives.

In my imagination, I pictured Ellen and her new husband flying away on their honeymoon, loving each other, and finally coming home to Dale's beautiful house. I pray they are as happy as I have been, first with Dale, and now with Niko. And, no matter how lonely I am for Ellen, l would not exchange what I have with Niko for any reason.

It is six o'clock and dinner is almost ready.

Nicholas is reading aloud to Niko in the family room. His high-pitched voice is confident. Niko's bass chimes in only when Nicholas needs help sounding out a word. When they laugh together, a frequent event, my heart soars.

When I call them to the table, they stand together for a moment in the open doorway. They are smiling. Nicholas is Niko in miniature. Then Nicholas runs to me, ready for a hug. Over his head, as my arms enfold him, my eyes meet Niko's, and the space between us vibrates with love.

**Continue the saga of the Grants
and their friends with a brief look at
Book #2 of the Doors of the Heart
Series:**
WOLF AT THE DOOR.

North Georgia, Summer, 1837

The forest was silent. Slowly, softly, Jacob crept toward the small, secluded clearing. It was noon, time for him to unpack the bread and cheese his mother had given him that morning, but he had another urge, and it was more powerful than the ache in his empty stomach.

He had seen them in the clearing every day for a week, two Cherokee girls. The elder looked to be about his age, the younger probably her little sister. They were always busy with some task, gathering mushrooms, herbs, or berries, before stopping to eat a midday meal. Today, they were sewing something. It looked, from his distance, like pieces for a quilt.

The older girl was beautiful. Her unbound black hair fell down her slim back almost to her waist. Jacob thought her face was as lovely as a flower, though he had not yet decided *which* flower. He knew only one thing for certain. He wanted to be near her for the rest of his life.

Jacob was sixteen. He longed to bury his hands in her hair, to tilt up her face to capture her lips with his own, to hold her in his arms, and to protect her always. He had never felt this way before.

He knew how to hunt for food, how to clear the land for crops, and how to build a cabin suitable for a family. He and his father had done all that after they claimed their farmland in the recent land lottery. But now, he was at a loss. He had no notion of how to approach her. Frightening her was the last thing he wanted to do.

He wished he knew her name. He called her Belle in his imagination, but her Cherokee name would be quite different. Though he had mastered only a few words in the Cherokee language so far, he knew that much. His father often traded with the Indians, while Jacob listened and learned.

Lately, there was worrisome news. The Congress in Washington had passed a bill giving white settlers the right to seize Cherokee lands for their own use. There was a rumor that if the Cherokee refused to sell their land to the new settlers, American soldiers would be sent to drive the Indians away. A small band of Cherokee had already traveled to Oklahoma Territory to settle in land that had been set aside as their new country, but most had stayed in their ancestral home places, here in the eastern mountains and forests.

Jacob was unsure how he felt about that. Yes, the land rightfully belonged to the Cherokee, but they should be willing to sell it to the white settlers. The Indians who sold their land would have to leave, of course. He hoped his Belle and her family could find a way to stay.

He knew where her village was located. He even had seen her father when he followed Belle and her sister home one day. The man looked fierce. Jacob had backed away quietly, and then, as soon as it was safe, he had run all the way home.

⤫

"I see you. Come here."

Jacob almost dropped his hunting gun. She was looking straight at him. He was crouched behind a tree, but it had failed to hide him.

"I see you. Come here!" she repeated, more loudly this time.

He stood slowly, and cautiously approached the clearing.

"Why have you come here to spy on us? We have seen you here each day this week."

Jacob lost the ability to speak. He choked, cleared his throat, and tried again. "To see you. Wait, you speak English?"

"We attend the Mission school. Why are you spying on us?"

He hesitated, and then decided he might as well tell her the truth. "You are beautiful. I wanted to get to know you, but I didn't know how. I didn't know you could speak English."

"Of course. We speak Cherokee when we are alone, but even my little sister speaks English. But, I do not understand. Why did you want to meet us?"

"I was out hunting a few days ago, and I saw you. I wanted to get to know you, that's all. I thought we might like each other."

"My sister, too?"

"Yes."

"Well then, come and sit with us. It is time to break our fast."

A dusky, rose-colored flush flooded her cheeks. Now, Jacob believed, she was even more beautiful than before.

Over the next days, turning to weeks and then months, they met as often as possible, and Jacob learned her name. Translated from the Cherokee into English, it was Rose. Her namesake was the wild white rose he had seen blooming in the forest. It fit her perfectly.

They each had chores to do, tasks that were sometimes hard, even dangerous. Even so, they tried never to miss their rendezvous. Soon, the little sister sat apart from them, so they could talk privately together. As their friendship blossomed, so did the love in their hearts.

And finally, Jacob achieved a part of his heart's desire. Each day, for a brief time, whether in the heat of summer or in winter's chill, he could hold Rose in his arms, kiss her beloved lips, and bury his hands in her thick, beautiful hair. She loved him too, and Jacob knew he was tasting heaven.

It could never last. When Jacob's father discovered them one day the following summer, he was outraged. How, he thundered to Jacob, could he "take up" with a "savage"? Those "filthy Indians" were going to be gone soon, and good riddance. The soldiers were coming at last.

And they did. U.S. Army soldiers brutally chased and captured Cherokee individuals and families, burning their homes and businesses, destroying their farms and villages. The soldiers drove their captives into stockades, where they held them with little food or shelter until more Cherokee could be caught.

Over the following months, stretching to two years, the soldiers forced group after group of Cherokee to travel more than twelve hundred miles westward to Oklahoma Territory. Many were sent on foot, and others in wagons, on horseback, or by river boat. The Cherokee were allowed only to bring as much as they could carry.

Once on the trail, the soldiers pushed the people relentlessly over rugged terrain, in blistering sun, soaking rainstorms, wind, sleet, and snow. Horses and people died, wagons broke down, and boats sank.

Many of the once proud and strong Cherokee people, especially the old and the very young, perished of starvation, exposure to the elements, exhaustion, and diseases that included whooping cough, typhus, dysentery, and cholera.

Of the approximately fifteen thousand Cherokee who were forced to travel along what came to be called the Trail of Tears, more than four thousand died.

Jacob was frantic when the soldiers came. He raced to Rose's village, only to discover that he was too late. It had been burned. The ground was littered with broken and blackened tools, weapons, and pottery. If there were survivors, they were gone. The village was deserted.

Jacob was devastated. He wandered in the mountain forests for three days, desperately searching for Rose and her family. Unable to imagine living without her, he ignored his body's demands for water, food, or sleep.

At last, at dusk on the third day of Jacob's desperate search, Rose's little sister, who had been out hunting for berries, found him as she was hurrying back to her hiding place. Her family were among several hundred Cherokee who refused to leave their homeland, finding refuge in remote mountain hideaways.

Carefully, she took his hand and led him there. When Jacob finally saw Rose, he collapsed at her feet. She and her family nursed him, and kept him with them until the soldiers at last were ordered to stop their pursuit of rebellious Cherokee, and leave the area.

By that time, Rose's family had accepted Jacob and consented to their marriage. Jacob was a valuable asset for them. He could trade with the white settlers, find jobs that paid good wages in goods or currency, and most importantly, bring the latest news back to Rose's family.

Though he often saw one or both of his parents in town, they refused to acknowledge him. They were angry, and ashamed of him, and they instructed Jacob's younger sisters and brothers to shun him also. Jacob was saddened by their attitude, but he was happy with Rose and their growing family. He loved them too much to ever think of leaving them.

He and Rose worked hard and they saved every spare penny Jacob earned. Finally, they were able to buy a small farm of their own.

The spark of love that first ignited in that quiet forest clearing in the summer of 1837, lived on through their children, their grandchildren, and down through the generations until the present day.

Fannin County, North Georgia
Six Generations Later

CHAPTER 1

I checked the clock on my rental car's dashboard. The last thing I wanted was to be late.

The sun glinted off the rear window of the car I was following. Blinded for a moment, I blinked hard and the road reappeared, climbing steadily through the mountains. The driver ahead was taking his time, and I was beginning to be anxious.

I took a deep breath and tried to relax and enjoy the scenery. Around almost every bend there was another view of the lush green valley below. Though it was a cool day for late April, I lowered the car's windows a few inches. The spicy scent of pine trees filled the car, and over the engine's soft growl, I imagined I could hear birds calling in the forest that cloaked the mountains on either side of the road. There were a few dogwood trees in bloom, and deep within the forest, I caught glimpses of large shrubs, bright with orange and yellow blossoms. I wondered what they were.

The GPS chirped, pulling my attention back to business. *"Turn left in point two miles, and your destination will be on the left."* I checked the clock again. Relieved, I saw that I was going to be on time after all.

I was rarely nervous when meeting new people, but though the man I was to meet today had been highly recommended to me, I was uneasy.

His name was Thomas R. D. Wolf and, in the photo on his website, his professional smile seemed appropriately predatory. His teeth were blindingly white against his bronze skin and his long, straight black hair fell well below his shirt collar. His face was lean, with prominent cheekbones, a large hooked nose, sparkling brown eyes set off by arched black eyebrows, and a strong chin. He was not classically handsome, but there was something compelling about his face in that photo, and a bit disturbing.

I hoped this journey to see him, the main reason I had come to Georgia this week, was not a mistake.

I continued up the narrow road, turned into a gravel driveway, and parked near a rambling, two-story log home. Next to the driveway, attached to the fence that held his mailbox, was a small sign: Thomas R. D. Wolf, Real Estate.

The log home looked rustic, but it, and its surrounding property, were fastidiously neat, with freshly mown grass and orderly split rail fences. I could see a large, red-painted barn set back and to the right of the house, and I guessed there were other outbuildings just out of sight.

A gravel path led from the driveway to the house, and pots of colorful pansies were set on either side of the front steps. Two white-painted rocking chairs, with red and gold plaid cushions, sat on the deep porch. There were wide picture windows, as well as narrow sidelight windows on either side of the red-painted front door.

A large coal-black horse, in a corral a short distance away, was eyeing me and dancing restlessly. In the pasture beyond, two other horses grazed peacefully, ignoring me completely.

The door opened, and a man stepped out. He stopped in the shadow of the porch roof.

I got out of the car and swallowed hard. Squaring my shoulders, I strode up the gravel path to his porch. My bravado slipped when I tripped on the first step, and almost fell.

The man, Thomas Wolf, presumably, had stood immobile as I approached, but now he moved quickly. He caught me by my upper arms, and pulled back slightly as though surprised. Then, he grinned the predatory grin I had seen in his website photo. Did he think my almost falling on his steps was funny?

"Well, hello. I'm Tom Wolf, and you must be Suzanna Smith. You need to watch that first step." Laughing softly, he escorted me up the remaining steps, keeping one hand under my elbow.

My cheeks burning, I struggled to regain my composure. "Yes, Mr. Wolf, I am Suzanna Smith. I believe you were expecting me?"

Of course, he was expecting me. Was I losing my mind? My arms were tingling where he had caught me, and so was my elbow, as though he had given me a small jolt of electricity.

Safely on the porch, I thrust out my right hand to shake his. As he took it, I felt the strange electricity again. I glanced up at him, wondering if he felt it too. If so, he was hiding his reaction. He was still grinning that wolfish grin.

I looked away, but not before I noticed the way the skin crinkled at the outer corners of his dark brown eyes, and that he was at least six inches taller than my five-feet-nine. He was lean, though he filled out his jeans and tucked white Oxford shirt extremely well. His rolled-up shirt sleeves displayed muscled forearms and large, well-shaped hands. His website photo had lied. He was much better looking in person.

His black hair was amazing: straight and thick, shining with health, and even longer than in his photo. Brushed back from his forehead and tucked behind his ears, it reached almost to the middle of his back. Millions of women would love to have hair like his. I longed to touch it.

"Just call me Tom," he drawled. His voice was deep and probably unintentionally sensual. I shivered. I was going to have trouble with his voice, and his thick, almost musical, Southern accent. I hoped I could avoid swooning at his feet.

"Cold?" Of course, he had seen me shiver. "Come on inside where it's warmer. These late April days can be chilly."

I nodded. He let go of my arm to open the front door, and ushered me in.

As I stepped into the foyer, my first impression was that the house was as rustic inside as out, but my first impression was wrong. A few steps farther, and I gasped. The house was more spacious than it looked from the outside, but that was not what surprised me. I turned around slowly to take it all in.

I was standing in an open-plan great room. The walls were painted the color of buttery cream, the flooring was polished oak.

Opposite the front entryway, a huge, grey stone fireplace took up most of the back wall. Over it, two large paintings depicted on the left, native warriors dancing in a circle, and on the right, two native women cooking over an open fire. I was not a trained connoisseur of art, but I thought they were both magnificent. It looked as if they had been painted by different artists, and I wondered if they were Cherokee.

Facing the fireplace was a massive couch, covered in rich, dark chocolate leather, and flanked on either side by two matching easy chairs. A glass-topped, wrought iron cocktail table sat in front of the couch with a colorful woolen rug on the floor beneath it.

Wrought iron and glass end tables between the couch and each easy chair held different but complimentary Tiffany-style lamps. A woolen blanket in a red and gold plaid adorned the back of the couch, and interesting, country-style accessories were placed around the room for maximum effect.

To the right, against the wall, there was a wide, floor-to-ceiling bookcase filled with books, geological specimens, and other natural objects, including a bird's nest. Hanging next to the bookcase was a dressed deer hide and, next to that, there was a hallway and stairs to the second floor, leading, I guessed, to bedrooms and baths. To the right of the hallway, there was a handsome oak desk with a matching file cabinet and swivel chair, obviously Tom's office area. The desktop was arranged neatly with stacked file folders, a laptop computer, and another Tiffany-style lamp.

On the front wall to the left of the foyer, under a large picture window, there were two wrought iron chairs upholstered in chocolate leather for Tom's clients. On the other side of the foyer, under a similar window, there was a wrought iron bench, covered in matching leather, but more deeply padded.

Along the side wall opposite Tom's office area, there was an enormous glass-topped wrought iron dining table with a huge Tiffany-style hanging lamp centered over it. The table was surrounded by a dozen wrought iron armchairs, their seats and backs upholstered in dark red and gold plaid wool.

To the right of the table, a large granite-topped island with a built-in wet bar separated the dining area from the kitchen. Four wrought iron stools were pulled up to the island, their padded seats covered in dark red wool.

The kitchen was fitted with what looked like professional-grade stainless steel appliances, granite countertops, and country-style oak cabinets. A flat screen TV was attached to the wall above one of the countertops and was visible from the island.

At the back of the kitchen, there was a sliding glass door. I could see a few feet of red brick paving through the glass, probably a patio and a walkway to the barn.

This was country chic at its finest. Tom seemed especially taken with Tiffany-style lamps.

I had not yet seen the rest of his home, but the entire great room was drop-dead gorgeous. Who, I wondered, had decorated this room? If not for the fact that this was Tom's domain, and of course, that it was more than eight hundred miles from my job in Manhattan, I would have been thrilled to move in. I was especially envious of the kitchen. My tiny New York City condo was severely limited in that department.

"Come by the fire and have a seat," said my host, indicating the couch. "You'll soon warm up. Okay if I call you Suzanna?"

I nodded, glancing up at him. "Most people call me Suzi."

His stare was both intense and appraising, and I felt my cheeks warming again.

"Nah. I'm goin' to call you Suzanna."

I shrugged my shoulders and moved to the fireplace. I stood staring into the flames for a few minutes, warming my hands and trying to get my bearings. Now that Tom had directed my attention back on himself and not on his stunning home, I was feeling oddly crowded and more than a little off balance. I had never met anyone like him before. His presence seemed to fill this large, beautiful room to bursting, leaving me feeling slightly breathless.

When, at last, I turned around, he gestured toward my jacket. "Are you warm enough now to take that off? If so, I'll hang it on a peg in the foyer."

He waited, and when I was slow to respond, he spread his hands, and with elaborate patience said, "Okay?"

I nodded again, and began to unbutton the light jacket I had put on that morning. I had assumed I would be taking it off as the day warmed, but the temperature had remained a little too chilly for that. I moved a few steps closer to him and handed it over.

He stood holding it, letting it dangle from one long bronze finger, while he looked me over slowly from head to toe. He seemed not to miss anything I was wearing, and I was certain he was mentally undressing me. He chuckled again. "You'll need to get used to wearin' warmer clothes up here this time of year. And, it's a lot colder at night."

"I'm not going to be here at night!" I crossed my arms over my breasts and clutched my upper arms defensively. What was he assuming?

"Oh, excuse me," he drawled. "I didn't mean to offend you."

I nodded curtly, and sat down in the closest armchair. Oddly enough, I realized that I was not offended, exactly. I was proud of my body. I always had been athletic. I visited a Manhattan gym regularly, and I liked to walk. I preferred to get around the city on foot whenever I had time to do so.

Tom returned from the foyer and sat on the couch near my chair. "So, what can I do for you?" He leaned toward me, still grinning that grin.

"As I mentioned in my email, you were recommended to me by Daniel Hardy, a genealogist I consulted in New York. According to him you're a realtor and an amateur genealogist, as well as a student of local history." I hesitated a little. "He also said you're Cherokee."

"That's right. Is that important?"

"It might be. I want to trace my grandmother's people. She claimed to be part Cherokee, and was born here in Fannin County. I don't have much information about her parents, and I'm hoping to find out more about them, and go back further, if possible.

"I intend to take a ten-week leave of absence from my job this summer, from early June through the beginning of September, and I'll need to find a place to rent for that time. Mr. Hardy told me you probably could help me with both. I want to get to know this area a bit, and if you can help me trace my grandmother's line back several generations, I'm planning to write her story."

"Are you a writer?"

"Not really. I work in public relations, and that involves quite a bit of writing. But, this would be for me and my brother and our children, so they can know a little about who we are and where we came from."

"Oh? You have children?"

"No, but I hope to one day. My brother and his wife have two boys."

"I see."

I doubted that. "I'll explain. Last year I spent a few days in Wilkes County, Georgia, researching my grandfather Kelly's side of the family. It was a great experience, and I met so many helpful people. I was surprised to learn that both my great-grandfather and great-grandmother Kelly are buried here in Fannin County, in the Methodist cemetery in Epworth. So, you see, all roads led to Fannin County."

"Really? That's interestin'. That cemetery's not far from here. I'll take you there when you come back this summer."

"Thanks. We'll see. Right now, I'm kind of pressed for time. I'm on a one-week vacation from my job in Manhattan. This is a scouting trip, really. I flew into Atlanta and spent the first few days visiting friends and touring the city. I drove up here to Blue Ridge this morning, and just had time enough to check into my hotel and grab some lunch before driving up here. I have to fly back home the day after tomorrow."

"Okay. I should be able to find you somethin' to rent before you need to leave. But, in the meantime, why don't you tell me a little bit more about yourself and your grandmother."

"Okay, well… my last name is kind of unusual. Not, of course, because Smith is an unusual name, but because of an odd circumstance. Smith was my Grandmother Rose's maiden name which, for reasons unknown to me, she kept after her marriage to my grandfather, John Kelly. My mother also kept Smith as her surname when she married my father, James Walker, and when I was born, she bequeathed it to me. I thought I might have a hard time combing through all the Georgia Smiths to find *our* family of Smiths. I'll need help."

Tom nodded, probably hoping I would hurry up and get to the point.

"Grandma was the eldest of seven sisters, and as I mentioned before, she claimed to be part Cherokee. She seemed to have mixed emotions about that, proud, but also slightly ashamed. Her attitude toward her heritage has always puzzled me."

Tom looked closely at me, and gave me a slow nod. "Sure, Suzanna. I'll be happy to help you," he drawled. I was having trouble both with his voice and his slow, sexy accent. They were making me, alternatively, both shivery and much too warm.

"But for now, tell me what you have in mind for a rental. Do you want a condo in town, or somethin' more rustic here in the mountains? I'm guessin' you'll want somethin' completely furnished."

"Yes, I don't want to have to buy or rent furniture for such a short time. But, as to condo or cabin, I don't know yet. Can you show me examples of both? My budget isn't very large, but it's somewhere in the mid-range for this area. I've done a little homework."

"That's good. No surprises, then. And it's good you've come now. The best seasonal rentals are goin' fast as we get closer to summer."

He thought for a minute, and then nodded. "I can show you five different condos and at least four cabins. None of 'em is very big, but they have all the essentials. They're fully furnished with heat, hot and cold runnin' water, workin' appliances, pots and pans, dishes and utensils, bed linens, and towels. You'd have to stock soaps, bathroom tissue and other paper goods, and whatever lotions and whatnot you use." He was grinning again by the end of that statement.

"Of course," I said. He probably had no real intention of insulting me, but there was something about the way he spoke, and the way he looked at me, frankly assessing, that set my teeth on edge.

He made me uncertain whether I wanted to do business with him. But realistically, I had little choice. There was no one else in the area who was both a licensed realtor and an expert in local history. That he was also Cherokee was a huge bonus. It would be great if he was able to help me learn about my possible Cherokee ancestors.

I sighed. I would have to try to get along with him.

"Look," he said. "Have dinner with me tonight, and I'll bring some brochures to show you. If you like the looks of 'em, I'll take you around to see 'em tomorrow. Okay?"

"Dinner? Where?" I had not expected that.

"I'll pick you up at your hotel and take you to Billy's BBQ. Billy Jr.'s a high school friend of mine. He served as an Army Sergeant in Afghanistan and was wounded. He got a medical discharge and as soon as he healed enough to get around again, he headed back up here to help his dad run the family restaurant. The décor is pretty basic, but you can't get better barbeque east of Texas. Or, you could stay here and I could cook dinner for you."

"Stay here?" I croaked, trying to clear my throat. I glanced at my watch. "It's not even two-thirty yet!"

"Dusk still falls pretty early now, and it gets colder, as I mentioned before. I usually try to serve dinner between four-thirty and six, dependin' on the season, so my guests can get home before it's pitch dark. There aren't any street lights on these mountain roads. Much later than six o'clock, and people sleep over. I have five bedrooms."

I stood, poised to leave. "It won't be necessary to cook for me. I really don't understand why you won't show me the brochures now, and take me to one or two places this afternoon?"

He stood too, still smiling. His height was intimidating, and he was standing much too close for comfort. I shivered again and my stomach did a flip-flop.

"Because," he said, "I want to have dinner with you, and spend some time goin' over the brochures this evenin'. I have chores to do this afternoon before dark, but tomorrow we can get an early start. I can show you just the condos and cabins you've chosen to see, or all of 'em if you want. Once we nail down the right rental, we can start workin' on your family's history. You only have one full day left, right?"

I nodded.

"So, we need to get goin' as soon as possible tonight."

I sighed. He was right about needing to get going soon. "Okay. If you'll tell me where this restaurant is, I'll meet you there."

"Oh, I don't think so. It's kind of out of the way. I'll come get you at six-thirty."

He grinned that grin again, with predictable results to my insides. I was sure my face was turning pink, but this time it was partly in anger. I took a deep breath and tried to relax. Realistically, I would be much better off not looking for a hard-to-find restaurant in the dark.

"Okay. I'll be ready by six-thirty."

We moved to the door and he helped me into my jacket. "I hope you have somethin' warmer than this to wear tonight." He kept one warm hand on my shoulder while he opened the door with the other.

"Yes, I have a coat with me."

"Good. You'll need it." He moved his hand to my elbow and escorted me down the porch steps and out to my car. He waited there until I was in the driver's seat and had my seatbelt fastened before he stepped away.

"See you at six-thirty," he called.

He stood watching me back out of his driveway, and then headed for his corral as I drove away.

I was still feeling the effects of the final jolt of electricity between us when he squeezed my hand in parting.

CHAPTER 2

Back in my hotel room in the town of Blue Ridge, Fannin County's largest municipality, I surveyed my scanty wardrobe. I wished I could pick something to wear tonight from my closet in Manhattan. For this trip, I had packed only as much as would fit in an airline-sized carry-on suitcase.

There was a pair of blue jeans I liked to wear with brown loafers while traveling. I decided they would be okay for a barbeque restaurant. The jeans fit well, and looked presentable. I also had a soft woolen turtleneck sweater in my favorite shade of cinnamon brown. It looked terrific with my dark red hair, and my thick cardigan sweater, which was striped with dark blue, beige, and more cinnamon, was a perfect match for the turtleneck. I would bring my coat for later, in case it really got that cold.

At least, I would be able to dress more casually here than in Manhattan. I could leave most of my business clothing and evening wear in storage.

With that subject covered, I decided to go for a walk in the town's business district, only a few blocks away from my hotel. I sat down on the bed to change into walking shoes and yawned. The bed looked so inviting. It must be the mountain air, I thought, as I lay back with my hands behind my head... and fell asleep.

I sat up with a start, wondering what had awakened me. I checked the bedside clock. It was five-thirty already!

Panicked, I stripped off my clothes, and headed for the bathroom. I would have barely enough time to shower, dress, fix my hair, and apply a little makeup. I wanted to be ready before Tom arrived to pick me up.

Forty minutes later, I stepped into the lobby. Tom was there already, leaning over the counter to flirt with the receptionist, a pretty, petite blonde.

She looked up over his shoulder, frowned at me, and said something to him that I was too far away to hear. He straightened, murmured an answer to her, and turned around.

He looked me over carefully and, I guessed, approvingly, because he was grinning the wolfish grin I was beginning to expect. Expecting it, though, did nothing to stop my physical reaction to it. My face was warm. I knew I was blushing again.

"Well! Hi, Suzanna," he said. "I didn't think you'd be ready this early. We'll have to take the long road to Billy's. Our reservation is for seven o'clock. But, that gives us time to get to know each other better. Come on. My car's just outside."

When I glanced back at the receptionist, she was still scowling at me, her pretty face distorted by an expression that bordered on fury. I wondered why she seemed so angry. Mentally, shaking my head, I took the arm Tom offered me.

He behaved like a perfect gentleman. He held the lobby door open for me, guided me to his white, two-door convertible sports car with his hand under my elbow, and opened the car door. Taking my coat, he laid it gently on the back seat, and pushed the passenger seatback upright again so I could get in.

He waited for me to settle myself and fasten my seatbelt before closing the door and going around to the driver's side. He got in, and looked me over again. "Comfortable?"

I nodded, and glanced around the interior of the car. It was an unfamiliar, to me, make and model, sleek and spotless. The dark gray leather seats were soft and smooth, and the dashboard looked like it belonged in an airplane cockpit. The engine purred and whined as he skillfully shifted gears. Obviously, the real estate business in Fannin County was booming.

He must have read my mind, because the next thing he said was, "Don't get the wrong idea. I'm not filthy rich. I just like nice things, and as I live alone with no dependents, I can put most of my income into investments that make money. I've saved, even scrimped, to get where I am today."

"Really?" I was skeptical.

"Really," he replied, nodding his head. "My best friend in college became a whiz kid on Wall Street. He gives me advice from time to time, and it usually pans out. I've been lucky so far. Also, I don't let everythin' ride on one investment."

"That's smart." I was impressed. His immaculate and beautifully decorated home, and now this car, seemed much too expensive to belong to a local real estate agent. This was not Manhattan, after all, or even a large town. The total population of Fannin County was fewer than twenty-five thousand souls, and it was clearly not the most prosperous county in Georgia. I was certain his yearly income would be too small to support what I had seen so far.

"But enough about me," he drawled. "Tell me about what you do in Manhattan."

"I'm a public relations executive and special events manager at a large public relations firm. We handle accounts for both corporate clients and not-for-profit foundations. I can't tell you about individual accounts or name our clients, but it's one of the most prestigious PR companies in the city."

"Have you worked there long?"

"About five years. I majored in Communications in college, and worked for several years in smaller companies before I moved up to the job I'm in now. I put in long hours to earn my pay. Maybe you'd be willing to share your Wall Street whiz kid's expertise some time. I could use some good advice to enhance my income."

As Tom negotiated a tight turn, I noticed that it was already dark. Now, I could see what he meant about the dangers of driving at night in these mountains. One needed to know the roads very well. We had been steadily climbing and I judged we were already at a higher elevation than at Tom's house.

"Where did you go to school?" Tom glanced over at me. "My alma mater is a local campus of our state university. Nothin' fancy."

"I went to Williams College in Massachusetts. It's located in the Berkshire Mountains. The Berkshires are tall hills, really, and tame by western standards, but the area is beautiful. I did a lot of cross country skiing while I was there."

"Wow. I'm impressed. Isn't that a hard school to get into?"

"I was lucky. I got good grades in high school, and I guess they liked my resume. I had done quite a bit of community service and took several AP courses. Everything added up, and I had a good interview. The woman who conducted it was nice, and put me at ease right away. I know that doesn't always happen."

"I think you're bein' too modest. You sound like a brain. Did you get teased a lot? Anybody call you a nerd?"

"No! Of course not! I didn't go to school with kids like that." I laughed self-consciously.

In the dashboard's glow, I could see Tom's face well enough to notice the skeptical look he gave me, one expressive eyebrow raised. Though the light was dim, I could see that his eyes were smiling, the crinkles around them deepening attractively. I laughed again, more softly this time. I was somewhat relieved. He was easier to talk with than I had anticipated.

"Oh, okay." I shrugged. "Pretty much everyone was a nerd at my school. Of course, I've been called that, and worse, but I've never cared. I set my goals early and studied hard to achieve them."

This time, in the low dashboard light, I saw him eye me appreciatively and nod. I seemed to have won some points with him.

A moment later, he said, "We're almost there. I hope you're hungry. The portions are big, and it's not exactly health food."

"Don't worry. My lunch is a distant memory. I should be able to cope."

He swung the car around the last curve and pulled into a large, gravel parking lot. I thought it looked like it was full, but Tom found a space that was too narrow for the huge pick-up trucks and SUVs already parked. There was plenty of room for his sleek sports car.

He came around to open the car door for me and help me out. His touch, as usual, sent tingles up and down my arm. I shivered, and wondered if I would ever get used to that odd sensation between us. Not that I expected to see much of him this summer. Once our business was finished, he would be busy with other clients. At least, I was not blushing this time.

He saw me shiver, of course, and reached for my coat.

"It's okay. I'm not cold. I'm just not accustomed to the climate here."

He looked unconvinced, but closed the car door and led me into the restaurant. The proprietor, Billy, Sr., came bustling up to seat us.

"Hey, Tom. You're a little early, but your table's ready for you. Sit down, and I'll bring you a beer. What will the little lady drink?"

Little lady? I was unsure whether to take offense at that, but Tom read my mind, or maybe it was my face.

"Don't mind Billy. Every woman who comes in here is little to him. See the size of him?"

I looked up at Billy. He was even taller than Tom, and three times as wide. I saw Tom's point.

I took a deep breath and said, "For now, just a glass of water will do, thank you."

Billy looked shocked, but nodded. "Comin' right up. Do you want lemon with that?"

"Yes, please."

Billy waddled away and Tom led me to "his" table.

As we sat down, he said, "Billy always says this is my table. It started a few years ago when I helped him secure a business loan and he's felt obligated ever since. I keep tellin' him there's no need, but he keeps doin' it. I must say though, this place has become so popular, especially in tourist season, it's good to know I don't have to wait for a table."

"There's a tourist season in Fannin County?" My tone was teasing, but though the county's website listed tourist attractions, mostly outdoor activities, I had trouble believing in a *real* tourist season.

"Of course. We're not all hicks. People, sometimes rich people, come for fishin', water sports, hikin', and campin'. Our tourist season runs from late spring through early fall, and then, there's huntin' season after that. We've got other attractions too. We actually do a very nice tourist business."

"Sorry. I didn't mean to offend you. It's just that it looks so… 'un-touristy' here, if I can use that word." I looked around for a menu.

"Well, we do try to keep up the folksy traditions people expect of us. There aren't any Wal-Marts here, but no Saks Fifth Avenues either, and we don't have any big fancy hotels or office buildin's. But the folks around here are not *all* like the characters in that old movie 'Deliverance.' We have some very well-educated people livin' here. Not everyone wears overalls, and some of us even have all our own teeth!"

He was laughing by the time he ended that speech, not really offended by my teasing. If I lived here this summer, I would find out for myself whether he was exaggerating or not. A young, apron-clad waiter hurried up to deliver our drinks. Tom thanked him, and told him we would have "the usual."

The waiter nodded and grinned at me before heading toward the kitchen. I stared at Tom, surprised and shocked at his nerve. How dare he order for me without my even seeing a menu!

"Wait! I haven't even seen the menu. How do you know what I want?" I was annoyed but, I realized, I was more surprised than angry.

Tom was off-hand about it. "Oh, Billy doesn't have a menu. He just barbecues whatever meat he has on hand and the vegetables come from his own garden or from local farmers. It all depends on what's in season. Tonight, we'll probably get pork ribs, with boiled new potatoes, early peas, and cornbread. You'll see. Billy knows his way around a barbeque kitchen. His cornbread is somethin' special. And wait 'til you taste his sauce. You'll just have to trust me."

I must have looked dubious and still a bit annoyed. "Please don't be upset," he said. "I apologize. I should have told you about the no-menu part in advance." He was grinning again. I was sure he was aware of how that grin would affect most women. Much to my annoyance, it certainly had an effect on me!

As soon as I thought I could control my voice, I said, "Okay. Okay. Don't worry. I'll get over it, especially if the food is good."

"Oh, it's good all right," he assured me. "You'll see."

I took a steadying breath and looked around. We were in a large room with a weathered look, as though it might once have been part of a barn. The high ceiling was crisscrossed with heavy dark beams that looked hand hewn, and the walls were wainscoted, painted dark green below and creamy white above. There were sturdy wooden booths and tables, both with padded seats upholstered in a forest-green, leather-like material.

Each table was covered with a green and white checked fabric tablecloth, and set with matching napkins and a small vase of daffodils, elegant touches I would not have expected here. The lighting was discreetly dim, especially near the bar, which was in a far corner.

Every booth and table was taken, as well as all the green-upholstered stools at the bar, where other patrons were standing three deep. The place felt homey and smelled delectable. I could hardly wait for the food to arrive.

While I was inspecting the décor, Tom sat watching me, occasionally sipping his beer.

I was beginning to feel more comfortable with his scrutiny. Would I still feel comfortable if he wanted to become friendlier? But wait a minute. He was a beautiful man who could probably have any woman he wanted. Even if I wanted him, there was no guarantee he would want me.

"While we're waitin', tell me a little about your background. Where did you grow up? Was it in Manhattan?"

"No. On Long Island. My Grandma Rose and Grandpa Kelly raised my brother, Ron, and me after our parents were killed in a car crash. They burned to death before they could be rescued."

I stopped, but I was not going to cry, not now, not in front of Tom. I looked down. Tom had reached out across the table and enfolded one of my hands in his. There was an expression of compassion on his face. I smiled shakily at him, and withdrew my hand.

"I was three years old and Ron was six. My grandparents lost their only child and their son-in-law in that crash, but Ron tells me they hid their grief from us, took us back to their big Long Island house, and poured all their love into raising us.

"Grandpa died when I was twelve, after a long illness. Grandma's stories about growing up on her parents' poor dirt farm in Fannin County kept Ron and me fascinated when Grandpa's health problems made it necessary for us to be quiet."

"Your grandmother's still alive?"

"No." I looked down at my hands, now in my lap. It was still hard to talk about her illness and death. "Three years ago, she lost her final battle with cancer. I'm still not over it."

"Of course. I understand." There was that compassion again. He really did look as though he understood. "What about your brother? Does he still live on Long Island?"

"No. We sold the house when Grandma got so sick. The proceeds paid for her care in a nursing home in Houston, near where Ron and his wife and my two young nephews live. Now that Grandma Rose is gone, I rarely see them. We're very close, though. We call or text each other every week and share our memories on social media."

Tom made a sympathetic noise.

Uncomfortable now, I took a sip of my water. Thankfully, the waiter appeared with our food just as I was putting my glass down and searching my mind for another topic of conversation. I wanted to be done with talking about illness and death.

The food looked wonderful and smelled even better. It was a welcome distraction, but I was shocked at the immense amount of food on my outsized plate.

"Oh, this is too much. There is no way I can eat all this!"

"Don't worry. Just eat as much as you can. That's all Billy asks of his customers. There are lots of us who can handle Billy's portions just fine. And if you can't, it won't go to waste. He feeds any leftovers that folks don't take home to his pigs."

I laughed skeptically, not sure if he was kidding.

"Don't laugh. He does. And what goes around comes around, to borrow an overused expression. One day, probably soon, those pigs will be barbequed."

I gasped.

Tom shrugged. "That's just the way it is here, and in lots of other parts of the world, too. Don't let it get in the way of your appetite."

Billy Jr., a younger and thinner version of his dad, appeared at our table, and Tom introduced me.

"Well, now, Miss Suzanna," he said, with a small bow and friendly smile. "Welcome to Billy's BBQ. Dad's in the kitchen right now, but he'll come out to check on you in a little while. How do you like our mountains, and more importantly, how do you like our barbecue?" He loomed over us, smiling expectantly.

I put a bite of barbeque into my mouth and savored the complex flavors. It was delicious, the best I had ever tasted. And, just as Tom had predicted, there were boiled baby potatoes and early peas. In the center of the table, fluffy yellow cornbread and a small container of whipped butter were nestled in a green wicker basket lined with a white cloth napkin.

I chewed blissfully and swallowed. "Billy, it's delicious. I've never had better. Thank you. And the mountains are beautiful!"

"Thank *you*," he responded, his grin now spread from ear to ear. "I'll tell Dad. He'll be pleased." He looked around and nodded to other diners. "Well, enjoy yourselves. I've got to keep movin'." Turning away, he greeted the people at the next table.

I had sampled everything, by now, including the cornbread. Tom watched me closely, nodding in satisfaction at my obvious delight. I thought maybe I could finish everything on my enormous plate after all.

By some sort of unspoken agreement, both of us turned our full attention now to the food. There was little conversation as we began to work our way through the abundance.

Eventually, I had to stop. I was sure there was no room for another bite. Even Tom was slowing down, though he had done better than I could. We looked at each other, and both of us grinned the grin of satisfied defeat.

"Wow, Tom! That was truly awesome."

Our waiter returned to take our plates and ask about coffee and dessert.

I shook my head. "Sorry, I just can't eat or drink another thing."

Tom said, "Okay, Johnny, you heard the lady. Just bring the check, please."

Johnny hurried off, while I reached for my pocketbook.

Tom held up one large hand. "Oh, no. This is *my* treat. You're goin' to earn me some serious money if you rent a place from me for the summer. So, this is the least I can do."

I was dubious. I hated to be in debt to anyone, and always split restaurant checks with my friends. Tom looked as though he would insist, however, and I decided not to make an issue of it. Not this time, at least.

"All right," I said. "Just this once though, okay?" The last thing I wanted to convey was a willingness to let him have his way with me, in anything, not just dinner checks.

Back in the car, we were mostly quiet on the way down the mountain. When we arrived back at my hotel, he parked near the door and helped me out of the car. Reaching into the back seat, he took out a briefcase and my coat. Then, with his other hand under my elbow, he escorted me into the lobby.

The blonde woman Tom was talking with when I came downstairs to meet him was gone, replaced with a young black man.

"Hey Frankie. How's it goin'?"

"Great, Tom. It's good to see you. How's Sheila?"

Sheila? Who was Sheila? Oh well, it was none of my business. But if that were true, why, suddenly, was I feeling so let down?

"She's fine. Workin' hard. We'll have to get together with you and your lady one of these days soon."

Frankie smiled and nodded. "Any time, Tom."

A small fireplace burned brightly in the lobby. Sleek furniture was grouped nearby, but for now, at least, we were the only people interested in sitting there. We warmed our hands at the fireplace before taking seats, with me in an easy chair and Tom on a couch. He was close enough to show me the brochures he had brought, and point out the features of each, but clearly, he was dissatisfied.

"Come on over here so I can show you these folders without gettin' a crick in my neck."

I shook my head, but he persisted. "Oh, come on. I won't bite."

I was unsure of that, but I decided to do as he asked. It would be more comfortable for me too. With a small show of reluctance, I sat beside him.

He handed me information on a few more condos and cabins than he had mentioned earlier, each with a different combination of features, and patiently answered my questions. Most of the condos were in, or at least close, to the town of Blue Ridge, though one was in a village not far away. All the cabins were in the mountains that surrounded the town. The proximity to Blue Ridge, the county seat of Fannin County, was important to me, as there were essential amenities here: a supermarket, a once-a-week greenmarket, a laundromat, the public library, a bank, and county records offices, among other things. Most of the condos had laundry facilities on site, but neither of the cabins did.

After discussing the pros and cons of each one, I decided to look at three condos and two cabins. Tom seemed to approve my choices, though I wondered why his approval was important to me. Of course, I would make up my own mind! Though I hated to admit it to myself, I was close to surrendering to his charm.

He put the rejected folders back into his briefcase. "Let's help ourselves to coffee. You've probably noticed there's always a pot goin'. And the owner's wife, Sherry Wilkins, bakes terrific cookies. I'm ready to have some. How about you?"

"I don't know if I can eat any cookies, but coffee sounds good." We stood and moved to the counter in the courtesy breakfast room where there was a full coffee pot and a covered plate of cookies.

"Who are Frankie and his lady? Not that it's any of my business."

Tom finished pouring coffee into our cups and put the pot down before answering. "Frankie and I played on the same sports teams in high school and were good friends, though I was a couple of years ahead of him. He had a football scholarship to Georgia Tech, but he was badly injured in practice durin' his junior year and had to stop playin'. His scholarship ran out, of course, and he had to leave school."

I shook my head in sympathy.

He added milk to his coffee and asked me how I liked mine. He followed my instructions, handed me my cup, and continued. "I was able to lend him a little money to help him finish college. He's almost done payin' me back. He's a full-time accountant durin' the day, and works here part-time at night. His wife, Mandy, just gave birth to their first child a couple of months ago. I know it's difficult for 'em, so I keep in close touch. They're really nice people."

I was beginning to see what a good friend Tom could be. He had the resources to help people when they needed it, and did so. The money was not a hand-out, just a little financial aid toward an achievable goal. I had seen two instances of his generosity this evening.

I realized that I might have misjudged him. Apparently, he wasn't simply a handsome hunk ready to take advantage of his looks. There might be an actual thinking person with a good heart inside that gorgeous exterior.

"That's very kind of you," I said. The coffee was hot and delicious. I was trying to resist the cookies. They were chocolate chip, my favorite. After eating so much at dinner, I could hardly believe I wanted cookies now.

Tom gathered his coffee cup, some napkins, and the plate of cookies and headed back to our couch. "I'll need to go soon, but I want you to know how happy I am that Mr. Hardy recommended me to you. I met him only once, but we've corresponded by e-mail several times. He knows his business."

"He spoke highly of you, too. I hope you'll be able to help me find out more about my grandmother's family."

"We'll see. There are some excellent resources in the library here, and there are more on-line. We'll go as far back as we can. Your grandmother told you she was part Cherokee?"

"Yes, though she didn't seem to be very pleased about it. I didn't understand her attitude. I'm very proud to be part Cherokee, though I guess it's only a very tiny part. She told me her great-grandmother was full-blood, so you can see how far back we need to go. Do you think it's possible, especially since we don't even know her great-grandmother's name? That's six generations counting me, a very long time."

"Assumin' we're successful, tell me again what you plan to do with the information."

"I'm going to write the story of our family's history this summer, or at least to get started on it. I want to do this for myself, for my brother, and for our children. He has two boys, and though I don't have any children of my own yet, I hope to one day."

He gave me a long considering look, took one more cookie, and drained his cup. "I must go. I'll pick you up at nine o'clock sharp tomorrow mornin'. We should be done by noon and then we'll go back up to my place so we can finalize your rental, have some lunch, and talk about your family. Bring all the information you have now: names; birth, marriage, and death dates; deeds; wills; and anythin' else you have. Genealogy is like a puzzle. The more pieces we have to start with, the better the chances of completin' the picture."

"Yes, I can see that," I said, nodding. "I'll bring everything I have."

He picked up his briefcase, and carried the cookie plate back to the breakfast room. I followed with our cups, and walked with him to the door.

He said goodnight to Frankie and turned to me. "I look forward to seein' you tomorrow. I hope you'll find a rental you really like."

"Me too!" I held out my hand to shake his, but he surprised me by taking it and brushing it gently with his lips.

I gasped, and wrenched my hand away. "What are you doing?"

This was not playing fair. He must know how susceptible most women would be to hand-kissing. They would find it, and him, irresistible! How dare he trade on that?

I turned around and stalked away toward the elevator, pausing only briefly to collect my pocketbook and coat.

ACKNOWLEDGEMENTS

In 2004, a woman with whom I had once worked invited me to be her guest on a river cruise in Russia. I accepted immediately. It was a fantastic cruise. I'm grateful to all our interesting and informative tour guides; our river cruiser's officers, entertainment staff, guest lecturers, and crew (including the great cooks and servers); the passengers who made my mostly solitary journey so much fun; my boss for allowing me leave my desk for two weeks; and my colleagues for picking up the slack while I was gone.

In addition to Russian souvenirs for my family and friends, I brought home the idea for this novel. However, there was no time to write a book—I was busy with my full time job, volunteer activities, after-hours freelance writing, and the various needs of my family. Plus, after many years of writing only non-fiction, I had to learn how to write a romantic novel.

It takes a lot of people to help a novice writer produce a book that people might want to read. I am so thankful for everyone who took a chance on me, and agreed to read my first stumbling drafts. My first reader is, as always, my husband, **Larry**

Speciner, followed closely by my friend and the leader of my community's book club, **Marcia Attard**. They both read multiple drafts, and their helpful criticism was vital and invaluable.

There were many other readers as well. Some found typos, some made plot suggestions, and all of you gave me constant encouragement. Special thanks go to my daughters, **Lisa Khavkin** and **Rachel Speciner McNaughton;** my sister, **Judy Scott;** my son's mother-in-law, **Lucille Cazzetto;** my friend, **Joan Jaffa;** her daughter, **Randye Korte;** and my friends, **Hetty** and **Zack Davies, Sue Gorman, Marcia Grey**, and **Sara Bauman**. I am particularly grateful to my friend, **Doreen Van Gjin**, whose wise insights helped me transform my story into a real book. Without each and every one of you, I'd still be spinning my wheels.

Finally, my heart belongs to Larry, our three children, our two sons-in-law, our daughter-in-law, and our seven beautiful, smart, and fabulously talented grandchildren. Thank you for everything.

AUTHOR BIO

P.F. Spencer has a B.A. in Environmental Journalism, and has worked in many aspects of publishing, including more than 10 years at the National Audubon Society's *Audubon* magazine as Advertising Production Manager. In her spare time, she spent more than 15 years as a tour guide and lecturer at Old Westbury Gardens, a historic house and gardens in Long Island, New York, and later as their full time Director of Communications. A former Nassau County Long Island Master Gardener, she served as a board member and President of the Long Island Horticultural Society, and as their newsletter editor for more than 10 years. She has also written freelance feature articles for a regional magazine, local newspapers, and web sites. This is her first novel.

www.ingramcontent.com/pod-product-compliance
Lightning Source LLC
Chambersburg PA
CBHW061307170626
46817CB00001B/88